THE DAMSEL

A VILLAIN DUOLOGY SEQUEL

VICTORIA VALE

❀ Created with Vellum

PROLOGUE

When Lady Rosamund Stanley went into labor with her firstborn son, her husband—Baron Stanley—worked himself into a state. Pacing the corridor outside her bedchamber, he wrung his hands and chewed his lip until it bled. He flinched every time she screamed, but resisted the urge to rush in and ensure everything proceeded as it should. One might think he was anxious about the birth of his child.

Yet, anyone who knew Baron and Lady Stanley would be well aware that this was not their first child. After the loss of three children born prematurely, she had begun increasing for the fourth time.

Delighted by this development, she'd held out hope that, at last, she might provide her husband with an heir. The baron had most certainly *not* been delighted. He did not relish comforting her through the loss of yet another babe, nor did he like the risk of losing her. He'd sent for physicians from all over England to examine her, and all had given the same disheartening diagnosis. While nothing appeared to be wrong with her, she seemed incapable of carrying and birthing a healthy child. But his wife was determined to produce a son, despite his insistence that they could take measures to prevent his seed taking root.

"You are more dear to me than a title and estate," he'd insisted many times. "I would rather have you for the rest of my days than lose you and be forced to raise a child alone."

Determined not to give up, she had begged him to try again, heedless of the obvious dangers. Because he had always indulged her, he hadn't had the heart to refuse.

From the moment they had realized she was with child again, he had commanded her to take her bed. It seemed the only way to ensure she avoided undue stress. An army of servants was made to wait upon her hand and foot, seeing to her every need. Despite being miserable in her condition, Lady Stanley had taken comfort in the hope of finally birthing a healthy child. She had knitted baby things while praying nightly for the desired outcome. She even sent for samples of wallpaper and fabrics for the nursery, somehow orchestrating its entire renovation from her bed.

With each month that passed without a showing of blood or the telltale pains that had preceded the first three births, their hopes rose. Then, on a November morning in the year 1786—after hours upon hours of screaming and suffering—Lady Stanley gave birth to a chubby, red-faced baby boy. Ten fingers, ten toes, a smattering of downy blond hair, and a pair of lungs that enabled him to fill the manor with his cries.

At the first sharp wail, Lord Stanley forgot all rules of etiquette and propriety, rushing into the birthing room to have a look at his firstborn. He sent maids gasping and dashing about to cover their mistress and make her presentable; but the baron only had eyes for the red-faced babe squirming in the arms of a servant. Tears filled his eyes at the sight of his son, naked and furious at being removed from the warm safety of his mother's womb. He'd never seen a more beautiful sight in all his life. The fullness of the baron's heart swelled when he glanced at Lady Stanley—who looked exhausted but healthy, her face aglow with happiness.

"We did it, my love," she said, a bit breathless from her ordeal. "I told you we would."

Accepting the swaddled bundle of his heir, the baron had smiled through his tears. The boy opened his eyes for the first time, revealing them to be a vibrant shade of blue just like his mother's.

"What will we call him?"

Lady Stanley gave a happy sigh. "He is your heir, so he should have your name."

And so they named the boy William Tobias Warin Stanley.

After the traditional period of lying-in for mother and child, invitations to his christening and a lavish dinner went out with that stately name etched upon them in decadent gold foil. The baron boasted to anyone who would listen about the strength of his wife and the handsomeness of his heir, while his friends pounded his back and congratulated him.

Lady Stanley took this blessing of a son after the loss of so many daughters as an omen. God had finally smiled upon her, allowing life to grow where once there had been only death.

"There will be others now," she told the baron. "I have seen it in my mind as if it were a dream. Strong sons, born one right after the other, all healthy. You will see, my love."

Despite being skeptical of his wife's premonition, Lord Stanley no longer found it necessary to avoid impregnating his wife. After all, if she were determined to give him more sons, she would eventually have her way. So, following her recovery, she invited the baron back into her bedchamber, where they attempted to grow their progeny with much vigor.

And so it went that over the course of six years, three more sons were born to the baron and his wife. As arduous as the birth of William had been, each boy that followed gave their mother an easier time of it than the one who had come before.

Lady Stanley was able to remain on her feet for six whole months before taking to her bed with the spare to the heir. His birth lasted half as long as William's and by the end of the night, the baron found he had not abused his lip quite as much as he had the first time. This boy was born with the same blond hair and blue eyes as his brother, and was named Jonas Algernon Stanley.

The third boy allowed his mother to keep out of her bed until the final few weeks of her confinement. After feeling the first of her labor pains at dawn on the morning of his birth, he had come into the world in time for luncheon. Rather than abuse his lip with his teeth, the baron had helped himself to a plate of finger sandwiches, which he ate sitting outside the birthing room. Another towheaded, blue-eyed babe, they named him Andrew Bennett Stanley.

The fourth and final son of the Stanley progeny took his mother quite by surprise. Having thought she'd grown too old to bear another child, the baroness had been perfectly content with her trio of handsome, bright, mischievous sons. However, within a year of Andrew's birth, Lord Stanley's attentions bore fruit yet again. At his utter shock upon the revelation of her condition, the baroness only smiled and laughed.

"Didn't I tell you, my love?" she teased. "Shame on you for not believing in me!"

If Lord Stanley had ever questioned whether there were a God, the birth of their fourth healthy son put all doubt to rest. The baroness was radiant from the day she'd discovered her condition, until the day she labored to bring him into the world. She took walks and danced, remaining upon her feet until the moment her water spilled all over the library floor. She'd been energetic, limber, and happy all the way through, and from the first pain to her final grunt and push, the birth spanned a grand total of three hours.

This time, the baron had decided to see what this birthing business might be all about, brushing off the insistence of the midwife that men had no place in such an environment. And what a wonder it had been, to watch the baroness labor and bear a sort of pain he would never know. By the end of it, his fourth son arrived, and while he bore resemblance to his siblings he also proved quite different.

In fact, the differences became plain the moment he was washed clean and placed in his mother's arms. The baroness gasped, while the maids and midwife looked on in silent wonder. Even Lord Stanley found himself without words as he stared down at the most beautiful child he'd ever seen.

Unlike the thin, fuzzy down William, Jonas, and Andrew had been born with, this boy possessed a headful of shining, golden curls. His face could be likened to those of painted cherubs—plump cheeks flushed with a pink glow, the perfect pucker of a mouth, and big eyes ringed in a lush fan of golden lashes. And his eyes ...

"They are like the sky on a clear spring day," a maid whispered.

And so they were; quite a perfect shade of sky blue, open and clear.

"It is a good thing he was not born a girl," Lady Stanley quipped, smoothing a hand over those perfect blond coils. "Could you imagine a girl with this face and those eyes?"

Baron Stanley could, in fact, so he thanked the Lord that this heavenly-looking creature had not been female. Otherwise, he would drive himself mad worrying over the attentions of men.

"Well?" he prodded, perching on the edge of the bed and reaching out toward the boy. "What shall we name this one?"

He smiled, placing his finger in the babe's palm, never growing tired of that first clench of a baby's hand around it. This delighted him now just as much as it had the first time William had done it.

"I thought we could name him for my father," the baroness replied.

"Robert. I like that."

"Very well then. Robert Nathaniel Stanley."

FOR TWELVE YEARS following Robert's birth, all was well in the world of the baron and his family. From the cradle to the schoolroom, then off to Eton, the Stanley boys grew by leaps and bounds. William was the sensible one, being the eldest and the heir. Because of this, the other three could almost always be found in his wake, dancing to his tune and doing whatever he commanded. Jonas proved the most mischievous of the four, vexing those around him with pranks, sly jokes, and—as he got older—crass innuendo. Being the spare and resident troublemaker of the family made him the most likely to butt heads with William. The two argued incessantly, but would come to each other's aid should an outsider think to do or say something untoward. Andrew was the studious sort—always reading and asking questions. When he did not indulge in these pastimes, he often sat staring off into thin air, as if seeing things no one else could.

"He'll be a great philosopher someday, wait and see," the baroness would say.

"Or a clergyman," the baron would add.

And then, there was Robert—everyone's favorite Stanley boy. Oh, no one *tried* to show him favor over his brothers. It just so happened that the youngest of the brood also happened to be the sort of boy everyone liked. Sunny, cheerful, and so pretty he could make angels weep, he had none of William's arrogance, or Jonas' devilishness, or Andrew's brooding. If one tried to understand the purpose of Robert in the midst of four very different brothers, one might assume it was to provide a much-needed balance. He was patient with bossy William, laughed at Jonas while everyone else was shaking their heads, and made an effort to show interest in whatever had Andrew's attention at the moment.

The servants doted on him, his parents adored him, and his brothers often envied one another his company.

"He will marry well," his father predicted. "With a face like that, and such a personality, he'll have the wealthiest heiresses in London vying for his attention."

Lady Stanley agreed that he would have his pick of the litter while searching for a wife, though secretly believed no woman could ever be good enough for her Robert. He was too good and pure for any of those snooty debutantes and their scheming mamas.

Robert was made for the glittering ballrooms of London, for wealth and status and adoration. His birth order might have put him on the fringes of London high society, but he would not remain there, his looks and charm sure to propel him into the highest of social circles.

With all this cemented in the minds of the baron and baroness, life went on as it should for some time. The boys grew and changed, approaching adulthood at the breakneck speed typical of children. It proved an idyllic life, one in which the Stanleys raised their boys in the country alongside neighbors with children of an age with theirs.

Outside the schoolroom, or on school holidays, the boys spent their time romping the land surrounding their small estate, getting into all manner of mischief and making most of the years before they'd be forced to think of adult matters.

All that changed in the winter of 1798, when Andrew Stanley fell suddenly ill. William and Jonas had come home from school for Christmas, which had been quite exciting for the younger two, for they had yet to leave for Eton and were always keen to hear the elder boys' stories of life away from home. In the weeks prior, Andrew had fallen into sudden sneezing fits that seemed of no consequence at the onset. By Christmas Eve, he had taken to his bed with a fever and complaints of a sore throat. By the New Year, he'd grown delirious from the fever, and the sound of his labored breathing could be heard halfway down the corridor. And on a particularly frigid January day, Andrew ceased breathing altogether, choking and gurgling as his mother sobbed in the baron's arms. There had been nothing the physician could do. Within minutes he was gone, his face drained of all color, his lips a grotesque shade of purple.

To say that Andrew's loss had come as a shock to the entire family would be an understatement. Lady Stanley was especially distraught, unable to fathom how she'd been blessed with four healthy sons, only for one to be suddenly taken from her by a mysterious ailment. The inevitable departure of William and Jonas as they returned to school cast a heavy blanket of grief over the entire house, which felt even emptier without Andrew. This proved an especially difficult time for Robert, who now had no companion at home with his elder brothers away at school.

But the baroness had an even harder time of it, weeping without provocation and lying in Andrew's bed, clinging to his pillow because she claimed it still smelled like him.

When he was not with his governess, Robert did whatever he could to cheer her up, as was his nature. He could never abide standing back to watch someone suffer if there was anything he could do about it. So, each day, he put forth an effort to make his mother smile—bringing her bouquets of wildflowers he had picked, taking tea with her even though he detested tea and hated how she fussed over his clothes and hair, singing to her when she seemed sad, because she'd always told him he had a lovely voice. On the days when grief would not allow her to leave her bed, he would sneak into her room and climb under the coverlet, holding her hand and pretending that seeing her weep did not bother him. He would go off on his own to cry when seized with the urge, for he had learned that to see him weep only made her grieve all the harder.

"You are my dear, sweet, boy, Robert," she would say. "Mama does not know what she would do without you."

In time, things returned to normal—or, as close to normal as could be with the gaping hole left by Andrew's loss. William and Jonas returned home at holidays. Then, William completed his education at Eton with plans to go off to Oxford. A year after that, Jonas' eighteenth birthday marked a drastic change. Instead of following William to university, he wished to join the Royal Navy. The baron had been thrilled with such a development, and had begun spreading the word that his son was soon to be a navy man.

They sent him off with a farewell dinner, inviting many neighbors and friends to celebrate the occasion. William had been home for it, of course. It would turn out to be the last time the Stanley family as they knew it would all be together this way again.

Robert could remember exactly where he was and what he'd been doing on the day that death, once again, saw fit to visit the Stanley family.

He'd just returned from a romp through the woods with the young girl who lived on the neighboring estate. A lovely little thing with fiery auburn hair and a rebellious streak. She had to be the prettiest well-born girl in the county, and earlier in the summer he had begun to notice the changes taking her from girl to woman. Robert had delighted in wooing her, indulging in secret kisses and furtive caresses out of view of their parents.

After parting ways with her on the forked path leading to their respective houses, he'd whistled happily, his blood thrumming through his veins with excitement. He'd been unable to think of anything other than when he might sneak off to be with her again, his lips still tingling from her kisses.

Approaching the house, Robert had found his parents waiting for him on the front steps, their expressions grave. He'd faltered on the path, heart leaping into his throat as he'd realized the baroness had been crying. Her nose and cheeks flushed red, shoulders shaking as she came forward, something clutched against her bosom. As she stumbled down the stairs, he realized it was a letter, the envelope and parchment crumpled in her shaking hands.

Before he could even form the words to ask, he had known. He'd simply felt it, like someone had reached down into his throat and pried some essential thing loose. Something irreplaceable and precious.

As it turned out, that thing had been Jonas—the brother who'd always been able to make him laugh, who had filled their home with so much joy, even when exasperating them to no end.

"They say *The Intrepid* has gone down with all hands," she whispered, her voice breaking off on a sob before she pitched forward and into his arms. "There isn't ... they don't have ... his body is still out there ... Oh, God!"

Robert had nearly buckled under the weight of the crushing grief —his own, as well as his mother's. But, he'd held firm and clung to her, eyes stinging as he tried to make sense of this. But, it did *not* make sense. Jonas had been a force of nature, as brave and fearless as they came. It did not seem possible for him to cease existing in this world.

And for there to be no body, no evidence of his demise ... it was nonsensical. Glancing up at his father, he found that the baron looked old, his face weathered and drawn. His father was not a young man anymore, but the losses of Andrew and Jonas had only quickened the process. Like Robert, he seemed intent upon remaining stoic for the baroness, who wept as if some part of her had been ripped out, too.

"Perhaps it is a misunderstanding," he had managed, his voice hoarse from the sobs he contained. "Someone might be mistaken about what has happened."

His tone had turned pleading, as if the son in him needed her to tell him everything would be fine. He wanted her to comfort him for once, to tell him that of course Jonas could not possibly be dead.

"Oh, I pray you are right, Robert. God, please don't let it be true!"

Time proved Robert wrong, as his father's journey to London and a few queries turned up the truth. *The Intrepid* had run afoul of a storm and dragged its seamen into a watery grave. The splintered remains had been found by another Royal Navy vessel, and its crew had identified the lost ship by the lettering along a piece of its leftover hull.

From that day forward, a dark cloud seemed to hang over the Stanley estate, as if Jonas had been the sun and there could be no light now that he was gone. William, who'd spent the summer in London with friends from Oxford, had returned home upon receiving the news. In the fall, he would have to return, and Robert was scheduled to leave for another term at Eton. His mother spoke often of keeping him at home and hiring a tutor.

"I cannot bear to be without my little boy," she would say while clinging to him, tears wetting her face.

"He must have his education like the rest of them, Rosie," the baron would argue.

His mother would try to plead her case. A tutor would do to see him properly educated, and he would be at home, where nothing awful could happen to him. When she was not worried that he might go to Eton and never return, she fussed over him like never before.

"Robert, do get out of those boots and put on dry stockings. You could catch a chill!"

"Robert, do not eat so fast, love, you could choke to death!"

"Robert, no running on the stairs! You will break your neck and I would never survive it. Is that what you want?"

Each time she warned him of some new danger, guilt would assail him over having worried her.

"I am sorry, Mother," he would murmur, then tailor his behavior to offer her peace of mind.

He never ran in the house, he always promptly warmed himself after coming in from the rain, and whenever he felt the urge to cough, he left the room so she could not hear him. Leaving for Eton made things easier. When he was not at home, he did not have to be reminded every day that Jonas and Andrew were dead. He could make friends and dedicate his time to his studies. Letters from home came filled with cautions from his mother, of course. She worried that he might not be eating enough, that he could not rest well sharing a room with three other boys, or that the classrooms were too drafty. Every time he wrote back, he would fill his letters with reassurances, doing his best to soothe her from afar. Yes, he had plenty to eat every day and had even grown quite a bit since the last time she'd seen him. He slept fine and liked the boys he roomed with. There was plenty of coal for their fires, so no, she did not have to worry he would freeze.

Yet again, life arranged itself into some semblance of order. When he and William came home on holiday, they spent as much time together as possible—partly to escape their mother's incessant worrying, but mostly because death had bonded them like never before. The first son, and the fourth who had now become the heir's spare.

"There are only two of us now," William would say when overtaken by melancholy. "We must always stick together, Robert. No matter what. We cannot let petty squabbles come between us. Andrew would not want it, and neither would Jonas."

Were Andrew here, he might have pointed out how inevitable it was for brothers to fight. Jonas would have joked that William was being bossy—as usual. Feeling the deep chasm of two dead brothers between them, Robert had done neither of those things.

He had merely nodded his agreement and murmured, "Yes, you are right."

The holiday before William's final spring term, he had repeated the sentiment to Robert for the last time. They'd stood on the front steps of the house, their breaths turning white on the winter air. Inside, his mother played the pianoforte while a gathering of neighbors joined her and the baron in their favorite Christmas songs.

"You'll be off for university soon," William had said, giving him a smile. "I suppose when you return, you might join me in London. It's a ripping good time, you know."

Robert knew only what William had told him, having never lived anywhere except home and Eton. "I suppose. We shall be two young bachelors about Town, chasing after the debutantes. Though, you ought to be wed by then, yes?"

William had chuckled at that. "God, I hope not."

Robert, who had discovered within himself a sense of romantic whimsy, had shrugged. "I do not know. Finding the right woman to wed might not be so bad. A love match … that's what I would want."

His brother had nudged his shoulder and laughed all the harder. "Oh, Robert … you were born with stars in your eyes, just like Mother always says. I pity the debutantes of London once you're old enough to be on the prowl. They will not stand a chance, not a single one of them!"

He'd smiled at that, studying his brother from the corner of his eye. While everyone thought him the 'pretty' brother, William was tall, with a broad chest and shoulders, and merry eyes. He could never be called anything but handsome.

"I hardly think they stand a chance around you, either."

William had frowned, dipping his head so he stared at his feet. "I have no interest in them."

"In debutantes?"

"In women," he'd whispered, glancing over his shoulder as if to ensure no one was about to overhear. "I never have been. My tastes are … different."

Shock had overwhelmed him for a moment. He had assumed William must be sowing his oats in London, helping himself to the Covent Garden doxies like every other man they knew. But then he realized he'd never actually seen William pursue a woman for any reason. Outside the obligatory dances and mundane conversation, he'd never shown romantic interest in *any* woman.

"Men?" he'd murmured, his eyes going wide.

William gave a swift nod, but seemed to have a hard time meeting his eye. "You cannot tell Mother or Father."

"Of course not! Your secret is safe with me."

No matter how unorthodox it may seem, he could never see William as anything other than his brother—his best friend. They'd grown close following the deaths of Andrew and Jonas, and nothing could change that.

"Is there someone you fancy?" he'd asked.

He'd wanted William to know he didn't disapprove or judge him for feelings beyond his control. If his brother could not speak of it with their parents, then Robert would be his listening ear.

William had flushed and finally met his gaze. "There is, but … he doesn't know. I've been too afraid to tell him."

"Oh, but you must tell him," he'd urged. "Does he … have the same inclinations as you?"

"I'm almost certain he does."

"Then you must—"

"I'm Father's heir, Robert," William had interjected. "That will require a baroness, a son, I can't …"

He'd brought a hand down on his brother's shoulder and squeezed. "Love is more important than any of it.You should be with the person you want most. If there is a chance he feels the same way, you *must* take a chance. I want to see you happy, Will."

His brother had nudged him in the ribs with a sly smirk. "Is it that you want me to be happy … or that *you* want to inherit the barony?"

"Perhaps I do," he'd said with a chuckle.

That had been the last time he had laughed with his brother. Within days of Christmas, he returned to them in a wooden box with a hole in his chest from a knife wound.

Having left to spend what remained of his holiday in London with a few Oxford chums, he had become the victim of a brutal stabbing. One of the friends who had been with him in Town had accompanied William's body back home. Standing in the drawing room with his hat in his hands, he'd explained to what was left of the Stanley family how their loved one had met his end.

"We were leaving a gaming hell when we heard a scream from down a nearby alley. William did not think twice—you should know that about him. He was brave until the very last, running right toward the scream intending to help. It was a lady under attack by some bleeder after her jewels. William wrestled him off her, and screamed at us to get the lady to safety. Two of us took her off to hail a hack and make sure she was all right. By the time I returned, William had been stabbed, and ... I am so sorry."

He hung his head and wept, while Robert choked on the tight knot of grief welling in his throat. For a moment, he wondered if this young man might be the one William had loved. The way he wept, as if mourning someone dear to him, Robert knew he had to be. It only made this all the more tragic, as he'd never know whether his brother had made his feelings known.

He clung to his mother, who sat staring into the hearth as if she hadn't heard a word. The baron buried his face in his hands to smother his own gut-wrenching sobs. The empty space that had opened within him after Andrew's death and grew all the more with Jonas', now seemed big enough to rip him in two.

Robert held the baroness in his arms and rocked her as he might a child, feeling how she trembled from the strain of it all, hearing the muffled whimpers of the sobs she tried her best not to let out.

William's friend declined an invitation to stay the night, stating he had family nearby and would lodge with them until he was ready to return to university. He would be near at hand if they needed him, and of course would attend William's funeral.

The shock of it kept Robert quite numb in the hours following, his mind reeling as the implications of this sank in. He was now the remaining son of Lord and Lady Stanley—the baron's sole heir.

Wandering into the drawing room where William's body had been placed for the time being, he felt the first sting of tears.

"It isn't supposed to be like this," he rasped, gazing down at William's corpse.

Even in death, his brother was regal and handsome—broad shouldered, tall, with the sort of rugged features the ladies swooned over behind their fans. Robert would never hear him laugh again, never suffer William's teasing over his softer, romantic sensibilities.

"I'm not supposed to be the heir. You are. And … and I am not supposed to be alone in this world. You should be here, damn it! You and Andrew, and Jonas …"

He went down to his knees, a sob ripping through him like the unfurling of a great storm. It was as if he felt it all for the first time—all three deaths and the horror of them crushing down upon him at once.

This was how the baroness found him, kneeling on the floor and sobbing so hard he could hardly breathe, his eyes clouded by a neverending stream of tears.

She stood at his side, one hand stroking his golden curls as he leaned into her, clinging tight to her skirts. Her own, softer cries mingled with his own, her hand shaking as she stroked his hair.

"Why has this happened? How … how have we lost them all?"

He turned his gaze up to hers, seeking answers but finding none. Her eyes were dark and hard, all the warmth he usually found there snuffed out by grief.

"I do not know why," she said, her voice rough and tortured. "But, I am thankful we ever had them at all, when there was a time none of you existed. You see, even in the midst of my pain, God has seen fit to smile upon me."

His face contorted into something like disbelief as he swiped his sleeve over his damp face. "How can you say that? He took them from us, all of them!"

She knelt beside him upon the floor, urging him to lean against her as he went on sniffling and trying to get himself under control. He had always been the one to comfort her, to bring her flowers and make her smile through her grief. But, just now he did not have the strength. So, this time, she held him and kissed his brow and did her best to reassure him in a way she never had.

"I can say that because you are still here," she murmured. "My dear, sweet boy. He made you special for a reason … because He knew I would need you when all was said and done. He might have taken Andrew, and Jonas, and William … and I may never understand why. His ways are mysterious to us. But as long as I have you, I can survive." He wrapped an arm around her and held tight, unable to respond with words. She held him back, trembling as if afraid he might slip away from her any moment.

"It's going to be all right," she whispered. "All will be well as long as we are together."

CHAPTER 1

LONDON, 1819

The Honourable Mr. Robert Stanley stood beside his barouche, watching the other carriage speed down the dark road. As it drew farther away, his heart began to sink, dropping deeper into his middle with every mile that separated him from the woman inside. Shoving his hands into the pockets of his greatcoat, he sighed. He barely registered the chill, or the wind mussing his hair. As he watched another man make off with the love of his life, all he felt was a deep, resounding grief.

His fingers brushed against something cold and hard, so he took hold of it and pulled it free. An enormous sapphire in a gold setting—a family heirloom passed down by generations of Stanleys—sat in his palm. The sight of the ring meant for the woman he'd hoped would become his wife only made the sensation in his gut worse. Now, along with the heavy weight of his heart, a churning maelstrom had begun, making him feel as if he'd be torn apart from the inside.

When he'd taken himself over to Fairchild House this morning,

Robert had been aware of the risks. Five years ago—or even one year ago—he would have approached proposing to Lady Daphne Fairchild with far more optimism. She'd been his friend since they were children, and in adulthood they had become lovers of a sort. While seeking privacy in the stretch of woods separating her family estate from his, they'd indulged in their carnal urges—Robert teaching her the sort of pleasure her untouched body could enjoy, Daphne engaging him with a sort of curiosity and passion that had enraptured him. They'd kissed and touched while smothering the sounds of their rapture, but he had always pulled back for fear of losing his head and ruining her.

Because, it had been the honorable thing to do and if there was one thing he'd always wanted, it was to live up to the title preceding his name. He was a gentleman, after all, and while he had never dreamed he might someday inherit the barony, he had always been aware of who his father was and what that meant. He'd also thought he stood in the perfect position to make Daphne his in truth someday, so had been content to bide his time.

He'd been courtly and polite and understanding. He'd been honest about the depths of his affections at all times, knowing she'd never care for aloofness in a man. And when he thought he would die from needing to be inside her, he'd taken himself off to the first whore with red hair he could find. None of them could ever match her in beauty, but if he focused on the parts of them that were like shadows of her, it would prove enough to help him keep a handle on his urges when in her presence.

It had brought him no end of guilt to lay with whores when his heart belonged to her. But, he'd have done anything to keep from ruining her before they'd been wed. It had felt like the right thing to do, taking the edge off his urges so he could keep himself in check whenever they were together. Once she was his wife, she'd be the only woman he'd want to touch ever again.

When she'd reached the age of her coming out, Robert had sensed she was not ready to wed, and so—true to form—he had done the noble thing. He'd withheld his proposal and stood back while she went off to London for her first Season. If what she wanted was to experience more of the world outside their little corner of Suffolk, then she deserved that much. Perhaps she'd even find she preferred the city and they would live there together after he'd made her his wife.

Idealistic dreams of appearing in London on a whim and winning her once and for all had sustained him in the years separating them. He'd been so certain of their destiny, and had convinced himself that they were fated to end up together. Nothing could stop that, not even a brief time apart. When the moment was right, Lady Daphne Fairchild would be his.

Except, when they'd finally found their way back to each other, someone else had already set himself firmly between them. The one person with the power to destroy the future he had thought to be set in stone.

Lord Adam Callahan, Earl of Hartmoor.

The man had cast his spell over Daphne, and while Robert had tried to convince himself that what the two shared could only be carnal, he'd been forced to face the truth. Hartmoor loved Daphne. That much had been proven when the earl had come to Robert only a few weeks prior, asking a favor of him.

"I am leaving London," he had told Robert while sitting in the small drawing room of his bachelor's lodgings in Town. "Daphne will not be coming with me."

That had come as a surprise, as the man had struck Robert as quite possessive, his obsession with Daphne obvious to anyone who paid even the slightest bit of attention.

"I see. Forgive me, my lord, but I'm afraid I do not understand."

"I do not like you, Mr. Stanley. I think you weak and simpering ... a milksop still latched onto his mother's teat."

He'd flinched, but said nothing, as he'd been well aware that Hartmoor thought these things of him. He might have said he found the earl to be crass and ill-mannered, that he was a conscienceless beast who'd preyed upon his Daphne in her hour of need, and that he wasn't fit to lick the soles of her boots ... but he refrained. Firstly, because the man was built like an oak tree and while Robert wasn't a small man he also was not daft enough to think he could survive being on the other end of Hartmoor's fists. Secondly, because he was still curious about why the man had come to him without provocation.

"But," the earl added. "You are as honorable a man as any I've ever known. You come from a good family and you have wealth, which means you can provide well for a wife. Most of all, you love Daphne. Do you not?"

Now more confused than ever, Robert hadn't known how to respond to the backhanded compliments other than to say, "Well, yes, of course."

Hartmoor had studied him in silence for a while, his gaze both assessing and intimidating. Had he been born small of stature, he would still seem a force to be reckoned with. That searing stare alone was enough to make any man feel two inches tall.

"You should give Daphne a bit more time … a few weeks, perhaps. Then, with me out of the way, you will be free to pursue her again. Ask her to marry you, beg her if you must."

Robert had frowned, his mind spinning as he'd tried to make sense of it all. This man had taken Daphne as a lover, ruining her in the eyes of society before casting her aside. Then, he'd followed her to London and publicly made her his mistress. Despite all that, the woman still seemed to care for him. Robert would be willing to bet she'd have Hartmoor as her husband despite all that.

It was obvious Hartmoor was mad for her. So, what was stopping him from putting them both out of their misery and marrying her himself?

"The last time we spoke, you made yourself quite clear where Daphne is concerned," he managed. "I did not miss your warning. You wanted her for yourself and did not appreciate my interference. Why the sudden change of mind?"

"It does not matter why. What matters is that I am leaving and I want her taken care of. Her reputation is in tatters due to the scandal her brother caused. Her attachment to me has only made matters worse. You can make her respectable again, and I know you won't abuse or neglect her."

"Of course not ... I love her. I have since I was a boy, and nothing that has happened can change that."

It had been shocking to find out that Daphne's brother had been getting away with raping the debutantes of the *ton* for years with no one the wiser. Many in their social circles would shun her now that he'd been put on trial, convicted, and executed for his crimes. That she had engaged in an illicit affair with the earl only thickened the dark cloud of scandal hanging over her head.

But, none of those things had been enough to put him off. His love for Daphne had gone deeper than any scandal or gossip, and he wanted nothing more than to be the one to save her from a life of loneliness and scorn.

And so, he had agreed to try his damnedest to make Daphne his once she'd had time to mourn the loss of both the earl and her brother —who had been executed just this morning after a lengthy trial. The wait had been easy enough—he'd been waiting for what seemed like his entire life to have her. He'd practiced what he would say, had his valet polish the ring for the umpteenth time to ensure it looked its best when he presented it to her. He'd even worn his best navy blue coat, wanting to cut a dashing figure for what would prove the most momentous day of his life.

In the end, he had not been able to go through with it.

Arriving at Fairchild House prepared to drop to one knee and plead his case, Robert had been ushered into the drawing room to find her standing before the hearth. She'd turned to face him, giving him his first glimpse of her lovely face in weeks. She'd been so much like the girl he'd always loved ... yet everything about her had changed. In that moment, Robert had seen for the first time what he'd refused to understand before.

He had lost her.

He could not pinpoint exactly when, but somewhere between letting her leave Suffolk and finding her again, he had given up his chance at happiness with her. Deep in the prisms of her dark blue eyes, Robert had seen her misery over Hartmoor, as well as her longing.

Yes, he'd wanted to be the gallant knight riding in to save her from a life of loneliness. And, he might have won her hand had he done what the earl suggested and proposed marriage. Now that Hartmoor had set her aside, she might decide to settle for a comfortable life with him.

But, Daphne was too good for that. She was too beautiful, fiery, and smart to settle for anything less than the passionate love she deserved. The sort of love she'd had with Lord Adam Callahan.

So, instead of proposing to her, he had suggested she try one last time to convince Hartmoor to take her with him to Scotland. He told her he still loved her, and would be willing to marry her if it was what she wanted. But, he'd been very clear that he understood she was in love with the earl, not him, and he wanted her to be happy.

That had led to this—standing on the side of the road, watching as Hartmoor drove away with the love of his life.

The earl had been right about him. He was a spineless, weak, mama's boy, unable to do anything other than watch with stinging eyes as Daphne ran off with one of England's most notorious rake-hells. To make matters worse, he'd even suggested that they stop off in Gretna Green on their way home. Within hours she would become the Countess of Hartmoor, putting her out of his reach for good.

"Fucking wonderful," he muttered, trudging back to his barouche.

His black bays stomped and snorted with impatience, undoubtedly tired of standing about and watching him brood. But, where was he to go? He had his suite of rooms in London, the rent paid up for several more weeks. His valet remained there, along with many of his things. Going back there was the last thing he wanted to do, for once he arrived he would have to face his man and explain that he'd come home without a fiancée. The pitying gaze of Felix as he took the ring to store it in the safe among his other valuables would only make him feel worse.

He supposed he could have dinner at his club, but he would surely be recognized by old school friends or some such. Knowing he would not be fit company, he ruled that out, along with the half dozen invitations resting on his desk.

Climbing up into his equipage and taking hold of the ribbons, he turned back toward London. He gave the horses their head, his mind wandering as they dragged him back toward Town. He was unsure what he would do once he got there, but could not very well stand about woolgathering on the side of the road. Or, maybe he could.

Maybe he could have stood there until he dropped dead.

It would kill Mother.

The thought always sprung forth the instant he considered that anything dangerous might befall him. He should not walk in the rain despite liking the way it felt on his skin, because he might grow ill and die, and it would kill his mother. He ought not drive his phaeton too fast, because he might crash it and break his neck, and of course it would kill his mother.

He should not put a pistol in his mouth and pull the trigger, succumbing to this swift, sudden, and painful loneliness opening in the depths of his soul … because it would kill his mother.

So, he drove at a reasonable pace and kept an eye out for rain clouds and uneven spots in the road, the careful son as always. Not that she would know the difference. When he had insisted on coming to London to pursue Daphne, she had remained in Suffolk with his father.

After a while, he came to a fork in the road. Pulling up on the ribbons, he wondered where the other path might lead. London and his empty West End flat loomed straight ahead. Wrinkling his nose, he veered right, deciding to avoid Town for at least a few hours more. Even if this road led him nowhere interesting, a nice, long ride would help him clear his head.

About half an hour later, he came upon a public house. It was not one he'd ever frequented, but from the outside it appeared much like any other he'd ever seen. Its edifice was plain but sturdy, its courtyard crawling with horses and conveyances coming and going. Smoke huffing from the chimney promised a warm fire, and if Robert was not mistaken, the inside would offer spirits in which to drown his sorrows.

Perfect.

He pulled into the yard, slowing his barouche behind a coach stopping in to rest its horses. From the looks of the driver—whose boots were caked with mud, and whose cape held a heavy layer of dust—it had stopped in the midst of a long journey.

"Afternoon, me lord!" a stable boy in filthy trousers and a threadbare coat called out as he approached. "I'll 'ave your beasts groomed and fed in a blink!"

Leaping down, Robert retrieved his purse from the breast pocket of his coat. Laying a shilling in the boy's dirt-smudged hand, he then proceeded toward the open front door.

"Take your time. I intend to be here for a while."

"Aye, me lord!"

Robert ducked past a man toting a valise, glancing up at the wooden sign hanging over the door.

"The White Cock," he murmured, interpreting the white rooster emblazoned across wooden signage. "Charming."

He did not care about the place's name—only that no one here would know him, and he could find oblivion in liquid form. A few heads turned as he strode toward the rough, wooden bar, but he ignored them, used to such. The men likely noted his fine clothes and recognized him as nobility, while the few scandalously dressed women lounging about on laps and against the wall wondered how much blunt they could milk out of him. Apparently, his expression indicated that he held no interest, because none approached him.

"Well, ain't you a sight," said the woman behind the counter, lips curved into an amused smirk as she eyed him.

Short and rotund, she wore a gown far too small to contain her oversized bosom. The apron tied about her waist had seen better days. A worn kerchief tied stringy, brown hair back from her round face, though a few stray strands clung to her forehead, damp with sweat.

"Good afternoon," he murmured, sinking onto one of the stools pushed up to the counter.

She laughed, the sound thick and hearty, her large bosom heaving with each chuckle and snort. "We're a humble establishment your Lordship. No need for your airs and manners around here. Say what you want an' I'll fetch it for you."

With a sigh, Robert went back into his purse. "Whisky … the best you have."

"Nothin' to eat?"

He hadn't eaten breakfast, but found himself without an appetite.

"No, th-"

He gritted his teeth around the 'thank you' and held it in. This woman would not appreciate it, anyway.

"Whisky, comin' right up."

She bustled away and returned a moment later with a pint-sized bottle. It smelled bloody fantastic when she uncorked it and poured a healthy amount into a clean glass. Glancing down the counter at the other men seated with their drinks, he noted that his was the cleanest tumbler to be found. He supposed his appearance and airs had earned him that, despite her insistence otherwise.

"Leave the bottle," he said, before she could take it away.

She held her hand out to him, accepting his payment. After retrieving a purse from within the bodice of her overstretched gown, she stashed the coins inside and nestled the money safely between her breasts.

"Shout if you've a need," she said before moving on to another patron.

He was certain the pint would keep him occupied for a while. Lifting the tumbler, he took a swallow—one so substantial it burned going down, making his eyes water. He gritted his teeth and bore the discomfort, knowing there would be numbness on the other side.

And while he sat here feeling as if someone had shoved a fireplace poker down his throat and pulled his heart out through his mouth, it was the best he could hope for.

He finished off the first measure far too fast, his head already spinning as he poured another. He took his time with this one, gazing around the taproom as the warmth of the whisky suffused through his body. The occupants ranged from shabby to well-dressed, a common enough occurrence in a posting inn so close to London. However, the two ladies he spotted seated at a table near the large hearth drew his eye, striking him as out of place.

Both finely clothed in carriage dresses, cloaks, hats, and gloves, they were accompanied by a lone servant. The man sat eying the occupants of the room as if ready to strike out at anyone who thought to accost either of the women under his protection.

Robert might not have stared for long if not for the sudden recognition that dawned on him as his gaze fell on one of the two. Funnily enough, it was not the most attractive of the two who achieved his notice. Another man might not have noticed the woman seated across from the ravishing blonde.

But this particular woman seemed to require closer inspection every time Robert laid eyes upon her, and now proved no exception.

Lady Cassandra Lane would be considered plain in comparison to the *ton*'s other eligible chits. A fair complexion seemed washed out by red hair masquerading as blond—strawberry, his mother would have called it. The shade did not have the vibrant luster of Daphne's auburn, or her companion's gold, falling into some muddle between the two. A light smatter of freckles lent a bit of girlishness to a face composed of sharp lines and angles.

He knew her to be a spinster firmly on the shelf. If she hadn't been, then the recent scandal embroiling her and several other young women would have placed her into the ranks of the ineligible.

He wasn't certain what it was about her that gained his notice. Perhaps it had something to do with the sullen expression she wore, and the fact that he'd never seen her smile. It could have something to do with the unflinching way she'd faced public scrutiny through what might be one of the beau monde's most scandalizing trials. Whatever the case, Robert found his curiosity about her reaching its peak.

Predictably, she perked up a bit, tensing as if she felt eyes upon her. A natural reaction to being watched, for certain. But, as she turned her head, eyes darting as if to ferret out the person watching her, Robert found himself unable to breathe. He sat as still as death and waited for her to find him.

That breath left him in a rush when her unsettling stare fell upon him and held. There, he found her hidden beauty—a pair of eyes in the most puzzling shade of pale blue. Much lighter than his own eyes, they seemed almost gray at times. Not that he'd spent much time staring into them, as the woman almost always kept them cast down as if loath to look upon anyone, or have anyone look at her. He'd bumped into her once at a soirée, and she'd had no choice but to look up at him while murmuring an apology.

They were mystifying, those eyes, like a clear stream one could see straight through. Yet for all their clarity, he still could not quite puzzle her out. They were as mysterious and shuttered as her expressionless face.

Robert blinked when she looked away, turning to speak to her companion. The hairs on the back of his arms stood on end when the blond woman glanced at him before turning back to Cassandra. The two exchanged words, and he held no delusions about the subject of their conversation.

Him.

The prickling sensation increased as Cassandra stood with a few last words to her friend. Then, to his utter shock, she turned and began to cross the taproom toward him.

WHAT THE DEVIL am I doing here?

The thought flitted through Cassandra's mind for the umpteenth time, yet she couldn't force herself to rise from her chair and vacate the taproom. Coming here had been a mistake, she realized that now. Millicent had insisted she was ready for this, yet her roiling belly and sweating palms proved otherwise.

"Cass," her friend snapped, pulling her out of her reverie.

She blinked and glanced up at Millicent, who might be one of the most beautiful women she'd ever seen. Why a diamond of the first water would want to keep company with a dowdy spinster like her was beyond Cassandra. The Ravishing Widow Dane, they called her. She'd been one of the most coveted debutantes upon her coming out, but had wed a baron old enough to be her father. Fortunately for Millicent, her husband had died within a few short years of their union and she'd been set free. Now, she boasted a fine London townhome and a tidy sum of money left to her by her deceased husband. She'd borne him no children, the lucky thing, and had no responsibility to anyone other than herself. It showed in her lifestyle, this woman who had gone unwed for years, despite boasting a slew of admirers from here to Scotland who would have given their two front teeth to call her theirs.

"I see so much of myself in you," the widow had said upon approaching her and offering friendship.

She'd been one of the only people to show Cassandra kindness following the scandal that had ruined her reputation. Since then, Millicent had given her far more than companionship, and she was grateful for all that the other woman had taught her.

That was why she was here … because Millicent had insisted she must take this final step to be free of the demons of her past. She had agreed to this, realizing she might never find the strength to move on with her life otherwise. The past several years had passed her by in a blur, as she'd walked about beneath a cloud of constant rage, despair, and fear. She didn't want to feel that way anymore, so had leaped at the chance to free herself from it.

"Yes?" she replied, finding her voice after a long pause.

"Are you certain about this?"

Millicent did not appear annoyed at her for woolgathering, or for her reluctance. Concern creased her brow, her gaze penetrating Cassandra and probing deep.

"Of course," she stated, her words coming out clipped. "I just haven't seen the right man yet. You were the one who insisted my selection would be crucial to ensuring success."

"Naturally," her friend agreed. "What about him?"

She followed Millicent's gaze to the rather plain-looking man who had just entered the taproom. He did not look as if he stood quite as high on the social ladder as Cassandra, but that was not altogether a bad thing. She could see why her friend had suggested him: his unassuming presence, average stature, and well-tailored but plain clothing. He would be forgettable, but also seemed nonthreatening. The sort of man she could use for her own ends and forget.

Still . . .

"He is too short," she grumbled, glancing down at the supper she had been picking at for the past quarter of an hour.

She had not eaten all day, and the offerings on her plate smelled heavenly. But her stomach churned and she felt as if swallowing one bite would make her sick.

Millicent snorted. "My dear, perhaps I ought to have warned you to lower your standards in that regard. If you use a man's height against him we may never find the right one."

Cassandra rolled her eyes, but had to admit that her friend was right. She'd been convinced for quite some time that God had played a cruel joke while creating her. Why else would he make her so plain to look at, then give her such substantial height—as if wanting to make her stick out in a crowd so everyone could stare and notice how unremarkable the rest of her was?

Still, it was her decision, and on this she would not be moved.

"I'd like him to at least stand tall enough for me to look him in the eye," she argued

Millicent sighed. "Very well. What about that one?"

She followed the discreet point of Millicent's finger to the tall man making his way toward the stairs. She wrinkled her nose while raking her gaze over the man's near emaciated form. While she could see he might not be strong enough to harm her, his spindly limbs proved offputting.

"Too thin."

"Very well. Hmm ... oh, he looks charming."

"Millie, he's clearly a servant."

"When did you become a snob?"

She had never been one despite her high birth, but wouldn't admit her true reason for turning her nose up at a servant. Men who worked for a living were always stronger than those who didn't—which meant if she needed to fight him off she'd stand no chance.

"Not him, I said."

Her friend heaved an exasperated sigh. "Cass, you must choose someone, darling."

"I know that," she snapped.

Still, as she gazed about the taproom, she found not one man who would meet her needs. Or, maybe they would, but she could conjure no desire to approach them.

And then, she saw him.

Seated at the counter with a pint of spirits and half-filled tumbler in front of him, he was staring right back at her. As if he'd been looking at her already.

Their eyes met, gazes holding as Cassandra wondered how long he'd been watching her. She was not accustomed to being the object of a man's scrutiny—especially one who looked like the Honourable Mr. Robert Stanley.

It was a wonder she had not seen him sooner, as he was the sort of man who drew notice. She might have been too anxious to pay him any mind, or he'd entered when she'd had her back turned. Whatever the reason, there was no escaping it now—the essential *thing* about Robert Stanley that drew the eye.

To call him beautiful would be an insult, and to compare him to an angel would be offensive to God himself. He was tall—at least an inch taller than her—with a form that was not too slender or too wide. The fit of his clothes flaunted broad shoulders and a proportional chest tapering into a trim waist. His limbs displayed the athleticism of a man accustomed to country life—but he was not so large as to be intimidating.

His valet might have styled the array of pale blond curls that morning, but the wind had made a mess of them. But, even the tousled strands were alluring, more artful in their disarray than unkempt. His face was the sort that inspired a painter's brush—pretty yet still masculine, his angular jaw complemented by full lips, an aquiline nose, and eyebrows so perfectly shaped women everywhere must envy him.

The sight of him might have caused other women to swoon, blush, or giggle. But, Cassandra was not like other women and hadn't been for some years now. In truth, the sight of him filled her with heat composed of equal parts primal attraction and rage.

Attraction, because ... well, one had only to look at him to explain that visceral phenomenon. Not hard to determine why contemplating what he looked like under his clothes made that elusive warmth spark deep inside her.

Rage, because men of his sort never ceased to stoke that emotion in her. Handsome, titled, privileged, overindulged. Lords and their sons who thought they could do whatever they wanted, with and to whomever they wished, simply because they'd been born with cocks and all the rights she'd ever been denied. She endured their presence all around her—in the park where she walked, at the occasional soiree, at her favorite coffee house, in the museums and shops she frequented.

They disgusted her, the lot of them, the emotion as acute as it had been from the moment Lord Bertram Fairchild's attentions toward her had changed from romantic and gallant to nefarious and painful.

She gritted her teeth so hard they ached, as the sensations of anger and lust warred inside her. Heat flushed the back of her neck and her hands itched to strike him, hurt him, make him bleed. Simultaneously, an incessant tingle began between her legs, originating from the bud of her clit. Her mouth watered from the desire to sink her teeth into his neck until he writhed and screamed beneath her.

Making matters worse was the way he stared at her—as if he wanted to peel back her brittle layers and expose the weakest parts of her. As if he wanted something from her she was not willing to give.

This time would be different. Cassandra resolved to prove to herself that she wasn't the same weak girl she had been upon losing her innocence in the most base and brutal of ways. She was in control, and no man—especially not the insultingly beautiful Robert Stanley—would get the best of her ever again.

Turning back to Millicent, she smiled. "Him."

She inclined her head just enough for her friend to know whom she referred to. Millicent's took Robert in from the corner of her eye.

Then, her brows lifted, an expression of shock flitting across her face.

"Robert Stanley?" he whispered. "Well … that is surprising."

Cassandra stiffened, her hackles rising so fast she could barely think before she'd lashed out. "What is that supposed to mean?"

That Robert was too handsome to even think of dallying with her? That she stood no chance of getting what she wanted from him? That she'd aimed too high and ought to reconsider the servant?

Millicent's hand came over hers and the other woman gave her a soft smile. "Only that I hardly expected you to choose a peer. Avoiding them was quite the point of us coming here … aside from the need for discretion."

She deflated, ashamed of herself for her reaction. Of course Millicent hadn't meant anything by her remark. The woman had never been anything but kind and understanding. Besides, the stories of her past proved nothing if not that they were very much alike despite the difference in their appearances. No one understood her like her friend.

Closing her eyes, she took a deep breath. "Of course, I'm sorry. Do you think it's a terrible choice?"

"No, actually. If it were any other man of privilege … perhaps. But Mr. Stanley is known for his charm and kindness. There isn't a soul who's disliked him after coming to know him. I've never heard any whispers of him acting in an ungentlemanly way toward anyone … and you know I'd have heard if there were anything of note."

That was true. Millicent's popularity ensured she kept a constant finger upon the pulse of the *ton*. She was never without news of the latest gossip and kept her share of salacious secrets, unless it served her to reveal them.

Still, she wasn't entirely convinced of Robert Stanley's goodness. She'd only known one man who would have done anything for her without ulterior motive. But then, a girl's father could almost always be counted upon to treat her well.

Robert couldn't be as pure and good as the stories claimed; and if she hadn't already decided he would serve for her own purposes, she might have set out to prove it. However, it did not matter if he were as pure as Christ, or as evil as Lucifer … not when she intended for this night to be the one and only time she ever spent in extended company with him.

"Very well," Cassandra murmured. "It's him, then."

Millicent folded her hands before her and nodded. "I will not insult you by asking whether you are certain, for I know that you are. I will simply wish you luck and remind you of what I have taught you. You are in control, and Peter and I will be here if you have a need."

Her gaze flitted to the large footman seated beside Millicent. She'd quite forgotten Peter in all this, but the man was good at being unassuming when he needed to be, and now proved no exception. He was one of the few men of large stature who did not make her uneasy—mainly because he'd been the one to teach her how to defend herself with a knife as well as a pistol. Millicent's servant and lover seemed nice enough, and he'd never done anything to hurt her outside their sparring sessions.

Her friend had offered his services as a protector of sorts for the night—just in case. That he would be near at hand eased a bit of the tension winding her belly into a knot.

"Thank you," she replied, before standing from her chair.

If she did not act now, she might lose her nerve. Millicent said nothing, freeing her to make her sojourn across the room toward the man who had continued staring at her through their conversation.

He looked shocked as she approached, those bright blue eyes of his widening as if in a panic. That brought a little smirk to her face as she realized she had caught him off guard. Of course he hadn't expected her to so boldly approach him, even after he'd stared at her for so long.

You had better get used to it, Robert ... I am not the sort of woman to simper and recoil from your sort.

To prove it to herself as well as him, she made her way to the stool right beside him and sank down onto it. Facing him with an assessing stare, she arched one eyebrow and stared him down.

"G-good evening, Lady Cassandra," he stammered, obviously caught off guard.

From across the room, she hadn't been able to see how haggard he looked, but now the evidence of a hellish day showed itself upon his face. But, even with his mouth tight and drawn, eyes bloodshot with the hint of dark circles underneath, he was infuriatingly handsome. The urge to slap his smooth cheek and watch it blossom with a crimson stain overwhelmed her, but she refrained. She wouldn't hurt him ... yet.

"Mr. Stanley," she replied. "What are you drinking? Whisky?"

He gazed down at his tumbler, then back up at her with a slow blink. His eyes began to show the glassiness of a man well on his way to being foxed.

"Yes."

"Oh, good ... I love whisky."

If at all possible, his eyes widened even more when she pried the tumbler out of his grasp before lifting it to her own lips. She held his gaze while taking a sip, enjoying the rich flavor of the whisky as well as its sting going down. Amusement curved her mouth as she set the glass back down on the counter. It was so delicious, toying with him before they'd even really begun. She began to feel akin to a predator stalking a helpless doe ... and how very doe-like Robert was, all wide eyes and parted lips, his breath hitching a bit as she edged closer to him.

"Now, then," she said. "I'd like to discuss something with you, Mr. Stanley ... a proposition of sorts."

Curiosity overtook his features, and he picked up his glass once more. "A ... a proposition?"

He frowned, and she could practically hear the wheels turning in his head as he tried to puzzle out what she could be talking about. They'd been formally introduced years ago, but had only a passing acquaintance of one another. As a young debutante, men like him had often intimidated her. That had been before Bertram, of course. After the horrific incident that had changed her life, she had avoided them out of a sense of preservation.

They'd never exchanged words outside of mere pleasantries, so of course she must seem quite mad to approach him this way. That did not matter to her. All she cared about was convincing him to give her what she wanted—which should not be difficult. It was appalling how easily a man could be led about by his prick. Millicent had taught her that.

"Yes," she replied. "I will not mince words with you. There is a room upstairs that I have rented for the entire night."

Curiosity morphed into shock once more, and he looked as if he'd tip off his stool and swoon in a dead faint.

"I beg your pardon?"

Pursing her lips, she bit back her annoyance, deciding that berating him so early in their conversation would not work in her favor.

"An upper room. I've rented one."

He shook his head and frowned as if trying to decide whether this could truly be happening. "Lady Cassandra, I must insist you allow me to escort you out of this place. A woman of your breeding could not know—"

"I know very well what those rooms are for," she interjected.

At one time, that knowledge would have shocked her, and she'd have never even thought of looking in the direction of that staircase.

Now, she was far wiser in the ways of the world.

Robert cleared his throat. "I see."

"I'm not certain you do, so allow me to make this clear to you. The room is secured, and all I require now is someone to accompany me upstairs."

This time, she felt certain he might suffer an apoplexy when he flushed from his neck to the roots of his hair. He opened his mouth, then closed it, looking very much like a fish out of water. A pretty fish with perfect eyebrows and pouting lips, but a fish nonetheless.

Cassandra helped herself to more of his whisky—this time straight from the bottle—while she waited for him to find his voice. After a moment of gaping and sputtering, he finally managed to respond.

"My lady, I don't think … surely you cannot mean …"

Corking the whisky bottle, she looked him in the eye and delivered the words that would either kill him off altogether or make him hers.

"I do mean it, Mr. Stanley. I want to take you upstairs and fuck you."

CHAPTER 2

She could have knocked Robert over with a feather, he was so shocked by her declaration. Had she left it at 'the room is rented, and all I require now is someone to accompany me upstairs', he might have convinced himself she couldn't mean what he assumed.

However, she'd driven it home with frank—albeit crass—speech.

I want to take you upstairs and fuck you.

His blood heated at the way the words fell from her mouth, particularly the way her voice had cradled the word 'fuck'. In her cultured tones it should have sounded odd. Instead, it struck a chord, some primitive part of him reacting to the sound of that monosyllabic word.

On top of that had been her odd phrasing. He'd had whores whisper all manner of filth into his ear, and not one of them had ever declared that she would be the one doing the fucking. It was always 'fuck me', 'take me'. Despite knowing that if he accepted her offer, he would be the one inside her, her wording left him wondering what her offer might entail otherwise.

He would have assumed a lady would refer to it as intercourse, or congress, or even attached some flowery connotation by saying 'make love'. But, he realized a well-born lady would never refer to it at all, let alone accost a man this way. Even so, he'd always known there was something about Cassandra that set her apart, something that had caught his attention during the trial of Lord Bertram Fairchild.

And, damn it all if he wasn't more curious about her now than ever, wanting to delve deeper and find out just what that 'something' was.

"Well?" she prodded when he did not respond.

He blinked, glancing up at her from his whisky. This close, the impact of her eyes was even more potent. He'd never looked into them from such a close vantage point and could now see why they appeared gray from a distance. Striations of the color spread out from her pupil, before fading into blue on the outer edges, as if storm clouds had gathered over a dreary sky. But, there was nothing drab about them. Quite remarkable, those eyes.

Clearing his throat for what felt like the hundredth time, he forced himself to hold her gaze. "Well, I … I'm really quite flattered …"

"Don't be," she said, that sharp voice of hers piercing him like the edge of a knife. "I want someone in my bed for the night. Any other man in this room will do, but as we are already acquainted I found approaching you more pleasing than any other option."

His face burned from the insult, but once the initial shock of it faded, a new thought sprang forth in his mind. That any man would do rang false. He'd watched her scan the room, her gaze falling on several other men before landing on him. That they were familiar actually increased the chances of her reputation taking a blow from this encounter, which ought to be reason enough for her to stay away.

There was a reason she had chosen him, and he became overwhelmed by the desire to discover what it was.

"I do not believe that any other man would do. You specifically chose me. Why?"

A brief flicker of surprise showed upon her face, before she replaced it with the previous mask of apathy she'd been wearing through their conversation. So, she was not quite as confident as she appeared.

"Does it matter why? I am offering you a single night with me, no questions asked, no demands to be made of you afterward. Most men would not think twice about accepting."

Most men of their acquaintance would be as shocked as him by such boldness from any woman, let alone a prim, reserved spinster such as Lady Cassandra Lane. He chose not to point that out, and instead blurted the next burning question weighing upon his mind.

"Why are you doing this, my lady?" he asked, keeping his voice low so they were not overheard. "You are a lovely young woman, and had you approached someone else—someone with no scruples or morals—he might have taken advantage of you ... it could end badly."

She scoffed, rolling her eyes in annoyance. "Spare me your gentlemanly concern, as well as your flatteries. I am five-and-twenty years of age, and besides that we both know I now lack the pristine reputation of some virginal debutante. We also know I am not 'lovely'. So, you may keep your false words behind your teeth where they belong and stop speaking to me as if I'm some dimwitted girl incapable of thinking for herself. I wish to fuck you, and I wish to do it now. You need not worry that you must behave with honor or spare my girlish sensibilities, as I have none. Think of this as a purely transactional encounter, one that ends the moment you've spent. It is no different from an agreement you'd make with any Haymarket strumpet, only I do not want or need your coin."

Robert finished off the whisky in his glass and refilled it, certain he'd need all the fortification he could get when dealing with Cassandra. A dozen arguments against her proposition rattled about in his mind ... That she might have a sullied reputation, but it was no fault of her own ... That he still saw her as a lady above reproach and wished to respect her as such ... That while she might be called plain by others, he found her to be far more intriguing than some other whey-faced debutante ... That even as they discussed a transactional agreement, he could not bring himself to compare her to a whore.

She seemed to think him still resistant, because she spoke again while he went about draining yet another tumbler of whisky.

"As for why I am doing this … I want something that I've been taught I ought not desire. Unlike a man, I cannot go walking Covent Garden to find what I need, nor can I hire a mistress or some such. There is only this … me choosing the man I want with a mutual understanding of what it will entail."

Robert supposed that when she put it that way, he could respect her motives. Women experienced desires just like men; but whereas those of his sex were allowed—and even encouraged—to pursue those needs, a woman's reputation could be destroyed for similar behavior. And Lady Cassandra's reputation could not afford another blow. In truth, he could think of no reason to refuse her.

Daphne.

Her face flashed through his mind, as it always did whenever he thought of things like passion or desire. Consorting with whores had been one thing, but he'd never allowed himself to be with any woman outside such encounters. He'd never courted anyone else, never so much as kissed another woman's lips in all the years he'd spent pining after Daphne.

Daphne belongs to Hartmoor now.

The reminder doused him like a bucket of frigid water, chilling him and settling a heavy weight in his middle. What was there for him to hope for now? What cause did he have for saving any part of himself, when Daphne might be speaking her vows to another man over the blacksmith's anvil as they spoke?

Suddenly, he wanted her in a way he hadn't at the start of their conversation. He wanted what she offered, if for no other reason than the prospect of losing himself in something else. Even if it were only for one night. Even if the woman in question had never displayed interest in him. Even if she was the last woman in the world he would ever have considered doing this with.

He bolstered himself with another sip of whisky, and before could lose his nerve said, "I accept."

Something like relief seemed to soften her features, a bit of the tension in her back and shoulders easing. "Very well. Before we adjourn upstairs, there are a few things you need to understand and agree to. I will have rules, and you must follow them if you want the night to end well for you."

His eyebrows shot up as he found himself taken aback yet again. This woman really was unlike any he'd ever encountered. Instead of being put off by her candor, he found it refreshing. After all the time he'd spent trying to woo Daphne with limited success and then heartbreak, he could appreciate a forthright lady. He didn't think he would have to worry about being strung along or given hope where there was none. They would go upstairs and fuck. That would be the end of it.

"All right," he said. "What rules?"

"First, you are to be bound by your wrists to the bed," she stated as if remarking upon the weather. "Second, you are to follow my lead. There will be no attempts from you at dominating the encounter or ordering me about."

It was a good thing he'd already swallowed his whisky, or he might have choked. She wanted him to allow her to tie him up and lay there while she ...

Now her assertion that she would fuck him made sense.

"I see. I suppose I can agree to that, though I typically prefer to be a bit more ... active, when I'm with a woman."

Her gaze dropped to his mouth and lingered there as she inched closer, just close enough that he could detect the scent of cloves and oranges—a fragrance he might not have found feminine until he registered it on her. It made his cock twitch in his breeches.

"I promise you will not regret it," she whispered, her voice lowering and taking on a husky quality that grew his cock to half-mast. It made him wonder how she'd sound moaning her pleasure, whispering his name.

What the devil was she doing to him? It had been some time since he'd had such a strong reaction to a woman. Not since ...

You will not think about her. Not tonight. You came here to forget, and that is what you will do.

"Any other rules for me to observe?"

It seemed absurd—rules regarding intercourse. Yet, he knew without being told that she'd rescind the offer if he didn't agree to them.

"Only that Peter there will remain outside the door … for my protection. I am certain you understand."

He followed her gaze to the large man who had accompanied Cassandra and her friend, and found the man watching them. He had no doubt the chap would break him in half if he so much as sneezed in Cassandra's direction. As much as Robert wanted to balk at the idea of him lurking outside the room, he supposed he could understand why she'd want protection.

The idea put a bitter taste in his mouth, made all the more sour by the knowledge that she'd been hurt once before. If he did nothing else tonight, he would make sure she enjoyed it.

"Understood," he agreed.

She nodded. "Very well. I will go up first with Peter. Wait a few moments, then follow."

Without giving him a chance to reply, she swiveled with a swish of her skirts and bounded toward the shadowed staircase with long, graceful strides. Peter followed at a discreet distance.

Robert remained for a long while, the effects of the whisky causing his head to swim, though his mind raced with surprising clarity. His decision to bed a lady in a roadside public house did not fit with his usual gentlemanly ideals. He might come to regret it.

As he pushed aside the tumbler in favor of finishing his spirits straight from the bottle, he pushed that thought aside. Caution and gallantry had gotten him nowhere with Daphne, so what use were they? Tonight, at least, he could forget the pain of his loss.

What did he have to lose?

CASSANDRA PACED AWAY from the small hearth, which Peter had lit before going to stand guard in the corridor. He would remain out there until she emerged, unless she cried out for help—at which time he would charge in, prepared to strangle her bedmate to death. She hardly thought she'd need to call on him, given Robert's amiable nature, which ought to have relieved her.

However, she was more anxious than ever, her hands sweating and shaking as she paced the cramped but clean chamber.

She only felt this way because she stood so close to her goal, and Millicent had assured her being nervous was normal. But, was she supposed to feel as if she might be ill, or swoon in a dead faint? Despite the frigid weather outside, this room emitted a stifling heat, causing her to snatch off her cloak and toss it aside.

That he hadn't refused her outright had been a relief, which helped ease a bit of her tension. One part of her mission—getting a man to agree to spend the night with her—had been accomplished. Now, she must get through the rest. She must touch him and taste him and ... take him inside her body.

She closed her mouth, bile rising to the back of her throat at the thought. Then, she took a few deep breaths and attempted to calm her racing pulse.

She could do this. Millicent had urged her to try pleasuring herself first, so she'd know what she liked best. She'd even given Cassandra a box of implements she had called 'dildos'; phallic shaped things made of lacquered wood, ivory, jade, and glass. She'd made use of the small ones first, unable to even look at the larger without succumbing to panic. Once she'd learned to use them and found she enjoyed it, she'd moved on to the larger ones and liked them even more.

Millicent had told her to keep them, and so she had—and often used her favorite, the ivory affair with a particularly large tip. So, it was not that she couldn't abide penetration. It more to do with the thing going inside her belonging to a flesh and blood man.

Her heart kicked up its rhythm, pounding against her breastbone as she braced her hand against the wall and doubled over. She felt as if the wind had been knocked from her as memories came unbidden to her mind—recollections of Bertram pinning her with his weight, the brutal invasion of him battering his way through her.

She heaved, but nothing came forth, her body convulsing and her stomach twisting as if wrung like a dishrag.

It is over and behind you ... it has been five years. You can get through this ... you can move on with your life.

For so long she had lived in a state of perpetual anger and fear. She'd thought helping Bertram's other victims take him down would help, that seeing him tried, found guilty, and hanged would help her sleep easier at night. As of this morning, her assailant no longer drew breath, giving her a bit more peace of mind. At least she knew he could never hurt another woman again.

Now she must face the thing that had terrified her since the day Bertram had raped her. As a young, idealistic debutante, she had listened to her elder sisters whisper about what went on in the marriage bed and experienced excitement. She'd thought she would marry someone kind, who would initiate her gently. Perhaps she would even enjoy it.

Bertram had robbed her of that, but Millicent had insisted all was not lost. She could learn ways around her fears and overcome them. She could know what it was like to be with someone of her own free will, and maintain control the entire time.

So far, so good, she thought as she straightened and turned just as the door to the room swung open.

Robert stood there. He had waited before following her, just as she'd asked. She supposed others might call him spineless, and perhaps he was, but a man who would bow to her wishes was exactly what she needed. As he closed the door and turned to face her, she couldn't help but wonder at his reasons for saying yes to her. Millicent had insisted that no man would turn down such an offer, yet Cassandra had noticed the way he'd seemed to give this much thought before agreeing. He'd seemed intent on finding out her reasons for making such an offer, as if he actually cared to know and understand.

Nonsense. Since when has any man other than Papa cared about your thoughts or feelings?

She'd once thought Bertram did, but of course that notion had turned out to be false. Robert would be no different.

He began striding toward her.

"That's far enough for now," she barked.

He paused mid-step, now halfway across the small room, brow furrowed. He seemed bewildered by her, but Millicent had told her not to worry about that. That he might not understand all her actions would add to the mystery, and once his prick was wrapped in her cunt, he'd cease caring.

She came away from the wall, clenching her hands behind her back so he wouldn't see how they trembled. Raking her gaze over him from head to toe, she could not avoid the realization that he might be the most beautiful man she'd ever laid eyes upon. If nothing else, her boldness had earned her a night with one of London's most coveted bachelors. If word of this ever got out, no one would believe it.

"Undress," she commanded, raising her chin.

Then, she backed toward the bed and sank down, bracing both hands on the edge of the mattress. He watched her while working at the knot of his cravat, his gaze far too assessing for someone who'd finished off an entire pint of whisky almost entirely on his own. But he was looking at her in that way of his again, making her skin tingle and her hackles rise.

Hurry up and undress so I can maul you.

Her mouth went dry at the sight of his throat. Such an innocuous body part, but it was long with tender cords begging to be bitten, and she could see the way his pulse hammered at the base of it. She bit her lip and forced herself to remain seated. That he could affect her this way proved a good sign. She would want him bad enough to go through with it, no matter her trepidation.

His coat came next, joining the neckcloth upon the floor. As he flicked open the buttons of his waistcoat she watched his hands, which were as perfect as the rest of him. Long-fingered and dexterous, they would probably be soft and nimble.

It was too bad she did not intend to let him touch her.

She didn't trust him enough for that, so she focused upon something other than his hands. Looking at them would only tempt her to make him use those fingers to toy with her nipples, or even stroke her clit.

No touching.

It was the one rule she meant to hold firm to, and tying him to the bed would ensure he did not forget himself and do it anyway.

Dropping the waistcoat, he then pushed his braces off his shoulders, letting them hang from his breeches while he worked at the buttons of his shirt. A fluttering sensation began low in her groin as he revealed a wide swath of his chest, the smooth skin sprinkled with downy-looking hair the same light blond shade as the strands on his head.

Then, he jerked the garment free of his breeches and pulled it off over his head, causing the sensation between her legs to go from a flutter to a steady pulse.

He was well-formed, his chest wide, his slender torso displaying light lines of definition, and that enticing trail of hair leading down to his fall. Against the fabric, she made out the intimidating outline of his cock.

The bile began rising again, but as he bent to attack his boots, he did not see her close her eyes and take a few deep breaths and work to calm herself. It was just a prick. It was no different than any of her dildos, with the exception of being softer and warmer. She thought of the way she could make herself spend using her favorite ivory phallus, and decided this would be like that. She would use him and get what she needed.

By the time he straightened to open his fall, she had recovered, sitting up straight and watching as he unveiled the rest. She clenched her thighs together at the revelation of his cock—a long thick organ already half-hard, rising up from a swirling nest of dark blond curls.

His bollocks hung heavy between two sculpted thighs, his calves sturdy and defined from riding.

Robert Stanley unclothed certainly proved a pleasant surprise.

He stared at her, raising his eyebrows as if to ask 'what now?'

Right. She was supposed to be maintaining control of this encounter. Rising to her feet, she gestured to the bed, where two short lengths of rope lay coiled near the headboard.

"Lie down."

She moved away from the bed as he approached, turning to face him as she reached for the fastenings of her gown. She had been intentional in selecting her clothing, opting to wear a carriage dress that buttoned down the front so she would not need help taking it off.

Robert's rapt gaze followed the motion of her fingers as she opened the garment to reveal that she wore nothing but a chemise underneath. She'd gone without stays or a petticoat, despite the cold weather, wanting to make this as easy on herself as possible. Fewer layers to remove meant less time undressing, and therefore a limited window of opportunity for her to back out.

The gown fell to the floor, and she kicked out of her slippers before reaching for the hem of her chemise. An audible intake of breath came from where Robert lay on the bed as she hiked the undergarment up over her hips, her belly, her breasts. A little smirk pulled at the corner of her mouth as she tossed the chemise aside to discover that he'd grown even harder, his prick now standing straight up from his groin, the tip glistening. His chest heaved as he stared at her, propped up on his elbows as he drank her in.

She might not be considered a diamond of the first water, but had known she had the necessary goods to make him want her. If the way his pupils widened to eat up the blue of his irises was any indication, her long, lithe form pleased him. She had to admit the way he looked at her heightened her need, causing her nipples to pebble as if he were touching them, and the slow throb took up an incessant cadence between her thighs.

After untying her garters and removing her stockings, she

approached the bed. His posture was all wrong, his upper body still propped up by his bent arms. Instead of telling him to correct it, she'd simply show him what she wanted. Best he learned early on that she meant to be the one in charge.

His breath rushed out on a shocked huff when she put a hand to the center of the chest and pushed, flattening him to his back. The awe in his gaze amused her, but even more telling was the way his cock twitched in reaction.

So, Mr. Stanley enjoyed being pushed around, did he? She might have missed it if she had not been watching him like a hawk, alert for any sign that he meant to jump up and try to take control of her.

Emboldened by that knowledge, she braced a knee on the bed and reached for one of her ropes. He didn't resist when she took hold of an arm, lifting it over his head and deftly tying him to the headboard. Millicent had taught her the proper knots for use in bondage, and she put that knowledge into practice now.

Climbing up over Robert, she straddled his torso and reached up for his other arm, lashing it to the wooden rails of the headboard as she had the other. Then, she took a moment to inspect her handiwork, making sure the bonds weren't too tight, but still properly knotted to keep him from slipping free.

Then, her gaze fell on his face and she found him watching her, a bit of curiosity in his expression. He opened his mouth as if to speak, but clamped it shut, seemed to think better of it, then tried again.

"Your hair," he murmured, his voice a near whisper.

She stiffened atop him, a thread of uncertainty winding through her as she reached up to touch her simple coiffure. The odd hue had been the bane of her existence her entire life, not blond enough or red enough to be called pretty, too strange not to draw notice.

"What about it?" she snapped.

He gave her a little smile, the motion blinding in its intensity, its beauty. He had probably disarmed countless women with that smile.

It made her want to slap it right off his face.

"Would you ... take it down?" At her bewildered expression, he cleared his throat, then added, "Please."

What game was this? Such an odd request, yet she supposed it couldn't hurt. He'd gone along with her rules thus far, so she supposed she could give him this one thing.

"Fine," she huffed, reaching up to begin plucking the pins from her hair, making it fall down her back in unsightly coils.

Despite her own distaste for the ridiculous hue God had cursed her with, Robert gazed up at her as if pleased, giving a little nod once she had finished and dropped the pins into a pile on the floor.

She leaned down and let the curtain of strands fall over one shoulder, the ends of it brushing his bare chest. His eyes grew heavy-lidded and he shifted beneath her.

"Happy?" she asked.

He raised his head, his breath tickling her cheek. "Lovely."

She reared back just before he could kiss her, his mouth brushing against hers. He made a little sound of frustration and tried again. This time, she rewarded him with a slap, her hand stinging as it made contact with his cheek. He gasped, his head whipping to the side as she settled her arse onto his chest. A flare of heat surged within her at the sight of her fingerprints marring his perfect complexion, a flush spreading over his face and neck as he looked back at her, eyes gone wide with shock.

She slammed her palm into his jaw, taking hold of his face with unrelenting fingers. "Let me make myself a bit clearer. You are not to do a thing unless I tell you to. If I want you to lay here like a corpse while I ride your cock to my own satisfaction, then that's what you will do. Do we understand one another?"

His harsh breaths hissed out between clenched teeth, and he looked as if he hovered somewhere between outrage and arousal. His cock must have won the battle, because despite his clenched jaw and flaring nostrils, he nodded his agreement.

"Good," she said, releasing his jaw and grabbing a fistful of his hair.

He grunted when she dipped her head and bit at his mouth,

catching his lower lip between her teeth, then groaned when she gave it a hard tug. Yanking harder on his hair, she tipped his head back and rose up onto her knees.

"You've such a pretty mouth, Robert," she said, shifting her body so that she straddled his head. "I can think of a far better use for it."

Robert took to her meaning without hesitation, opening his mouth as she lowered herself within reach of his tongue. His lips brushed against her quim, his sharp breaths tickling her curls. Then he flicked his tongue at her, aiming at the seam of her mons and seeking the delicate flesh hidden within. She drew in a swift breath and held it, her throat and chest burning as she waited for him to do it again, to heighten the little frisson of pleasure that single stroke had caused.

He lifted his gaze to hers, holding it without blinking as he went back for more, his tongue darting at her opening and then stroking upward, landing on her clitoris. Her breath came out on a low groan and she tightened her hold on his hair, surging her hips in a silent command for more.

Robert licked her again, the slow, burning lap sending a jolt of pleasure through her like a lightning strike. Then, with a ragged growl, he raised his head, pulling his hair out of her grasp and pressing his open mouth completely against her. Cassandra trembled, reaching out to take hold of the rough headboard as he began to devour her like a starving man, his mouth pulling and sucking, his tongue lashing the pulsing bud at her center with relentless insistence.

This … this was nothing like what she'd been led to expect. Millicent had explained the act to her, and it had sounded nice enough. She'd known she'd gain pleasure from it, probably enjoy it more than being filled by a cock.

But this wasn't simple pleasure. This was like falling and flying all at once, like coming alive, all her nerve endings sparking and creating sensations in places she'd never even known existed.

Tightening her fingers on the headboard, she threw her head back and released the last of her reservations. This was what she'd wanted —this feeling of power and pleasure, all of it overshadowing any fears she'd entered this room with. She rode his mouth with abandon, adjusting to the angle that resulted in perfect pressure against her clit. For all she knew, she was suffocating the man, but couldn't find it in herself to care … so long as she came off before he drew his last breath.

She was so close, something deep inside her winding up tight, a building sense of urgency making her movements more erratic, less controlled. Glancing down at Robert, she found him completely engrossed in his ministrations, eyelashes lowered over his cheekbones as he worked her with his mouth. He was even prettier like this, head between her thighs, hair mussed, and her hand print in a pink outline on his cheek. It made her want to strike him again, yank his hair, bite him places that would mark him further. Her perfect little canvas.

His eyes snapped open as if he'd felt her looking at him, though he never ceased driving her mad. Gaze locked with hers, he surged his head up and latched onto her clit, pulling on it with strong, belly-quivering sucks.

"Oh," she exclaimed, her thighs trembling on either side of his head as the first tremors of a powerful release began to sweep through her. "Oh … fucking hell!"

Robert groaned, applying himself to her pleasure even more, strumming her clit in swift circles and sucking in perfect unison. She splintered, digging her nails into the headboard and holding on for dear life as climax tore through her like a raging storm. Her clit tingled and deep pangs of poignant and near painful pleasure stabbed through her inner thighs and deep within her womb, until she nearly collapsed on top of him.

She held herself up, riding out every second of her finish, trembling as Robert went on kissing and licking her. His attentions were gentler now, as if he knew she'd become even more sensitive to touch. As if he knew that one more slow drag of his tongue over her clit might actually kill her after such a powerful release. So intent was he on his task, he seemed genuinely shocked when she began to pull away.

He chased her with a little huff of annoyance, his tongue skimming in her a hurried stroke. "I wasn't finished, yet."

She couldn't help a smile at the petulant disappointment she found on his face. "Eager little thing, aren't you?"

He raised his head, trying to capture her in his mouth again, but she'd moved farther down his body, straddling his chest and putting herself out of his reach.

"Come back here," he groused, narrowing his eyes at her.

She grasped his chin again, gentler this time. Apparently, the spectacular things he could do with his mouth had stoked her softer side.

"That was marvelous, but I have other plans."

He gasped as she moved down his body until the tip of his cock brushed against her sopping wet entrance.

"Yes," he sighed, surging his hips upward, trying to get closer to her, get inside her.

She moved out of his reach, skittering back to crouch between his legs. It was difficult not to laugh at the look on his face, equal parts desperation and frustration. The sound came out completely foreign, low and throaty, as if from the lips of some sort of seductress.

Completely unlike her.

She liked it. She liked everything about this experience—the thrill of being in control, the heady feeling following a climax, the feel of his eyes on her, expectant and pleading for more.

Why had she ever been afraid?

"Please," Robert whispered, bucking his hips again.

The motion caused his cock to brush against her knuckles, his skin silken and soft, but scorching in its heat. The word he'd just uttered fell on her like the stroking of his tongue, bringing her arousal back to life with surprising force.

"Say it again," she urged, staring at his mouth so she could see the word form there. "Beg me for what you want."

He squirmed, his arms pulling at the ropes, the flesh around them turning pink. It must hurt, but she didn't care. Hell, he didn't seem to either, his arousal becoming worse by the second. He was hard and straining upward, the tip of his prick an angry red, beads of mettle gathering at the slit.

He liked this—his own helplessness, her control, perhaps even the pain of the ropes biting into his wrists, made so by his own thrashing.

"Please," he said again, the word coming out heavy and breathless. "Please, touch me."

She obliged him, no longer able to hold back. This would be her first time touching a real cock with a willing hand, and she realized with some degree of shock that she actually wanted to touch Robert's.

He hissed when her fingers closed around him. The organ in her grasp was rock hard, a vein along its side pulsing as if the thing had its own heartbeat. As she studied it with an untamed curiosity, he began to move, hips shifting to create friction between his cock and her hand. He seemed mindless with need, practically fucking her fist as he strained against the ropes.

It would seem he'd grown impatient. She couldn't have that.

Giving his cock a tight squeeze, she simultaneously brought the heel of her free hand onto the crease where his thigh met his pelvis. Pressing down, she found the mass of nerves and tendons Millicent had told her about—ones that, when pressed, would cause a flare of pain that could subdue even the strongest man.

It had the intended effect, Robert letting out a bellow and shuddering beneath her before going still. He stared down at her with wide, wild eyes, his chest heaving as he struggled to breathe through what she felt certain must be a good degree of pain. Yet, his cock was as hard as ever, his bollocks drawn up tight, another telltale bead of moisture making his head gleam in the light of the fire.

"Bloody hell," he whispered with breathless awe. "I don't . . . I don't understand how . . ."

"You like the pain," she told him, smoothing her thumb over the pressure point she'd just tortured, noting the way it made him shiver. "Adversely . . . I like hurting you ... more than I ought to."

He wrinkled his brow, seeming to wrestle with himself, with her words. She could practically hear the wheels turning in his mind as he tried to rationalize what was happening between them.

Cassandra didn't have time for that. She'd come to terms with who she was, the things she wanted. Robert could do the same on his own time … right now he was hers.

She bent her head and flicked her tongue over the tip of his prick, which seemed to tear him away from his distracting thoughts. He moaned, and she went back for more, lapping at him and dipping her tongue into his slit. The salty taste of his seed invaded her palate—not altogether unpleasant.

"Christ," he groaned, arching his back as she enveloped him into her mouth.

She took him in until he hit the back of her throat, then withdrew before trying again, taking up a slow and steady rhythm. He seemed to have a hard time keeping still, and Cassandra wondered if she ought to have tied his ankles as well, spreading his legs and making it harder for him to thrust at his own pace. But then, she found she didn't mind it so much now that she'd found a rhythm … now that she realized he couldn't be still because of her.

Laying her thumb over the bruise that had begun to form over his pressure point, she pushed against it while drawing her lips up his shaft in a long, slow drag.

Robert bit back another loud cry, gritting his teeth so it came out more like a growl. She did it again, noticing the way it made the muscles in his belly clench and his arms jerk against his bonds. A dizzying sensation swept over her, as if she'd had too much to drink. Only she was drunk off the moment, off the thrill of having a man at her mercy. And not just any man. He was the sort her mother or sisters might have told her she'd never have; the sort she'd once been terrified of.

With the last of her reservations discarded, there was nothing left for it. She couldn't wait any longer, and it seemed as if Robert hung on by a thread.

It was time to finish this, to move past the final barrier holding her back, keeping her in that place of fear and revulsion. Robert muttered an oath when she released him from her mouth, but watched her with eager expectation as she climbed up over his body, positioning herself to take him inside.

He licked his lips, locking his gaze on the sight of her angling him so that his broad head rested right against her clit. She rubbed herself against him, using him to stimulate the little nub and coating him in her juices. A shudder wracked her as she increased her pace, rolling her hips and gripping his cock tighter to keep him at the right angle.

She could spend just like his, from the friction of his tip offering the perfect counterpoint to each surge of her hips. Robert seemed to be right there with her, his breaths coming out in harsh pants, hips flexing as he tried to push harder against her.

"Take me inside you, please ... please."

Her eyes slid shut and she trembled, that damned word wreaking havoc on her senses once again. She could listen to him beg until his voice had gone hoarse.

"Try again, Robert," she urged, placing him just inside, but refusing to slide onto him until she got what she wanted. "Beg me to do what I said I would when we first spoke downstairs. You remember, don't you?"

His eyes glittered with a feral light, all his good sense and notions of what might be right, wrong, or seemly washed away. He was a trembling mass of want and need, just like her, and would, apparently, do anything to be put out of his misery.

"Fuck me," he rasped, rocking against her, trying to nudge his way deeper into her. "Fuck me, please."

She sank down onto him in one swift motion, her eyes rolling up into her head as both his cock and his words filled her, making a liquid heat erupt from somewhere deep within. Bracing her hands against his chest, she gave herself over without a second thought, too far gone now to think about the past, her fears, her anger, any of it. She rode him at a maddening pace, her fingers pressing against his chest, thighs slapping against his. Her cunt stretched around him with a delicious and pleasant pull, the thick width of him pushing up against her most sensitive places.

Robert met each of her downward motions with upward thrusts of his own. She'd expected to tie him down and fuck him ... not for him to fuck her back with this sort of abandon and lack of restraint. He was a madman, panting and grunting, forehead broken out into a sweat as he drove up into her, stroking the sweet spot buried just within her cunt.

To her surprise, she was happy to let him, to meet him stroke for stroke and match his rhythm, to be as unbridled and unrestrained as he was. She clawed at him, dragging her nails down his chest and making him roar, swiveling her hips and taking him in deeper, so deep she felt stretched to her limit, full and bursting with him.

She had to grasp the headboard for leverage, which put her breasts within reach of his mouth. He took advantage without hesitation, lifting his head with a rough groan to take a nipple between his lips. The heat of his mouth and rasp of his tongue threw her over the edge, and she trembled atop him, her vision going dark at the edges as she fought for more time. She wasn't ready for this to end, for the heady rush of power, pleasure, and glory to be over. Yet, there was no stopping it, the scrape of Robert's teeth against the tender tip of her breast hurtling her into a dark miasma of pure, tortuous delight.

Relentless paroxysms shook her from the inside, and she closed her eyes to surrender to the waves of ecstasy steadily dragging her under. Her cunt squeezed around him, her belly clenching and her thighs twinging with the force of a climax the likes of which she'd never known.

"Oh God," Robert murmured against her breast. "I can't ... I'm going to ..."

She went limp on top of him, weak from the torrent of her own release, yet faintly registered his words, his jerky movements beneath her ... the desperation hinting at his own finish.

Cassandra managed to lift herself off him just in time, taking him in hand as his seed began to erupt from him in hot spurts. Throwing his head back, he jerked and groaned, his mettle splattering the back of her hand and his belly as she stroked him through till the end, working his shaft until she'd wrung him of every last drop.

He went limp, arms sagging in his bonds. Cassandra sat between his spread legs, leaning back onto her elbows as she closed her eyes and worked to catch her breath. Her limbs felt heavy, and keeping her eyes open proved a trial as a languid sort of calm washed over her.

She would soon have to rise and release Robert. But, he didn't seem in a hurry to break the thrall that had fallen over them both—their breaths ringing out in unison with the crackle of the fire, their legs touching as they lay supine on either side of the narrow bed.

And so, Cassandra tilted her head back and smiled, reveling in the warmth of sweet, ecstatic triumph.

CHAPTER 3

SUFFOLK, 1820 FOUR MONTHS LATER ...

Robert pulled the reins of his mount as he neared Briarwell Manor, his ancestral home. His time in London now several months behind him, he'd returned to the comfort of his familiar life in the country. A life in which he tended to the estate duties his father had fallen too ill to manage. A life in which he doted upon his mother, remaining steadfast as she counted the days until yet another man she loved took his last breath.

A life in which he did his best to pretend he had not been changed in the most elemental way by the night he'd spent in the upper room of a public house with Lady Cassandra Lane.

As he approached the stable at a brisk cant, he tried and failed to keep his mind from wandering back.

After the most satisfying sexual encounter of his life, Cassandra had untied his hands from the headboard to reveal the abrasions left from the rough twine. His wrists had stung, but he could hardly be angry at her when it had been his own squirming and thrashing that had caused the rope burn. She'd tossed him his cravat, which he'd used to clean up the spunk staining his belly. Then, he'd lain back and watched her, unashamed to admit that he was now more enthralled with her than ever. The things she'd done to him ... he'd never been with a woman so bold and raw, so aware of her own wants and needs.

As she'd gone to stand naked before the hearth, he'd followed her with his gaze and wondered how anyone could ever think her plain. He had been guilty of seeing her as a drab wallflower in the past, but that was because, like everyone else, he had only taken the most cursory of glances. Now that he was able to see her in her most natural state—with the masses of that red-gold hair hanging down her back in frazzled curls—Robert *saw* her. The long limbs sinewy from physical activity, perhaps riding. The flare of her hips, the jut of her sumptuous breasts, the curve of her back leading to a slender waist. The outline of her profile as she stared off across the room as if deep in thought.

Once the silence seemed to stretch on for an unbearable length of time, Robert had shifted on the bed and waited for her to speak, to say or do something, anything. This had been such untouched territory for him. With a whore, a man knew how to conduct himself. When he finished, he paid her and departed without a glance back, returning to his own life while she went off to prepare for her next tumble. With a woman he'd cared about or had any sort of affection toward, he might have lingered, pulling her into his arms and basking in the lingering effects of what they'd just done.

But, he'd never been with a woman like her before—one who tied his hands and requested he not touch her, who withdrew into herself when all was said and done.

Once it became clear that she did not intend to speak, he sat up and cleared his throat, unable to bear the silence any longer.

"I hope ..."

He trailed off when she turned her head to look at him, the lighting of the room making her eyes appear more gray than blue.

Disarmed for a moment, he paused, cleared his throat once more and tried again.

"I hope you got whatever it was you needed from me."

He held her stare, challenging her to deny his assertion. He wanted to believe she'd simply used him to sate an acute physical need, but something told him there was more to it. This had been about something more than simple fornication, and there was a reason she'd chosen him above the other men downstairs.

Inclining her head, she returned his gaze in a way that made him feel utterly exposed, even more so than having his nude body on display.

"Yes," she replied, staring back into the fire. "I did. And quite a bit more than I expected. So … thank you."

Her, thank *him*? He'd hardly done anything … at least, not compared to his typical fervor when taking a woman to bed.

Still, he could only reply, "It was my pleasure … quite literally."

She laughed, but the sound wasn't hearty or light. It was more a snort than anything, short and breathed out as she began picking up various articles of her clothing. As she bent to pull on her stockings, he wondered if he ought to offer her assistance. Did her edict against touching still apply now that they were finished?

He decided to err on the side of caution and dress himself, allowing her to do the same on her own.

Once he had finished, forgoing the cravat and stuffing it into the breast pocket of his coat, he'd turned to find her facing him. She'd donned all her layers again, including her gloves and cloak. She hadn't bothered to put her hair back into its coiffure, and a thick lock of it hung over one shoulder.

"Well, I must be off," she said, beginning to edge toward the door.

Something in him had lurched, forcing him forward, his hand reaching out before he could think better of it. She had tensed when his fingers closed around her arm, eyes narrowing as she stared at him with a heavy measure of accusation. He hadn't understood what possessed him to touch her that way; he'd only known he needed to tell her why he'd said yes.

"I've been in love with the same woman for most of my life," he blurted before he could lose his nerve. "In recent years, I'd come to see that I was losing her. She'd begun to slip through my fingers, and … well, perhaps she was never mine to begin with. I thought if I tried harder, if I fought for her, if I made up for the time we lost, I could win her back. But, today I watched her choose someone else—a man who is everything I'm not."

The annoyance in her expression had melted away, and understanding lit in her eyes. There was no pity there, thank God, but her gaze had told him she understood.

"Lady Daphne," she said—not a question, but a confirmation.

"Yes," he replied, a knot rising in his throat at the mention of her name. "She and Hartmoor … well, it hardly matters anymore. I only mention it so you'll understand … I came here tonight to forget her, to try to feel something else."

She'd seemed to try to smile, the side of her mouth twitching the slightest bit. Yet, her expression had remained as solemn as ever.

"And did you ... feel something else?"

He'd smiled at her then, a little laugh bubbling up in his chest. "I did not think of her once the entire time."

Now, the corner of her mouth did turn up a tick. "I am glad for you."

With a nod, he released her arm and backed away, content now to let her leave. He would linger for a bit to give her time before he exited himself. Now thoroughly exhausted, he had been more than ready to return to his suite of rooms in Town and turn in for the night.

To his surprise, she'd paused in the doorway, turning back to face him. He caught sight of the servant turned guard, Peter, lingering in the corridor. The man stepped out of view once he peered into the room and seemed to decide everything was as it should be.

"You asked why," she'd said, one hand resting upon the doorknob.

"And the answer is quite simple, Mr. Stanley. You see, there has been no one since … well, since Lord Fairchild."

He'd winced at the reminder of the man who had hanged just that morning for violating more than half a dozen of the *ton*'s young debutantes, Cassandra among them.

"I wanted to choose who it would be, how and where it would happen," she continued. "As for why I selected you … I hold quite a bit of disdain toward men of your sort. Titled, wealthy, pampered. And if you think to take offense to that, don't. It is simply a fact that men of the *ton* are a species all their own, and you are one of them. But, I can honestly say that you do not seem quite so much like the rest of them. In short, I chose you because I did not believe you had it in you to hurt me."

No, he'd thought. *But you have the capacity to hurt me.*

Aloud, he'd said, "I am glad I could be of some help to you."

Those flimsy words had not been adequate enough. Yet, how could he explain that he wanted what she'd given him again, and then again and again? How could he tell her that he'd do it as many times as she needed to wash the rancid taste of Bertram Fairchild out of her mouth?

"Good-bye, Mr. Stanley," she said, taking the matter out of his hands.

In those words, she'd made herself more than clear. She had told him this would be a one-time affair, and she meant to hold true to her word. They would part ways now and never speak of this again.

"Good-bye, Lady Cassandra."

He had not seen or spoken to her since that good-bye, having spent only another sennight in London before he'd given up his rooms and returned home. He never liked being away overlong, as he never knew when his father might take a turn for the worse.

"I'll take good care of 'im for ye, Mr. Stanley," said the stable groom who accepted the reigns of Robert's gelding once he'd dismounted.

"Thank you," he replied, turning to tramp along the pathway back to the manor.

The chill of an early spring morning had given way to a pleasant warmth, the sun high overhead in a cloudless sky. He'd been going out of his mind trapped inside the house this past week, near constant rain making outdoor activity impossible. Upon arising this morning to find the ground almost dry and the clouds abated, he'd set out for a morning ride. He had hoped it would offer a reprieve from the constant state of agitation that had plagued him since parting ways with Cassandra at the White Cock.

He had thought the craving for more of the tortuous pleasure Cassandra had opened his eyes to would abate over time. After all, he'd been quite the same after wetting his cock inside a woman for the first time. He'd been insatiable, wanting more and more, whenever and wherever he could find it. That sort of persistent arousal had gone away with age and experience, and he'd moved forward with his life able to go longer than five pitiful minutes without thinking about fucking.

But, this proved a different problem altogether. It wasn't simply that he could not stop thinking about fucking … it was that he couldn't stop thinking about fucking while being tied down, slapped, and dominated. Cassandra's fingerprints had faded by the next morning, but he could swear he felt that strike every time he thought back to that night—the vibrant blossom of the sting over his jaw, the surge of blood rushing through his veins as his heartbeat sped to a gallop, the way it had made his cock harden to painful limits.

Ruined. He was absolutely ruined.

He'd tried to capture that elusive feeling in other ways. But the whores in Lavenham—even the pretty red-haired one he'd always favored—could offer him nothing that appealed to this newly discovered part of himself. One had tied his hands for him, another had even bitten him a few times. Neither had affected him half as much as Cassandra, and he'd left both encounters more frustrated than ever.

In the past month he'd given up altogether, even as the memories plagued both his waking hours and his dreams. As a result, he now walked about with a constant feeling of mounting pressure from someplace deep within. Yet, no matter what he did, he could never find relief from it.

The irony of it, was that he'd been so grateful for that night, for the way it had helped to offer him an escape from the reality of his heartbreak, his enduring loneliness. Now, he hardly ever thought of Daphne at all, which ought to have been a blessing. News of her unexpected elopement had spread far and wide, whisperings of what had led to her union with Hartmoor making the rounds in London drawing rooms and country manor parlors alike. But, aside from the periodic twinge in his chest at the thought of his lost love, Robert found himself growing increasingly indifferent toward what he'd first thought of as a crushing loss.

Now, a different woman dominated his thoughts, and try as he might, he could not free his mind from the snare of her trap.

"Good afternoon, Mr. Stanley."

He blinked, finding that he'd entered the house and come face to face with the housekeeper. Concern knit her brow as she studied him —a look he was growing used to. He was different now, and it seemed everyone around him could sense it. The usual sunny smiles and amiable nature that had once been a trademark of sorts for him were now distinctly absent.

"Good afternoon, Mrs. Godfrey. Have you seen Mother?"

Before he made his way into the study to answer the correspondence he'd let pile up on his desk, he ought to look in on her. Things had been a bit strained between them since he'd gone off to London to go after Daphne.

"Yours is a fool's errand," she had warned him. "That woman is damaged goods and is not fit to become your future baroness. In truth, she never has been."

"You don't know her," he had argued. "She's a good woman … the woman I love. You'll see. When I return, it will be to announce our betrothal."

Of course, once he returned empty-handed and heartbroken she'd been all-too happy to declare that she'd been right the entire time, though she did wrap it in the guise of sympathy.

"My poor, sweet boy," she had crooned, reaching out to cup his face with a gnarled hand. "I told you she was never good enough for you. She couldn't possibly be if she cannot see what a wonderful husband you will make."

He'd brushed off her hand and walked away, refusing to give in to her constant need to coddle and fawn over him. Most times, he tried to be understanding of her feelings. He was her only remaining child, after all, and had become the recipient for all the love, concern, and meddling one mother contained inside her for four sons. But, he hadn't had the patience to endure it, and found even now that his forbearance began to run shorter and shorter.

"I believe she is visiting with your father," the housekeeper replied.

"Very good, thank you."

Breezing past her, he took the stairs two at a time, his body still thrumming with the excess energy that seemed to take up every crevice and corner of his being. The ride hadn't been enough. He needed some other way to occupy himself, but for the life of him could not figure out what to do. Perhaps riding out again would help. It had been some weeks since he'd visited with tenants, and he supposed he ought to ensure that the repair of several cottage roofs was going as it should. His father had always been an attentive landowner, an easy task considering that theirs was a small holding. While the baron had not yet died, the task of ensuring the people depending upon the estate for their welfare were taken care of now fell to him.

The door to his father's chamber hung ajar, so he pushed it open, peering inside to find the baron abed reading, his mother seated in an armchair nearby with an embroidery hoop in her lap.

He'd seen them this way so often over the years, it proved difficult to imagine entering any room in this home to find his mother there without his father. They were quite a pair, his mother petite with a rounded figure, his father's slender frame having gone rail thin due to illness. His dark hair, and her wheat blond had both gone completely white, with his father's bald pate showing through the thinning wisps on top. The baron's dark eyes still twinkled with cheer, despite his weakened and ravaged body, though his mother went about with a perpetual scowl marring her face, twin lines permanently etched between her eyebrows due to her furrowing them.

The two had lived through the trials of youth, marriage, birth, and death together, settling into age and growing into one another like two trees with their roots entangled underground. It seemed the only thing they would not do together was die. While his father's health had been declining for years now, his mother remained as healthy as ever.

The floorboards creaked as he entered, the sound capturing their attention. His father glanced up from his book, eying Robert over the rim of his spectacles, his cheeks wobbling as he offered a smile. Even so small a task seemed to require a great deal of strength, and he could not maintain the expression for long.

"Well, good afternoon," his father said as Robert approached the bed. "I see you've been out enjoying the fine weather."

His mother glanced up and took in his attire and the state of his mussed hair with a disdainful sniff. "Still far too damp for my liking, and the air still holds a bit of a chill. You ought not go traipsing about under such conditions, Robert. You could fall prey to fever or pneumonia or some other such thing."

"Leave the boy alone, Rosie," his father admonished. "He is young and healthy. He ought to be enjoying his life, not cooped up in this old house with us. Did you have a good ride, son?"

Before he could open his mouth to reply, his mother had risen from her chair and put her embroidery hoop aside. Approaching the bed, she began fussing over the baron, pulling the bedclothes up to his chest and tucking him tight, brushing the meager strands of hair back from his forehead and then pressing the back of her hand there to check for clamminess or fever.

"Really, William, you mustn't encourage such behavior. My Robert isn't like those reckless fools with their carriage races, and over-imbibing and wenching and the like. He's a good boy, aren't you, Robert?"

"Of course, Mother," he murmured, a force of habit.

He would always do his best to keep her anxiety at bay, conceding to how demanding and overbearing the loss of her sons had made her. His father did the same each day, submitting to her coddling and bearing it all in silence. His affection for her allowed him to see that it made her feel better to know the people around her were cared for and safe. She clung to them because they were all she had left.

If she ever found out about his night with Cassandra, she'd probably suffer an apoplexy. The thought brought a slight smirk to his lips as he wondered if she'd still think him such a 'good boy' if she knew he'd enjoyed having a woman tie him to a bed and straddle his face.

"Robert, have you heard a word I've said?" she snapped, pulling him out his reverie.

He blinked and shook his head, giving her a sheepish smile. "Sorry. What was that?"

"Dinner … tonight with the Fletcher's. You promised to escort me, remember?"

He stifled a groan and fought to keep his annoyance from showing. After all, he *had* promised to accompany her to the neighbor's residence for the evening, as his father was no longer able to leave his bed for long stretches of time without growing weak. However, he remained well aware that this entire affair was nothing more than a matchmaking scheme cooked up by his mother and Lady Fletcher, whose youngest daughter Lucy was unwed with a massive dowry. Never mind that Briarwell made more than enough income to keep them comfortable and a dowry wasn't needed; his mother obviously thought an heiress would prove the cure to his heartsickness over Daphne.

"Of course," he said, rather than tell her he'd rather suffer through having his teeth extracted one by one. "I cleared my evening of any plans at your request."

She smiled and nodded, using a damp cloth to mop at the baron's forehead. His father didn't seem to need any such attention, but bore it in placid silence.

"Very good. I cannot wait for you to become more acquainted with Miss Fletcher. She's such a lovely girl, and quite accomplished, I understand. Her mother says she sings, plays the pianoforte, and is quite adept with water colors."

So was every other English chit fresh from the schoolroom. One couldn't throw a stone around these parts without hitting a debutante with a mother standing by ready to titter on and on about how 'accomplished' her daughter was.

But, he couldn't tell his mother that such women did not hold his interest. Not without her pointing out that his pursuit of a more unconventional woman had ended with him being tossed over for another man. Such women were fickle, she would insist, and to pursue a safer option such as Miss Fletcher would be in his best interest.

"I look forward to meeting her."

SEVERAL HOURS LATER, Robert found himself wishing he had found some way to back out of his obligation. He might have faked a cough, throwing his mother into a fit of panic as she shooed him off to bed and sent for a physician to ensure he didn't have croup. He might have thrown himself down the stairs and broken his ankle, so his mother could not coerce him into going anywhere for several months.

Or, he might have told his mother to sod off altogether before striding out of the house, throwing himself onto the back of his horse and racing off to someplace where she couldn't follow and try to drag him back—like a gaming hell, or a brothel, or an opium den.

That last one might have been a bit dramatic and unnecessary. But, after suffering the company of the insipid Fletcher family and their bland daughter, he'd begun to wish he had done anything other than act the dutiful son.

Now, there was nothing for it but to get through the evening without succumbing to the urge to bash his head against the Fletchers' drawing room wall.

They had arrived early on his mother's insistence—an entire hour before dinner. Lady Fletcher, a woman who proved a match for his mother in age, stature, and overbearingness, had been thrilled at the chance to put her daughter on display. After settling them into a drawing room and offering him a brandy and his mother a cordial, she'd bustled off in search of Miss Lucy Fletcher, whom they'd been assured was almost finished dressing for dinner.

Robert had taken half his brandy in one swallow, determined to begin dulling his senses as early in the evening as possible. After ten minutes of waiting while his mother remarked upon and criticized every element of the drawing room's decor she found to be in bad taste, Lady Fletcher appeared with her daughter.

He tried not to judge anyone based on appearance alone, after all there were many who often took one look at him and thought him shallow and empty-headed as if the Almighty could not have blessed him with a brain to go along with his pretty face.

Miss Lucy Fletcher was not unattractive, but neither was she a stunning beauty. That might not have mattered if not for the vacancy he found when he peered into her eyes—as if she were nothing more than a doll being propped up and moved about by her mother. She even spoke with her mother's voice, a low near-whisper he had to strain to hear. He supposed the girl had been taught that it was demure and ladylike, but he found it a trial to hang on to a single word she said when he could hardly hear them.

After the introductions were made, Lady Fletcher had taken to guiding the conversation, doing everything she could to highlight her daughter's attributes. The baroness had acted as the consummate accomplice.

"Robert, isn't Miss Fletcher's gown the most lovely shade of white?"

All the debutantes wore white, and white looked the same to him no matter who was wearing it. Still, he had nodded and smiled, telling Lucy she looked fetching, not mentioning that the sheer number of ruffles on the frock made her look as if she ought to be adorning a table as an ornament.

"Lucy, dear, tell Mr. Stanley about the watercolor landscape you've been working on," Lady Fletcher had prodded.

The girl had flushed and then began explaining to him, in her whisper of a voice, every aspect of her countryside painting with painstaking detail—right down to the technique she'd used on the sheep.

"They're difficult to paint realistically, you see, for sheep are known for being white, while in truth they aren't entirely white at all. They appear rather gray at times … dirty, you know. Well, I didn't want my sheep to appear *dirty*, but not pure white either. So it took me hours to find the right combination of paints to get it just right."

Dear God, if ever you thought to strike me dead for some transgression or another, now might be a marvelous time to do so.

His prayer had gone unheeded, and he'd had to suffer through several more minutes of watercolor talk. Such conversation shifted to horses when Lord Fletcher and his son entered the room, a topic that Robert held a marginal interest in. But, right as they'd begun discussing the latest offerings to become available at Tattersall's, Lady Fletcher had coaxed her daughter to the piano, insisting they ought to enjoy some music before dinner. And yet again, Lucy was thrust back into the spotlight.

She played well enough, but Robert yet again noticed the emptiness in her eyes as she stared off at some point across the room, her chin tilted at an angle just so. The move seemed practiced—as if her mother had shown her how to flaunt her profile to its advantage.

Insipid, the both of them.

Cassandra's confused muddle of blue-gray eyes flashed through his mind, turbulent and filled with a thousand secrets. No one who had looked into those eyes for more than a few seconds could call her bland. No one who had studied the contours of her face, searching and not just seeing, could call her forgettable.

Tightening his hand around his tumbler, he'd knocked back what was left of his brandy and did his best to tear his thoughts away from her. It would not do to work himself into a state of unquenchable arousal in the company of others. Best to save it for when he could be alone and revel in it, taking his cock in hand and stroking himself off to thoughts of Cassandra on top of him, mastering him, bringing him to life.

Dinner had bored him to tears, with the food proving to be more interesting than the company. He'd done his best to be a good guest, forcing smiles at the right moments and answering any questions that were thrown his way—all while wishing he could devote his entire attention to the veal on his plate.

It was truly good veal.

His mother nudged him beneath the table at regular intervals, her way of letting him know he wasn't paying enough attention to Miss Fletcher. His responses were mechanical, his head swiveling to the woman seated at his side each time his mother's elbow made contact with his ribs.

"Miss Fletcher, do you not think these mashed turnips to be quite the most delicious thing you've ever tasted?"

"Why, yes, Mr. Stanley, Mother says Cook makes the best turnips in all of Suffolk!"

"Miss Fletcher, you played the pianoforte very well. You must have worked quite hard at it."

"Oh, yes, Mr. Stanley ... but I enjoy the practice ever so much. Mother says I'm the best she's ever heard."

"Miss Fletcher, have you ever been to London?"

"No, but I've always wanted to go. Mother says I may have a Season next year ... if I find I do not like my prospects here at home."

She'd given him a sidelong glance at that, batting her eyelashes and seeming to try to coerce him into something that would lead her into believing he held any interest in her prospects. As he wasn't at all interested, he simply smiled and went back to his veal.

Now that dinner and dessert had ended, and Lady Fletcher had urged them all into the drawing room for after-dinner drinks and conversation, Robert found himself counting the seconds until they could make a graceful exit.

He'd reached one thousand, two hundred and ninety-four seconds, when a bit of the conversation finally piqued his interest.

"They're calling him the Masked Menace. He's become quite notorious for his escapades along the Great North Road!"

"Martin, really!" Lady Fletcher huffed, clicking her tongue at her son. "Such conversation isn't appropriate in the company of ladies."

"Oh, but tales of highwaymen are ever so romantic," Lucy murmured, perking up at bit.

"There is nothing romantic about a criminal terrorizing London's lord and ladies, pilfering their jewels and such," his mother had declared with a disdainful sniff. "He sounds like an awful miscreant to me."

Robert frowned, rising to join Martin at the sideboard for more port. "What are you all talking about? Who is the Masked Menace?"

"You haven't heard?" Martin asked, filling Robert's cut crystal glass first, then his own. "He's a highwayman who's made quite a name for himself over the past several months. They say he's like a specter— coming and going while dressed all in black—complete with a mask and domino as if he's attending a masquerade. Can you imagine?"

"I can, and it sounds like a perfectly horrid nightmare," Lady Fletcher declared. "I heard he even used a knife to cut the solid gold buttons off a man's waistcoat."

Martin guffawed, spilling a bit of port onto the back of his hand. "Whoever heard of such a thing ... solid gold buttons on a waistcoat?"

"The man was one of those fops, you know ... high heels and ruffles, and patches and all that," Lady Fletcher declared, turning up her nose as if said fop stood before them, sullying her drawing room with his flashy sense of style.

"Well, what's to be done about it?" Robert asked, enjoying himself more now than he had throughout the entire evening. He could imagine London ballrooms and clubs were ablaze with the gossip.

"What can anyone do?" Martin said with a shrug. "The man come and goes so fast no one can get a good look at him. I suppose the Bow Street Runners might have a go at hunting him down, but I'd be willing to wager they'll never catch him."

"I hope they do," the baroness said with an exaggerated shudder. "Until the reprobate is brought to justice, the roads will not be safe to travel. I am so glad you returned from London when you did, Robert. It is far safer here."

"Indeed," Lady Fletcher agreed. "Now let us talk of something else. The subject of highwaymen isn't fit for my Lucy."

The girl in question blushed and stared off into the fire, likely dreaming about some whimsical highwayman in a black cape come to whisk her away.

"Oh, have you heard we're getting a new neighbor?" Martin said. "The Duke of Penrose of all people!"

Now, he had Robert's full attention. The Duke of Penrose happened to be Cassandra's uncle, who had inherited the dukedom after the death of her father. The former duke had sired four daughters onto the dowager duchess, and so the title and all accompanying wealth and lands had been left to his brother.

"A duke as a neighbor?" Lucy chirped, sitting up a bit straighter. "Oh, that is marvelous news! But, why on earth would he come here?"

"He's just purchased Easton Park ... you know, the abandoned Fairchild estate."

Easton Park, the estate neighboring Briarwell, had belonged to Daphne's family until they'd been forced to abandon it due to strained finances. Of course, it had come to light during Bertram's trial that the family had been beggared by thousands of pounds paid out to the young lord's victims. They'd paid for the silence of the women he had assaulted, including Cassandra, making it easy for the rest of it to be wasted away—most of it squandered due to an uncle's terrible gambling habit.

"Lord Fairchild sold Easton Park?" the baroness asked, one hand coming up over her bosom. "I had no idea."

"Well, he's been beggared and disgraced by the scandal, and of course the property wasn't entailed, so it could be sold. Well, Penrose himself decided to purchase it and have it renovated. The tenants are in dire straits, so I suppose he means to set things right. The estate will turn a tidy profit once he gets it up and running again."

Robert had it on good authority that the vast majority of Easton Park's tenants had abandoned their homes, many of them seeking work and a better living situation at Briarwell. But, he did not mention that, far more interested in Penrose moving into the neighboring home. The man seemed to prefer dwelling in London, at his massive townhome in Grosvenor Square along with the dowager and her youngest, unwed daughter. Still a bachelor himself, he must be thinking of settling down if he were purchasing another large country estate so close to Town.

"Does he intend to take up residence there?" he asked, trying to keep his tone light.

Meanwhile, his heart had begun to hammer at the thought of Cassandra living so near he could walk through the woods separating Briarwell from Easton Park and reach her within minutes.

Martin shrugged. "Rumor has it, he intends to continue residing mostly in London, though renovations have begun on the property as well as the tenants' cottages. I've heard he's allowing a relative to take up in the dower house. The former duchess has no use for it, as everyone knows she prefers living in Town. So one of the sisters will be living there alone ... the unwed one ... the spinster."

Cassandra.

His pulse leaped, his blood racing in his veins and leaving a warm tingle in its wake. Cassandra was coming to Suffolk. She would live close enough that he might see her often, could talk to her, perhaps come to know her … submit to being tied to a bed again and ravished within an inch of his life.

A slow smile spread across his face, which he had to wipe away before his mother noticed. It wouldn't do for her to know he had any interest in Cassandra, who she'd likely find to be even more unsuitable than Daphne. Never mind that she was the daughter of a duke. She was tainted by a horrible scandal and had been shunned by the vast majority of the *ton*.

As if on cue, his mother made an inarticulate sound of scorn. "I cannot say I am keen on the idea of having such a neighbor. It is … unsavory."

Robert's hand clenched around his glass, and he bit back a scathing retort, trying instead to be his usual diplomatic self. "Mother, it is hardly her fault. She's been the victim of a terrible crime."

"Yes, but did she have to air it all out so publicly? It is vulgar."

Yes, it is so horribly vulgar for a woman to want her rapist to be held accountable.

"I understand what you mean, Lady Stanley," Lady Fletcher chimed in. "Of course no one blames her for what that despicable man has done. But then … one does wonder why she'd allow herself to be led off alone. A proper young lady knows not to go sneaking about with a gentleman. There are consequences for such actions."

"Precisely," the baroness said with a curt nod.

"Whatever her own mistakes, she has been through enough," Robert argued, trying to keep from throwing his glass across the room and asking his mother and her friend what the devil was the matter with them. "The scorn of the *ton* has surely been bad enough, so we ought to endeavor to be kind to her."

"Oh, but I have heard she is such a surly creature," Lucy said with a shake of her head, as if she couldn't understand a woman who wasn't constantly smiling or being biddable. Of course she wouldn't. "I don't think I could ever get along with such a woman."

Robert's face went hot, and he realized his agitation had begun to show when his mother reached out to pat his hand with a little laugh.

"Oh, very well, Robert. Of course we will try to be kind to the girl. Really, my Robert is such a gentleman. So kind and always thinking of others. I adore him for it."

"A wonderful trait in a young man, to be sure," Lady Fletcher agreed.

Across the room, Martin merely rolled his eyes and went back to his port.

Robert followed suit, refusing to be baited into an argument concerning Cassandra. The others could treat her how they pleased, but he could not wait to see her again.

He'd been unable to get her out of his head, anyway, so being able to see her, to find some way to sate this craving she'd created in him ... well, it had to be better than the way he'd suffered thus far.

CHAPTER 4

LONDON

Darkness shrouded Cassandra as she walked, the hem of her cloak flapping in the soft evening breeze. The chill of the night air required the covering, but she clung to the garment for a reason that had nothing to do with the cold—the way it helped her become one with the night, shadows clinging to its edges and obscuring her to an unrecognizable degree. With her height and the voluminous fabric veiling her, she might even be mistaken as a man. The breeches and boots she wore underneath helped the illusion, so she brushed past members of the *ton* coming and going from various soirees in Grosvenor Square without drawing much notice. They were as self-involved as ever, their laughter and insipid conversations about the night's events and juiciest bits of gossip of no interest to her.

There was a particular gentleman she'd come here to find, whom she had raced to intercept after spotting him at a musicale hosted in the home of the Marquis of Ashton. Invitations hardly ever came to her anymore—not since she had removed herself from the residence of her uncle, mother, and sister, thereby marking herself as even more of a social outcast. Ashton, however, was a friend of Millicent, and his wife was one of the few souls in this accursed city who did not turn their noses up at her.

She hadn't planned to attend the musicale; not until she'd learned of the attendance of a certain man. The Honourable Mr. Curtis Barlow, son of a viscount, had attended the event in the typical black and white evening kit, though his waistcoat had been a garish jonquil shade—the bright splash of color making it easy to follow his progress about the room as he'd sipped champagne and mingled with other guests between musical performances. Now, it would help her identify him in the dark.

Barlow disgusted her the way most of his kind did—the bright, charming smile masking his true nature, the underlying malice hidden under a thin veil of courtly manners. A viper slithering through a room filled with hapless victims who had no notion of the danger lurking amongst them.

It wasn't Lord or Lady Ashton's fault. They did not know what she knew—that Barlow was a man of low morals, a predator looking for his next kill. How could they know when he was so good at hiding it with a handsome face and amiable personality? Even she had not been entirely certain, not until she'd overheard a tearful conversation between two ladies in the retiring room during the interval of an opera performance. It never ceased to amaze her what people would discuss in such a place when they thought no one else could hear. She'd become adept at making herself invisible until she wanted to be seen, and had remained behind a privacy screen while listening to one lady's account.

She had invited Barlow into her country home for a house party, only to find him attempting to get beneath the skirts of a chambermaid. The servant had been in hysterics by the time the lady came upon them, tears wetting her face as she clawed and scratched and tried to free herself from his hold.

Cassandra had clenched her jaw and fought the urge to hurl the nearby chamber pot across the room in a fit of rage as she'd listen to the lady tell her friend how her fool of a husband had done nothing to aid the servant. Instead, he'd cast blame on the maid for being caught alone, and insisted his friend had done nothing wrong.

"I am certain he only misinterpreted her signals. That is what Paul told me when I insisted he do something. Mr. Barlow should not be allowed in our home ... I wanted him gone, but Paul would hear none of it. Oh, and poor Libby was in quite a state. I shudder to think what would have happened had I not found them."

Cassandra knew very well what would have happened. She had lived through the consequences of such a thing, and there had been no one there to come to her aid or defend her.

But she would defend Libby and her blubbering mistress. She would ensure that Barlow paid for what he'd done, and she would do it right now.

Just before the musicale had ended, she'd slipped from the drawing room and seen herself out of the marquis' home. Her driver, Randall, had circled the block at her command, ready for her to emerge at any time. He hadn't questioned the directive, even though it would require him to drive in a continuous circle for hours. Understanding her mission, he would do exactly as she asked, knowing it could prove the difference between success and failure.

And so, when he'd approached within seconds of her departure, she had promptly leaped into the vehicle and made haste changing out of her evening attire. While Randall pulled off down Duke Street, she'd exchanged her lady's finery and replaced it with her comfortable breeches, shirt, waistcoat, and boots, before shrouding herself in the cloak. A silk turban had covered her hair, but was now gone, the tresses brushed flat to her scalp and scraped back from her face.

He had let her off on Brown Street, right outside of Grosvenor Square, and from there she'd continued on foot. He left her on her own, taking the carriage off to Reeves' Mews where he would await her return.

She'd taken the walk back to Duke Street on swift feet, and she'd arrived just in time to find Mr. Barlow exiting the Ashtons' townhome. An infuriating smirk curving his lips, he trotted down the front steps with a spring in his step, an ornate walking stick twirling in one hand.

Her timing could not be more perfect.

She'd seen him arrive on foot, so had known he would leave the same way, taking himself off after the musicale in search of some other amusement. Where he was off to next was of no concern to her. As they left the well-lit Grosvenor Square, the shadows of the homes looming to one side kept her hidden, her steps silent as she advanced upon him. He remained oblivious to her pursuit, walking about free and clear with no regard to the danger he had placed himself in.

These pompous lords and their sons were all the same. They walked about with such freedom and lack of fear because no one would ever punish them for their crimes against others—their abuse of the women they were supposed to protect, their cavalier attitudes toward the less fortunate, their mistreatment of servants.

But, no more.

If no one would defend the defenseless, then Cassandra would.

She halted on Hart Street when he did, slipping back into a narrow space between two townhouses as Barlow held his walking stick under one arm and began rifling about in his coat pocket. Untying the cravat tied in a haphazard knot around her throat, she stretched it taut between both hands, waiting for the opportune moment. There was no one else about who might see, but that could change in an instant. It must be now, and she need only wait for an opening

It came when he retrieved a cheroot, head lowered as he remained oblivious to his stalker.

Moving with reflexes born from months of practice, she crept behind him on swift and silent feet, hooking the cravat around his neck and jerking him against her body. His surprised yelp died away into a choked gurgle when she tightened the linen around his throat until he could not draw breath. His legs kicked, one of his shoes slipping off and his walking stick clattering to the ground as she hauled him into the darkness.

He must outweigh her by at least two stone, but the strength leeched from his muscles as his air became trapped in his lungs.

She released him just before he lost consciousness, preferring for her prey to remain alert so it could squirm and whimper while she did what she pleased. Rushing back to the mouth of the alley, she crouched to retrieve his walking stick while he rolled about on the ground, coughing and wheezing and drawing in sharp breaths. She waited until he'd managed to rise to his hands and knees, gazing about in a daze. Then, she lifted her weapon with both hands and brought it down across his back. He went down with a grunt, the impact knocking the wind from him.

"What the devil?" he rasped as she neared, using one foot to push him over so he lay on his back.

"Hmm, I've never been called The Devil before," she mused aloud, moving to straddle him, then crouch down until she practically sat on his torso. "But I do like it … after all, I am here to punish you for your sins."

The whites of his eyes flared in the dark, the orbs going wide and his jaw slackening as he gazed up at her. With the moon at her back, she must look like some sort of specter, her face invisible in the dark shadow of her hood. Before he could attempt fighting her off, she retrieved the dagger she kept in her boot and held it up, letting the moonlight caress the metal's sharp edge.

"Sins?" he blustered, squirming beneath her and working himself into an indignant rage. "What sins would you accuse me of, a stranger who knows me not?"

She scoffed. "You spoiled little lords are all the same, you know. So predictable. Here is the part where you will puff up with righteous anger and rail at me. I do not know you, you'll claim, could not possibly have the right to judge you. But, what you'll fail to realize is that I don't need to know you … don't care to, actually."

He began to try to fight her, her voice having given her away as a woman. Typical. Planting herself more firmly on top of him, she kept the knife in her right hand while drawing back the left in a fist. He groaned when she made impact, snapping his head to the side and filling his mouth with blood.

"Do make this easier on yourself, Mr. Barlow. Fighting will only agitate me, and when I'm agitated ..."

She emphasized her point by digging the tip of her dagger into the meat right under his jaw. He whimpered when she drew blood with a single prick, the drop running in a bright rivulet down his throat.

"What do you want from me?" he railed, blood and spittle flying from his mouth to splatter her cloak.

Taking hold of his chin, she forced his head back down, leaning in close and trailing the tip of her dagger down the side his face from brow to cheek.

"Retribution," she whispered, before going upright and getting to work.

She took up the cravat she'd dropped nearby and forced his mouth open before stuffing it inside. His muffled cries left her unmoved as she began using her knife to slice away the buttons of his waistcoat, then his shirt. He twisted and swung, trying to fight her off, but she used her knife to subdue him—slashing at his arm when he tried to hit her. Then, she used her knees to pin his arms to the ground, taking away the use of his hands.

Seemingly resigned to his fate, he lay beneath her with tears in his eyes, shuddering and whimpering as fear began to truly set in.

"You must be terrified," she crooned, smiling down at him once she'd sliced his shirt open to bare the rest of his abdomen. "Trying to figure out what I'm going to do to you. I wonder if the poor maid you cornered during that house party felt such fear. And the ones before her ... do you think they were as afraid as you are right now?"

It took a moment for him to understand, but once he did, he grew louder, his lips moving as he seemed to try to plead his case through the wad of linen in his mouth. She pressed her knife against his lips.

"Shh ... hush now. You are a big, strong man, are you not? A titled lord with all the power and privilege in the world. What have you to cry about? Oh, I see ... you are worried that I'm going to hurt you like you hurt that poor maid—like you've harmed countless others?"

He issued a garbled sob as he nodded, squeezing his eyes shut. Cassandra laughed, the sound as hard and harsh as the heart beating inside her chest. She had no pity for this man, no care for his tears or the blood he would shed by the time she had finished.

"Do not worry, Mr. Barlow. That limp waste of flesh between your thighs is of no interest to me. No, I am interested in something else altogether."

"What?"

The single word was almost indecipherable, but she understood it through the linen sucking all the moisture out of his mouth. Positioning her dagger against his chest, she braced herself with one hand upon the ground.

"Ensuring that bastards like you never assault another woman ever again."

Then, she began to cut. She made long, deep gouges through his skin, watching with savage satisfaction as his blood welled up in the neat lines and curves. Barlow's eyes widened until she thought they might fall free of their orbits, his face going purple as he bellowed through his gag. She was quick and efficient, realizing she only had so much time before someone heard and came to investigate, or the city watch found their way down the alley.

When she had finished, she used his own cravat to wipe away the blood pooling over his chest and running in messy rivulets down his body. He had gone silent and pale, light whimpers the only sign that he was still alive. Resigned to his fate, just like the others she had done this to ... accepting of his punishment.

The crimson gore wiped away to reveal the word she'd carved into his chest with painstaking care.

DEFILER.

BY THE FOLLOWING EVENING, Cassandra had arrived at what was now her new home. Randall had been waiting for her in the mews as promised, and had conveyed her out of the city with the dark blanket of night still over them. They'd traveled until the sun broke the horizon, then found a small inn at which to rest the horses, take a meal, and relax for a short time. She had changed back into her finery in the back of the vehicle, earning her the best treatment when coming face to face with the innkeeper. She'd been offered a room in which to wash her hands and face and sleep for a bit. A hot meal had been sent up for her, and she'd been assured that Randall and her horses were well taken care of. By afternoon, they were ready to set out again, Randall driving them at a maddening pace on her command.

Now that she no longer lived in London, she could not abide remaining there any longer than necessary. Uncle Rupert had played a large role in helping her escape Penrose House, where he lived with her mother and youngest sister. She was grateful for it, for him and his understanding and affection. He was not her dearly departed papa, and no one could replace the former duke, but he was one of the few allies she had left—the only one in her family who did not blame her for the things Lord Bertram Fairchild had done to her, and the resulting scandal that had ensued when she'd revealed it all.

"You deserve to be happy," he'd said when pulling her into his study and informing her that he'd purchased Easton Park. "I can see that remaining in London, among all the people who look down on you with such pious judgment, will only wear on you more and more over time."

It hadn't been fair, the way the *ton* had turned on her once she and Bertram's other victims had bound together to expose and prosecute him. But then, she'd always known it would be this way. She was a spinster, after all, five-and-twenty years of age, unwed, unwanted, and unpopular. Even as she'd lain all her secrets bare to the world, testifying about the horrors of being lured into solitude and robbed of her maidenhead in the most brutal of ways, they'd judged her and found her wanting. The *ton* refused to see her as anything other than a desperate chit who'd gotten herself ravaged while trying to get him off alone to lay a marriage trap. What would a handsome, well-liked lord like him want with a plain-faced spinster like her?

And so, they shunned her. They warned their sons to stay out of her path, and used her plight as a cautionary tale for their daughters. The men leered at her as if she were fair game now that she was ruined, and the women held their skirts aloft to keep from brushing against her when they walked past.

London had become a miserable place for her as a result, even as she used it as a means to gather information and exact her revenge. She had taken Uncle Rupert up on his offer, demanding the inheritance that was her due now that she'd reached her majority. He'd given it up freely, urging her to take it and be happy, living however she saw fit.

Little did he know, she saw fit to become the avenging demon who lurked in the night, punishing unsuspecting lords for their abuse of women. Bertram had been allowed to prey upon debutantes for years, unchecked. Cassandra had been only one in a long line of victims, his wealth and powerful father proving enough to get him out of trouble each time an angry papa turned up on his doorstep demanding things be made right.

No more.

Never again would men like Bertram be able to do as they pleased without consequences. Not as long as she drew breath and was able-bodied. Wherever she heard whispers of ungentlemanly behavior, she followed the gossip to the truth, and meted out the sort of justice she had been denied following her own rape.

As she descended from her carriage and swept up the front walkway of her home, she hoped sleep would come easier to her knowing that another defiler of innocents had received his comeuppance.

The dower house at Easton Park had been referred to as a cottage, but did not fit the picture of a small and quaint dwelling such a word called to mind. Two stories high, the wide front of the house boasted picturesque windows, ivy vines crawling up the brick facade, and pointed peaks covered in stone tiles for a roof. The hedges lining the path to the front door had been wild and overgrown upon her uncle's purchase of Easton Park, but his money and an army of both indoor and outdoor servants had set that, and many other neglected things, to rights. The neat hedges now guided her on a perfect path to a front door that had been painted a bright white and boasted an ornate brass door-knocker.

Inside were two drawing rooms—a small one for her personal use, and a larger one for entertaining if she so chose—an elegantly appointed dining room, a small study lined with bookshelves, a water closet on the first floor, a kitchen, four bedrooms, and a circular veranda one could access through a set of doors in the large drawing room. Beyond it lay a small garden, which had been overrun with weeds, but was now almost bare in preparation for the new plants she'd sent for. In a small corner, her housekeeper—who also functioned as a cook—had begun cultivating vegetables and herbs.

Aside from the housekeeper, there was a single footman, a chambermaid who practiced at being a lady's maid when Cassandra needed her, Randall the driver who kept her horses and looked after Leon, a stable boy in training, and a scullion who assisted in the kitchen.

The footman opened the front door for her and welcomed her home before accepting her cloak. The housekeeper bustled in from the kitchen to ask if she would take dinner. Cassandra asked for it to be sent to her bedchamber, along with the tub and hot water for a bath. Then, she carried her weary body up the stairs to seek out solitude.

Once alone, she sat on the small, cushioned bench before her vanity and mirror and began plucking the pins from her hair. As she watched the unruly curls fall to frame her face lock by lock, a memory came floating back to her.

Robert lying under her, his bright blue eyes boring into her with curiosity, perception, even a bit of fear. That gaze tracing her every feature, caressing each curl as she'd freed it for him, much like she did now.

Your hair ... will you take it down?

Avoiding her own reflection, she focused on the clink of the pins inside the little porcelain pot where she stored them, trying to get a grip on her wandering mind.

Four months had passed since her night with Mr. Robert Stanley, and he'd dominated her thoughts ever since—much to her annoyance.

Millicent had warned her that once she overcame her fear of intercourse, she'd find herself yearning for more. She'd want to fuck, again, with the same man or even a different one. The urges she typically abated with the use of her dildos would become something else altogether ... something that only a real cock, attached to a real man could sate.

And so it had happened, that soon after her encounter with Robert at the White Cock, she'd begun to feel the stirring in her loins that hinted at a carnal need. She had been in the middle of gathering information on a certain gentleman, one who'd cornered a debutante during a visit to her parents' country estate and forced her to perform fellatio on him. Because she had been so focused upon her task, she hadn't had the time to go looking for someone with which to sate her craving. She'd seen to her own pleasure for weeks after Robert, and it had only ever taken a bit of the edge off. It never satisfied her in the way that tying him to the bed and fucking him while he begged for more had.

Once she had finished with her prey of the moment, she'd taken the time to find someone else, returning to the White Cock—alone this time—and assessing each man in the room as she had the night she'd found Robert. She hadn't needed Peter to look out for her, having grown more confident in the skills the large footman had taught her. So, she'd approached the man of her choosing, plied him with a bit of whisky, and had him accompany her upstairs. He'd agreed to her rules, even let her tie his hands and take charge of the encounter the way she liked.

It had been one of the most disappointing experiences of her life, leaving her unfulfilled afterward. Her bedmate had looked so pleased with himself, grinning up at her from where he'd lain with his hands tied up over his head.

"If you're game, I could—"

"No," she'd interjected while cutting him free of the ropes. "I've had quite enough, thank you."

He had laughed, as if she'd just told a hilarious joke. "Don't you want me to make you come off again?"

She'd rolled her eyes at him and pointed toward the pile of his clothes on the floor. "I didn't come off the first time, and that you're too dense to notice is why I'm done with you."

He'd glared at her, but said nothing as he stood to pull his clothes back on. He mumbled something under his breath as he departed, but she hadn't bothered to try to find out what.

Upon returning home, she'd promptly retrieved her favorite phallus from its storage chest. While using it to bring herself to the sort of satisfaction that her bumbling bedmate had failed to give, she'd thought of a different night in that same upper room of the public house. She'd thought of Robert bucking and arching beneath her, his cheeks flushed as he'd panted and groaned her name. She'd imagined the rough red abrasions around his wrists from the burn of her ropes, and the give of flesh beneath the heel of her palm. She'd pictured him under her, his cock filling her and stroking places so deeply hidden she hadn't known they existed until he touched them. She'd heard his moans echoing through her mind when she spent, thrusting the dildo in and out of her cunt and using her other hand to stroke her clit.

It had become her practice over the following months, frigging herself while thinking of him.

It wasn't the man, she told herself. Robert had simply been convenient, the only pleasant experience she'd ever had with a man and his cock. Bertram had been the first, and the one to almost ruin intercourse for her altogether. Robert had cleansed her palate, making it so she could experience arousal without the self-loathing and fear that had once come with it.

Then, why couldn't she find someone else to replicate the experience with? Millicent had taken Peter as her lover years ago and the two seemed happy enough in their arrangement. But before him, she happened to know her friend had experienced many paramours, and had enjoyed herself with all of them.

If it was possible for Millicent, then it was possible for her.

As Lila arrived with her dinner, followed by the footman toting the copper tub, Cassandra resolved to do something about her little problem. One mediocre experience should not be enough to keep her from seeking out someone else she might enjoy as much as she had Robert. As soon as she was able, she would try again ... and this time, she would not let the night end until she'd had her satisfaction.

SHE AWAKENED SOMETIME before daybreak with a start, her chest heaving as she fought to catch her breath and untangle herself from the remnants of her hellish nightmare. Sweat soaked her skin, making her nightgown cling to her body and strands of hair adhere to her forehead and the back of her neck. She had kicked the bedclothes aside, fighting in her sleep against a demon she only ever encountered when she slept.

Breath sawing through her parted lips, she squeezed her eyes shut and tried to fight off those clinging talons of terror, reminding herself that none of it was real. Not for her, not anymore. Bertram was dead, and had been these past four months. He could never harm her or any other woman again, and she took comfort in that.

Yet, she still saw his face some nights, still relived the painful moment when he'd transformed from doting suitor to soulless monster. In the few seconds it often took for her to separate dream from reality, Cassandra could swear she smelled him—the overpowering scent of sandalwood that so many men doused themselves with.

She'd come to hate the fragrance.

She could still feel him, stabbing between her legs like a flaming knife. She could hear him, laughing and rasping filth into her ear.

But then, she would blink and come to full wakefulness, and remember.

It was over and behind her. Her monster had been sent to the deepest pit in Hell, where he belonged.

Swinging her legs over the side of the bed, Cassandra rose, deciding there was no use in trying to go back to sleep. The sun would rise soon, and sleep meant the possibility of another nightmare. Instead, she put on the slippers she'd left near the armchair by the window, before shrugging into her warm dressing gown. Then, she crept through her bedroom door and toward the stairs, careful to remain quiet. Lila would be awake at this hour, ensuring each room with a hearth was stocked with coal. She didn't want any of the maid's questions or concern, nor did she want anyone thinking to follow her. If they knew what she was about, they would surely send word to Penrose House and inform Uncle Rupert that she ought to be locked away in Bedlam.

She made her way to the drawing room with the doors opening onto the terrace. The frigid air of early dawn bit at her hands and face, but she pressed on. Morning dew soaked her feet through her slippers when she stepped into the grass, ignoring the path leading into the garden and angling toward the trees. The dense woods characterizing this area was one of the reasons she enjoyed living at Easton Park—and also that her being here gave testament to the fall of the family whose son had wronged her. That her family now owned the property, and she could call a part of it her own, seemed like another bit of justice.

Moving through the trees, she made her way to her favorite spot not far from the dower house. She had discovered it while exploring the day after settling in, and when she was in residence visited the place daily. It was at its most beautiful at night, even in the darkest hours before dawn—the thick trees giving way to make room for a little pond that often reflected the light of the moon on clear nights. Just now, it was nothing more than a still sheet of black glass, its gentle glisten camouflaging the brutality of its coldness, its depth.

Her feet sank into the muddy ground as she approached its edge, the ground still damp from yesterday's rain. Standing on the bank, she closed her eyes for a long moment, taking several long, slow inhales—breathing in the scent of earth, grass, and trees. The water itself had its own scent, some unnamable thing mingling on the air with the rest of it.

Cassandra stepped out of her slippers, shivering when the mud squished between her toes and cradled her bare feet. That did not stop her, however. She carried on, untying the belt of her dressing gown and letting the garment slither down her body to rest atop her slippers. Then, she was walking toward the water, arms stretched out wide as gooseflesh appeared along her skin.

The water kissed her feet, then lapped up over her ankles, her calves, her thighs, her hips. She walked to what she knew to be the edge of the shallows, the discovery having taken her quite by surprise the first time. Now she knew where to pause in order to linger on the edge of the black abyss, a plunge with a bottom she could not see. She let her head fall back and raised her arms high, noticing the way the sky had begun to lighten, the darkest blue in existence fading toward navy, then cerulean in the distance.

One step, and she was plummeting, down, down into the darkness. Breath held in her chest, nightgown billowing about her legs, she let herself become formless and weightless, a ghost in the water.

She imagined that this must be what death felt like. The part after one took their last breath, at least. She supposed dying itself would be rather painful. But then ... there might be this. Darkness, quiet, a body that was lighter than air. No pain, no despair, no fear. No rage. Simply her, water, and the dark.

Her lungs burned, her throat clenching as her body began to fight against the submersion. Yet, she continued to let herself sink, testing her own resolve. She often contemplated letting go; taking in a long breath and filling herself with water until she choked on it, discovering if her theory about what lay beyond death proved true.

But, whenever she reached the point at which she must take a breath or die, the primal instinct toward survival urged her to fight. And so, she kicked her arms and legs, propelling herself upward, back toward life. Breaching the surface, she released the breath she'd been holding and dragged in a fresh one, tasting and smelling it all so much clearer than before she'd gone under.

When she pushed wet tendrils of sopping hair out of her eyes, it was to find the pink and orange rays of dawn bursting forth on the horizon.

She swam toward land and hoisted herself free, the chilled air of the morning biting at her wet skin. Her nightgown still clung to her, but no longer from the remnants of a painful dream. She didn't feel the pain, or *him*, anymore. The air prickled her arms and legs, pebbled her nipples, caressing her legs as she walked up the bank. Then there was the warmth of her dressing gown as she pulled it on and held it closed over her body.

Sliding her feet back into her slippers, she trudged back toward home—reborn, and renewed.

CHAPTER 5

Robert tramped through the woods bordering Briarwell and Easton Park, taking his time to avoid the snare of protruding roots. He peered through the trees and through the dark night, searching for the familiar property on the outer edge of the neighboring estate. He knew the lands well, having spent countless summers running through these very trees, chasing a ribbon of vibrant, auburn hair. As children, Daphne and Robert had been the best of friends, with Bertram rounding things out quite nicely. In the years after his brothers had gone off to school, Robert had reveled in their companionship, glad to have children his own age with which to play.

Catch me, Robert, catch me!

Daphne would run barefoot through these woods, her giggles floating on the breeze. The games hadn't gone away as they grew older—they'd only changed. They had gone from a trio, wading in streams and throwing stones, to a twosome—he and Daphne sneaking away from her brother. The transition from girl and boy to woman and man had altered everything between them, and the need for privacy became paramount to exploring the differences in their bodies, in their feelings toward one another.

Catch me, Robert, had turned into, *Kiss me, Robert,* Daphne's voice deepening from a girlish chirp to a sensual purr.

As he tread the familiar ground, he could swear he still heard her voice, could still see that streak of red hair just ahead. The memories didn't hurt as much as they had four months ago, though they did leave a bitter taste in his mouth. For years he'd pursued her thinking all his waiting and longing would eventually come to an end. It had been part of the game—her slowing down enough that he could overtake her, laughing when he swept her off her feet.

Reality had been nothing like the game, and Daphne hadn't slowed for him. She'd dashed headlong into someone else's arms, leaving him to put the pieces of his shattered heart back together.

The irony of his current position wasn't lost on him. He walked through these woods where Daphne haunted him, in search of a different woman. Or rather, in search of confirmation. He'd accompanied his mother on a visit to a neighbor's home for tea this afternoon and heard gossip stating Lady Cassandra Lane had settled in into the dower house at Easton Park. His pulse had raced at the mention of her name, the news that she was near enough for him to walk to her making his mouth go dry. Since he'd first heard the news of her imminent arrival, he'd thought of little else. He'd spent hours contemplating her reasons for leaving London, and the possibilities that her nearness could present.

Despite knowing he was foolish to think she'd even care—she had ended their night together by walking away without looking back, as promised—here he was. After lying abed for hours trying to sleep, he'd found himself too restless, his thoughts overrun by Cassandra. Even when he closed his eyes and began drifting off, memories of her tormented him—her scent and taste, the tight clench of her around him, the wide-eyed shock that had transformed her face the moment she'd reached climax.

Not that his thoughts were entirely comprised of erotic memories.

There had been her admission that no one had touched her since Bertram, the haunted look in her eyes as she'd given him that secret, the words seeming to come out against her will. Had she repeated the experience again with someone else? Had she chosen other men the way she'd chosen him, tying them up, hurting them, fucking them into oblivion?

He'd gritted his teeth, his mind rebelling at the notion, even as he realized how ridiculous it was to be jealous. Especially considering he'd tried to capture the intensity of their coupling with whores before giving up entirely. His failure meant that no one else could please him the way she had.

But, she had made him no promises, given him no indication she'd wanted anything more than his cock for that one night.

Yet, here he was, walking toward her new home just for a glimpse, for any sign that she was here, close enough to … to what? What would he do once he found her again? Tell her she'd ruined him for other women, beg her for more?

He'd had no clear motive when hurriedly dressing and tiptoeing through the house, praying he wasn't heard, slipping out a servant's entrance to make his way across the estate grounds. He only knew he couldn't deny the pull of something inside him toward that dower house, toward her.

Reaching the place where the woods opened into a little glen with a pond at its center, he paused, a flash of movement catching his eye. The swish of a white nightgown drew his eye, a brilliant splash against the dark of night.

It was her, he realized as he ducked behind a tree, peering out from behind it to watch her. She'd come to the water in only the thin garment, seeming not to feel the cold. Her hair hung in a riotous mess of curls down her back, her skin glowing pale in the light of the moon. She moved toward the pond like a ghost, her feet barely touching the ground as if she floated instead of walked. Looking like something out of a dream, she paused on the bank, arms raised high over her head as if trying to reach Heaven. From this distance, he could not make out all her features, but he imagined she had closed her eyes. She'd be serene, her bared arms broken out in goose bumps as the air caressed her skin with icy fingers.

She held his rapt attention as she began to move again, that ethereal grace carrying her into the pond. He shivered against the cold, imagining that the water must sting like the devil with nothing more than the protection of a flimsy scrap of cotton. Yet, she showed no sign of discomfort, walking toward the center of the pond, the white gown beginning to pool around her legs in an undulating cloud.

His mouth fell open, his grip tightening around the trunk of the tree as he realized she did not seem inclined to stop. He knew this pond, had swum in it many summers with Daphne and Bertram. A few more steps, and she would drop off into the deep center with nowhere to plant her feet. Seeming oblivious to this, she kept going, the water now up to her belly, lapping under her breasts.

A vise clenched his throat as he lumbered out of his hiding place right before she fell out of sight, the tips of her fingers the last bit of her he saw. He held his breath, waiting for her to reappear on the surface with a splash and a gasp. She wouldn't have walked into the pond without being able to swim ... would she?

His heart pounded against his ribs, seeming desperate to leap free of his chest. His held breath made his lungs burn while he counted the seconds. Five, then ten, and twenty. Panic overwhelmed him when thirty seconds passed without so much as a splash on the surface, the water like a dark sheet of ice.

"Cassandra!" he bellowed, bursting through the trees and stripping off his greatcoat as he dashed to the water's edge.

He gave no thought to how cold the water would be as he tossed the garment aside and went splashing into the pond. Her ankle must be caught in the reeds that grew along the bottom, or her body convulsing and jerking as she drowned, lungs filling with water. There was no time to take off his shirt or his boots, no time to think of anything but her as he dove, fumbling about in the dark for a limb, a lock of hair, any part of her he could latch onto. Even with his eyes open, he could see nothing in the dark water, not a flash of the nightgown or a flailing limb. There seemed to be nothing except darkness and silence, leading him to wonder if he'd imagined it.

He went back up for a breath, swiping water out of his eyes and gazing about to ensure she hadn't resurfaced on her own. No sign of her, so he plunged again.

He wasn't mad, and he hadn't been seeing things. She was here—she had to be.

Suddenly, something struck his shoulder—a hand or a foot. He swiveled and took hold of it, relief flooding him as he followed what turned out to be a hand along the arm attached to it. She thrashed in his hold, the strength she exerted telling him that she lived, if nothing else. Wrapping both arms around her, he kicked for the surface, struggling to keep hold of her as she fought his hold, panic making the motions uncoordinated. Tendrils of her hair lashed his face and tickled his jaw, while a glimpse of her nightgown showed itself amongst the black water.

Finally, she stilled, seeming to realize that her struggles would drown both herself and her rescuer. Keeping one arm tight around her, he propelled them up, up and out of the depths. Frigid air stung his throat and chest as they sprang free with a splash, his head spinning from so much time without air. Coughing and sputtering, she began twisting and writhing again, trying to break free of his hold.

"It's all right," he managed between coughs. "Cass, it's me! It's Robert."

She kicked free of him, beginning to swim toward the bank. Puzzled by the evidence that she was a strong swimmer, he followed, panting from the effort it took when his rescue attempt had leeched all the strength from his limbs.

"You!" she spat, glaring at him over her shoulder as she trudged through the shallows. "What the devil were you thinking?"

His feet found the spongy ground, the wet earth sucking at his boots. His skin stung as if thousands of tiny needles prickled him, while his shirt clung to his chest.

"Me?" he replied, his breath still coming in shallow spurts as he struggled to steady it. "What about you? How could you be so reckless, wading in a pool you aren't familiar with in the dead of night?"

She'd reached the bank now, shuddering and shaking as she swiveled to face him, hands balled into fists at her sides. "I am thoroughly familiar with this swimming hole, thank you very much. Furthermore, I wasn't drowning, you idiot. At least, not until you came grasping about down there and frightened me half to death!"

Teeth chattering, Robert wrapped his arms around himself and stared at her, disbelief flooding him in a confused rush. Several thoughts filled his mind at once, but he couldn't seem to form any of them into words.

She'd gone under on purpose, and stayed there for a full minute, possibly longer, without surfacing. While she insisted she hadn't been drowning, Robert couldn't fight the fear niggling the back of his mind. It told him she was lying, or at least not telling him the entire truth. She hadn't been drowning … yet. But, something told him she might have wanted to, that she had come out here tonight to contemplate ending her life.

The horror that seized him at the thought proved overwhelming, panging through his entire body from the vicinity of his chest.

"I couldn't h-have kn-known," he stammered, his entire body now trembling against the frigid air. "I c-came upon the p-pond and saw y-you go under. Wh-when you d-didn't resurface, I …"

She crouched to pick up a dressing gown, swirling it over her shoulder as she rose. Casting him a derisive glance, she snorted, thrusting her arms through the sleeves.

"You thought to come to my rescue like the perfect gentleman you are. How very noble."

He wasn't certain if it were the cold air or the contempt dripping from her words, but annoyance rose in him faster than he could squelch. Taking a few steps toward her, he clenched his teeth to stop the chattering.

"I r-risked my own neck jumping in after you," he ground out. "Even if I assumed wrong, a s-simple 'thank you' might be in order."

She snatched the belt of her robe into a knot, then stomped toward him, her face set in hard, harsh lines, nostrils flaring. His belly clenched when she drew near, his limbs tingling as his blood rushed as if preparing him to run. He held his ground and told himself he was still shivering from standing about in the cold.

Her upper lip curled back into a sneer as she came nose-to-nose with him, her voice a harsh growl.

"Other women may find your false gallantry and heroics to be romantic, but I do not. In short, Mr. Stanley, I am not some wide-eyed damsel in distress … I do not need saving."

She stood close enough now that he could make out her every feature, illuminated by the moonlight shining from a cloudless sky. The icy water had stolen the warmth that usually kissed her skin with a healthy glow. Her eyes seemed larger, gleaming a silvery blue in sharp contrast to her pale face. Her hair looked more red than blond, wet and hanging around her face in slick coils. She achieved the sort of spirals other women used curling tongs or papers for with no effort, making him want to toy with them, pull each coil and watch it spring and bounce back into place.

But, touching her would be a horrible idea, so he kept his hands to himself, despite wanting to pull her into his arms and kiss that disagreeable frown right off her face.

"What were you doing on my property in the middle of the night, anyway?"

"Technically, I was still on *my* property until I approached the pond," he retorted. "I am your neighbor now, in case you weren't aware, and I often walk and ride in these woods."

Her raised eyebrows seemed to ask if he always traipsed about in the middle of the night. After a while, her silent, probing perusal made it difficult to stand still. Before he could begin squirming under her scrutiny, he turned to walk away.

"Right, then," he muttered. "It's a long walk back to Briarwell and it's bloody freezing out here."

He began picking his way around the edge of the pond, keeping an eye out for his greatcoat. He had no idea where it had landed when he'd cast it off. He'd just located it when Cassandra called out to him.

"Mr. Stanley!"

He turned to find she still stood where he'd left her, clutching at the lapels of her dressing gown as she watched him.

"Yes?" he replied, shrugging into his coat.

His toes had begun to grow numb from the water pooled in his sopping boots, but his coat offered a bit of protection from the elements.

Cassandra's expression shifted as she stared at him, as if wrestling with annoyance and sympathy. Finally, she heaved a sigh and motioned for him to follow her.

"I cannot very well send you back to Briarwell in such a condition. The least I can do is allow you a place to warm up and dry off. Come along."

Without waiting to see if he would follow, she turned and began trudging up the sloping path through the trees and toward the dower house. For a moment he contemplated refusing, turning back the way he'd come and returning home, the cold and his wet clothes be damned. She hadn't seemed happy to see him, which only made the fact that he'd been thinking of her for the past four months all the more embarrassing. Besides, it was clear she was doing this because she didn't want to be responsible for the consequences of sending him out into the night in such a condition.

But then, that nagging curiosity about her reared its ugly head, prompting him to follow wherever she might lead. There was also the prospect of a warm fire and dry clothing, so the choice seemed clear enough.

He rushed to follow her, unsteady on shaking legs and numb feet. He blew warm air into his cupped hands to keep them thawed and followed her through the trees and toward the cottage.

Even in the dark, he could see that the abandoned property had been prepared for its new occupant, the overgrown yard and garden tamed into some semblance of order, the roof repaired, and the door freshly painted. The manor itself, several acres deeper onto Easton Park lands, would need a bit more attention before the Duke of Penrose could visit or invite guests. After Bertram's indiscretions had bankrupted the family, his father had attempted selling off all his unentailed property, including Easton Park. But, the destroyed reputations of the Fairchilds had kept any potential buyers away. So, the family had been forced to abandon the property, and here it had sat, crumbling and falling deeper into ruin while its tenants found new homes and the servants sought employment.

"Will your uncle take up residence in the manor soon?" he asked, the silence putting him on edge.

She glanced at him from the corner of her eye as they passed a small garden enclosed by a stone wall with wrought iron adornments along its top.

"Not anytime soon ... at least, not until after the end of the coming Season. Penrose is partial to London and so are the rest of my family. I wanted out of the city, so he offered the dower house."

They neared the back of the cottage, where a pair of doors hung open to a terrace.

"Have you found Suffolk to be preferable?"

"It is quiet and isolated without being too far from Town ... which is all I required. I suppose the manners of some of our neighbors leaves much to be desired, but I expected nothing less."

He scowled to know she might have been treated poorly, but was hardly surprised. His own mother had spoken of Cassandra as if she had the plague.

Holding a finger over her lips, she led him into a darkened drawing room. On the table near the door sat a taper in a brass holder. She gestured for him to close the doors behind them and took up her candle.

The place remained silent and still as they moved through a

narrow corridor toward the front of the house. Then, he followed her up a steep staircase to the second floor, careful to keep his footsteps as light as possible.

Cassandra's taper cast their shadows against the wall, oblong shapes stark and exaggerated in the circle of yellow light. Opening the second door on the right, she ducked into a bedchamber. Robert followed, sighing with relief as the heat of a crackling fire began warming his face. He still shivered a bit, but no longer felt as if he'd been stabbed in the heart with an icicle.

"Take off your clothes."

The command came so suddenly, her voice shattering the silence of the room, that for a moment Robert could only stare at her. He flushed, her words calling all sorts of erotic memories to mind. He thought of taking off his own clothes, then hers, then laying her before the fire and …

"So that I can lay them near the hearth to dry," she added, raising an imperious eyebrow at him.

Where before he'd been freezing cold, he was now burning up with embarrassment. He felt like an utter dolt for his wandering thoughts. Of course she only wanted to make sure his clothes were dry.

"Here. Wrap this around yourself once you've disrobed."

She offered him the counterpane from her bed, then began undressing herself. Robert laid the blanket over the back of a nearby armchair and began peeling off his clothes. While he let each garment fall into a pile on the floor, he could not help but stare at Cassandra, who neglected the privacy screen on the other side of the chamber as she let her dressing gown slip down her body. He paused, his fingers trembling at the buttons on his trousers as he watched her work the fastenings down the front of her nightgown.

The rapidly opening gap of the garment displayed the swells of her breasts, the wet fabric clinging here and there, leaving little to the imagination. Biting his lip, he lowered his gaze when she glanced up to catch him staring. Stilling his numb, shaking fingers, he began working his own buttons again.

"You can turn your back if it offends your sense of modesty to look," she said. "But ... well, you've seen all of me, haven't you?" God, had he ever.

"Right, of course," he replied, daring another glance at her.

She had moved to the fireplace and stood there in the buff, brushing her wet hair with smooth, rhythmic strokes.

His next words fell out before he could think better of them. "Not that I'd look away because I ... I mean, I like looking ... you ..."

No woman had ever robbed him of words. Even with Daphne he'd always had the perfect, honeyed words on the tip of his tongue.

Cassandra turned him into a bumbling idiot, and he wasn't certain he liked the feeling.

"I think you're beautiful," he finally managed.

She paused mid-stroke, the brush pressed against her hair. The curls began to frizz as they dried, leaving her looking like some wild goddess, the flames turning the blond tones to pure gold.

"Another thing other women might enjoy that I do not Mr. Stanley ... empty flatteries."

He frowned, taking a step toward her before remembering he stood there in only his drawers. Clearing his throat, he took up the counterpane and wrapped it around his shoulders. Then, using one hand to keep the blanket closed over his body, he used the other hand to push his small-clothes down around his ankles. Then, he knelt to gather the clothing and approach, careful to use the blanket as a shield.

And it was, indeed, a shield—against her probing eyes and her notice of the erection growing between his legs. The sight of her standing about nude affected him in the most primitive of ways, and he did not wish to flaunt it.

"I did not say it for the sake of having something to say."

He offered her his clothes, then lingered near the fire to soak in its heat.

Already, the feeling had come back to his toes and he was quite warm beneath his counterpane.

"The word 'beautiful' gets thrown about so casually, it has no meaning any longer," she said while spreading his clothes out over a small loveseat facing the fire, smoothing her hands over them as she did. "It's used against every empty-headed chit to make her feel special, when the same word is applied to trees and flowers and the sky. In truth, it reduces a person to being no more than an ornament to their surroundings, and I have no interest in that."

Her words spoke to a deep-seated part of himself—the part that had longed for people to see him as more than the 'pretty' Stanley boy, the one people only wanted to be around because he was pleasant to look at. He had very few close friends because of it, the interest of others proving shallow at best.

"I didn't mean to be cliché," he said. "It is just … well, instead of saying that, I ought to have said that I think your hair is quite the most interesting thing I've ever seen. Not quite blond or red … sort of gold at times. Your eyes, too … not blue, but not gray either."

To his surprise, she smirked at him, the expression both teasing and mischievous. "Mr. Stanley, are you calling me a conundrum?"

A little chuckle bubbled up in his chest. "You are, indeed. Which is why …"

Staring into the flames, he bit his tongue, cursing himself for almost embarrassing himself yet again. What was it about being in her presence that made him want to spill his every secret—even the deep, dark thoughts he'd never whispered to another soul?

She turned to face him, letting her hairbrush drop to the floor, the grayish glint of her eyes turning to molten silver as if heated by some internal fire.

"Why, what, Robert?" she asked, taking a step toward him, then another.

A lump rose in his throat, swift and hard, making it difficult to breathe let alone speak. Her breasts swayed with every step, the pink tips earning his full attention. They were the perfect caps for the teardrop-shaped orbs, and he remembered them being quite sensitive to the touch. Her reaction when he'd teased them with his tongue had been electrifying.

She took hold of the counterpane wrapped around him and gave it a sharp tug, yanking him even closer. He sucked in a sharp breath and struggled to stay on his feet, the throbbing organ between his thighs making it difficult to think. She was touching him, pulling him close and looking at him as if ready to devour him whole.

Heaven help him, he wanted to let her.

"Tell me," she demanded, a sharp command thinly veiled under a seductive purr.

And just like that, she'd snared him like she had that night at the White Cock. He'd do or say anything to have her touch him, command him, rule him.

"Why I haven't stopped thinking about you since … that night," he murmured, lowering his gaze to her lips. "I have tried for four long months, but to no avail. You have been like a fever in my blood, always raging with no relief in sight."

A cat-like smile curved her lips, and she used both hands to cast the counterpane aside. He stood naked before her, every bit of him exposed—including the cockstand pointing straight at her as if to indicate that the thing it wanted stood right there.

Her eyes glittered even more, her gaze sliding down his bare chest and abdomen before landing on his cock.

"Have you thought about how I fucked you?"

"Y-yes," he stammered, nearly doubling over when her fingers closed around his shaft. "God, yes."

"Have you stroked this cock to the memory, wishing for it to happen again?"

His head fell back and his eyes slid closed as she gave him one long stroke from base to tip, her thumb smoothing over his swollen head.

"Constantly," he confessed. "Almost every night since."

She met his gaze while still working his cock—up, down, that slow drag of her palm over his flesh pure torment as he fought not to thrust into her hand.

"What if I told you that you could have a favor from me? Anything you wish, in exchange for your attempt at saving my life tonight. I might not have been drowning, but you didn't know that. I think you deserve a reward regardless."

Your cunt wrapped around me, he thought. *That's what I want.*

But he kept that to himself, his mind racing as he thought over the other things he wanted from her. Obviously, he wanted more of the explosive pleasure she'd given him in the upper room of the White Cock. But, based upon the way she was looking at him and the grip of her hand around his cock, Robert could very well guess where this was going. He would have her cunt whenever she decided to give it to him. So, what else did he desire that she wouldn't give unless he made it his one request?

Recalling the one restriction she'd placed on him during their first encounter, he was struck with inspiration. There was one thing he wanted more than to be inside her.

"I want to touch you," he declared, never allowing his gaze to waver from hers.

Surprise flickered in her eyes, her brow furrowing. "That's all? You don't want to ask me to fuck you, or suck you off, or—"

"No. Only to be allowed to touch you wherever I wish. If you decide to allow me the rest after that … well, I certainly will not mind."

If he employed the correct strategy, she would allow it—he'd make certain of it.

Releasing his prick, she backed toward the loveseat where she'd spread his clothes. Pushing them aside to make room for her, she sank onto the cushion. Slouching a bit, she rested her arms over the back of the sofa and then spread her legs. His mouth went dry at the sliver of pink flesh peeking out at him from the swirls of reddish-gold curls between her thighs, slick and glistening in the firelight. He almost regretted not asking to taste her, but then thought of how that silky, wet flesh would feel against his fingertips and decided he'd chosen right.

"You'd better get on with it before I change my mind."

It was all he needed to approach her, his cock throbbing and aching with every step. He ignored his own need, focusing upon the task at hand. She was going to let him touch her, and he did not intend to squander the opportunity.

Going down to his knees between her legs, he braced his palms against the insides of her thighs and spread her a bit wider. She drew in a sharp gasp, her eyes growing heavy lidded as she watched him smooth his palms up the long limbs.

As he'd suspected, her body was all taut sinews, her thighs alluring in their suppleness as well as their strength. He exerted pressure on the tendons leading up to her groin, smiling at the little groan it produced from her. He smoothed his hands up over her hips and bypassed the offering of her vulnerable cunt altogether. The action seemed to surprise her, but he went on in his exploration as she watched, passing over the smooth plane of her belly. Her chest rose and fell with sharp breaths as he made his way to her breasts, his fingers itching for their first feel of that soft, perfect flesh.

He leaned in, the heat of her core pressing against his belly as he braced himself over her. Cupping both her breasts at once, he closed his eyes with a deep sigh. She felt just the way he'd imagined, heavy yet still somehow soft. The fit of her in his palms was so perfect it became difficult not to give in to the whimsical notion that she'd been made for him.

Glancing up to find her watching him, he met her stare and held it while smoothing the pads of his thumb over both nipples. Her eyes slid closed and she groaned, arching her back in a silent demand for more. He obliged her, strumming her nipples in slow circles and watching how they furled tight in reaction. His cock pulsed and leaked, droplets of his seed smearing his head as thoughts of all the things he could do with such magnificent breasts filled his mind with salacious imaginings. He could kiss them, lick them, bite and suck them, fit his cock into the cleft between them and thrust back and forth with all that flesh pressed tight around him.

He bit back a groan and tempered his own urges, doing his best to remain within the parameters of his request. She would let him know when she was ready to allow him more.

Tightening his hold on her breasts, he squeezed them, then pinched her nipples—gently at first, then with increasing pressure. She cried out, her legs clenching around him as she shuddered and writhed with each pull of his finger and thumb.

Once he'd driven her mad—thrashing and writhing about beneath his hands—he traveled back the way he'd come, playing his fingers over the expanse of her belly and watching the way it made her shiver. Keeping one hand braced against her lower stomach, he let the other one slip between her legs. She gasped when he stroked his first finger down her center, tracing the seam of her mons and the tender flesh concealed within. The slick heat of her arousal surrounded him as he delved deeper, testing her entrance with his middle finger and then sinking it deep. She sighed, gripping the edge of the sofa and raising her hips to take him in deeper, her wetness soaking his knuckles as he added his first finger to the second, both now enveloped by her hot, satiny sheath. The scent of her arousal made his mouth water for a taste, his position on his knees putting him in the perfect position to take it.

But, she was quite literally at his fingertips, writhing and bucking as he pressed his thumb against her clit. And she was so close to splintering—he could hear it in the harshness of her breaths, felt it in the tension thrumming through her and the tight squeeze of her cunt around his fingers. Her legs clenched, meeting resistance as her knees came against his shoulders. He wedged himself between them, keeping her legs open while working his fingers in and out of her and stroking her with his thumb. She threw her head back and let her hips rise up off the sofa, her limbs trembling as she released.

The rasp of her nails against the cushions intertwined with the ragged sounds she tried to keep trapped behind clenched teeth. Her entire body snapped taut, going still while her insides pulsed around his fingers. Then, she fell limp with a rough sigh, her head lolling and her body becoming pliant once more.

Robert slipped free of her, raising his glistening fingers to his lips. The scent of her clogged the air around them, exacerbating his already painful arousal. She was right there for the taking, legs spread, the glistening pink opening to her body exposed and beckoning to him with promises of pleasure and oblivion.

She glanced up at him just as he enveloped his fingers in his mouth, lapping up her juices and humming at the earthy taste of her. Her lips parted and her eyes widened, something dark and primal glinting in the depths. Sitting up straight, she reached out and took hold of his hair, urging him back to her with an unceremonious yank. His scalp stung, the sensation spreading to other parts of his body in an electric crackle that ended right at the tip of his cock.

"Fuck me," she rasped while wrapping both legs around him.

She used them to force him even closer, threading her fingers in his hair and raising her head to kiss him. Bringing one knee up on the sofa, he angled himself between her thighs, the tip of his cock brushing against her silken, hot quim. Her mouth claimed his, hard and demanding, her tongue thrusting deep into his mouth. He cupped her buttocks, tilting her hips at the perfect angle and pushing into her, moaning into her mouth. Keeping her legs tight around him, she took hold of his shoulders and held on, using his body for leverage so she could move against him. They collided in a swift rhythm, the cadence of her thighs slapping against his a staccato drumbeat matching the rhythm of his heart

He groaned when she bit his lip, the jostling of their bodies causing her to draw blood. Robert tried to pull away, but she growled into his mouth and used her grip on his hair to keep him in place. The metallic taste danced on his tongue, mingled with the flavor of Cassandra—primitive and wild.

The pain of the bite fizzled into something else, ramping up his pulse and sending a heady rush of blood straight to his head. His cock throbbed within her as if begging for more. Tearing his mouth away from hers, he stared down into her eyes, never losing their rapid rhythm.

"Hurt me," he growled. "Please."

A wolfish smile spread across her face, that predatory gleam in her eyes sharpening as she read the need and desperation in his words. Tightening her grip on his hair, she wrenched his head back to expose his throat. Bracing one hand against the back of the sofa, he slowed his pace inside her, holding his breath and waiting for whatever torment she would subject him to.

The breath left him on a hoarse shout when she sank her teeth into the side of his neck. His entire body jolted as the sharp burn of it overwhelmed him. His hips snapped, returning him to their frenzied rhythm. She moaned against his throat, her mouth still latched onto his neck as she suckled him like a vampire drinking its fill. The pulls of her mouth added heat to the original bite, sending acute tremors of pure pleasure rolling down his spine.

The sofa rocked beneath him as he fucked her like a madman, his mind going blank of its typical, endless thoughts. He did not care if anyone heard them, or if he was being too rough with the woman mauling him like a lioness. He did not care about anything other than the explosive ending looming closer and closer with every scrape of her teeth against the stretched tendons of his throat. Her heels dug into his arse, urging him deeper. He rolled his hips, grinding against her and digging as deep as humanly possible, desperate to take her with him when he climaxed. She shuddered, panting against his neck as the telltale fluttering began deep inside her. He gritted his teeth and fought back the simmering sensation in his cods threatening to erupt at any second.

Then, she was spiraling, groaning against his shoulder as her insides began to clench and spasm. She bit him again to muffle her cries, this time just beneath his collarbone, her fingernails dragging down his back. He jerked out of her at the last possible second, and his spend began spurting from him in powerful waves that made his legs buckle. Gripping tight to the back of the sofa, he lowered his head, feeling like a cad for the way his seed splattered her belly and thighs, but lacking the strength to remove himself from on top of her.

For a few moments, there was only the darkness and his heavy breaths mingling with hers. Then, her laughter reached out to him, soft chuckles that reminded him of a cat's purr. It stirred something deep within him, some part that warmed to the sound and craved more of it.

Opening his eyes, he found her relaxed beneath him, eyes heavy lidded and lips curved into a smirk.

"And here I was beginning to think that you would be the perfect gentleman even when fucking me," she said. "But look at you … you've gone positively feral."

His face blossomed with heat as he gazed down at his cock, gone flaccid in his hand and smeared with her juices. Then, he gazed at her inner thighs, reddened from his battering thrusts and splattered with thin rivulets of his spunk.

"Before you open your mouth to apologize … don't," she said, lifting her arms over her head and stretching with a soft sigh. "In case you hadn't noticed, I have no interest in false gentlemanly sentiment. I'm not a piece of glass and don't relish being treated as one. That was ... invigorating."

He finally found his way to his feet, staggering back and turning toward the privacy screen he assumed concealed a washstand. Ducking behind it, he was proven right, finding a ceramic bowl filled with cool water and a variety of bottles and vials along with a stack of folded linens. He took one up and dipped it into the water for Cassandra.

"You speak as if behaving as a gentleman should is somehow repugnant."

Her derisive snort reached out to him through the screen. "Because most gentlemen use the niceties of good manners and pretty speech to conceal the truth about themselves. I much prefer for people to portray their true selves, don't you? That makes it so much easier to know whom to trust."

He offered her the dampened linen. She accepted it and began wiping away the evidence of what had just transpired.

He found that his clothing had fallen to the floor in the flurry of their coupling, and bent to pick the articles up. While not soaked as they had been, they still proved quite damp.

"Not all men who act with courtesy and kindness are doing so with ulterior motives," he said, taking up the counterpane and wrapping it around his body once more. "Not every gentleman you meet is wearing a mask."

She went to the washstand, the linen hanging between her fingers. When she came out from behind the screen, she met his gaze and folded her arms over her bare breasts.

"Lord Bertram Fairchild was every inch the gentleman until the moment he was not," she snapped. "So, you will forgive me if I find that difficult to believe."

His mouth fell open, and for a moment he struggled to find words. "Oh ... I ... I'm sorry, I didn't—"

"Don't," she interjected. Her hands had balled into fists, her eyes gleaming like steel. "Don't do that. I do not need your pity."

Furrowing his brow, he swallowed past the lump in his throat. Did she think it was pity he felt toward her?

"I don't pity you," he replied. "I admire you. It couldn't have been easy, telling the world what happened to you. But, you did it with more grace and strength than I ever imagined one person could possess."

Her jaw hardened, working back and forth as she seemed to grind her teeth. Her gaze never left his as she shook her head and snorted, as if thinking him an utter dolt.

"Meanwhile, you and Bertram were the best of friends. Were you not?"

He flinched, his own guilt over not knowing the truth about his childhood friend never far from his mind. "I thought he was, but as it turned out I did not truly know him. In the few years leading up to the revelation of his … indiscretions, we drifted apart."

"And you must think it so singular, this wolf in sheep's clothing moving amongst the *ton*, preying upon the innocent and defenseless."

In truth, he had thought it beyond the pale—unthinkable. Obviously, he'd heard whispers of scandal here and there, but never anything so heinous as what Bertram had done. His ignorance of the things happening right in front of him had made him feel as if he were partly to blame.

"I am not like him," he stated. "We are not all like him."

Striding toward her bed, she gave him a pointed look over her shoulder. "That may be true, but you have no idea how many Bertrams there are amongst your peers. You'll never know if you're unable to look past the cut of a man's coat or the propriety of his speech."

Before he could say another word, she yanked back the sheets and gestured toward the bed.

"Your clothing won't be dry for hours yet, and it is late. You may as well get into bed and try to sleep. That is … unless you're afraid you might be missed. Wouldn't want to worry Mother."

The offer of a warm bed was welcome after his long and eventful night, but her comment had put his teeth on edge.

"I realize it is quite the thing amongst our peers to make fun of me for having respect for the woman who birthed me," he ground out. "But I do not find it so amusing."

She left the bed and reached out to take hold of the blanket, using it to yank him toward her.

"I am tired and I know you are, too. Let's go to bed."

Her closeness overwhelmed him—the heat of her body, her scent intertwined with his, the playful gleam in her eye. He had no desire to put his damp clothes back on and walk home in the cold and dark. The call of the soft, warm bed, and the soft, warm woman he'd be sharing it with was too great a temptation to resist.

They spread the counterpane over the bed together. Once settled in bed, he glanced over at Cassandra. She lay on her back, her bedraggled hair spread across the pillow. She stared at the ceiling, her gaze pensive. After a long moment, she turned her head to meet his gaze.

"I don't sleep much," she said. "When I find it difficult to rest, I swim … it helps me clear my head."

There was a lack of conviction in her words that had him wondering if there might not be more to it. She might protest if he pressed, but a part of him wondered again if she'd gone under the water with the intention not to resurface. Perhaps, if he hadn't dived to retrieve her, she might have changed her mind or let fear get the better of her. Or, she might have remained down there until she drowned. He shuddered at the thought.

"I do not sleep well either … most nights," he confided. "It has gotten worse, recently. And when I am restless, I walk. Tonight I happened to wander a little farther than usual."

Because of her … he'd walked to the edge of his family estate for a simple glimpse of her home. He was pitiful, sniffing about for pieces of her, because he suspected it was all she'd ever let him have.

Did he even want more than she'd given him? Months after Daphne had tossed him over for another man, Robert certainly wasn't ready to go throwing his heart into another woman's hands, nor did he think Cassandra wanted it. Why would she? Experience had taught her to see the worst in men, and there wasn't much he could say or do to persuade her otherwise.

But if there were … if he could …

No. The thought was preposterous. He liked her, and they suited one another well in the bedchamber. There didn't have to be anything more than that. With a woman as complicated as Cassandra—and he'd barely even scratched the surface—it seemed there never could be.

CHAPTER 6

LONDON, 1 WEEK LATER...

Cassandra paused before the front door of Penrose House, hand poised upon the knocker. Hesitation was not like her, but encountering her mother and sisters always required a moment in which to gird herself with the proper armor. The dowager duchess was a lot to take in all on her own—with her three favorite daughters surrounding her like a flock of birds, she'd be even more unbearable. The moment she said something insulting, it would become like a frenzy of sharks. One drop of blood in the water, and Cassandra would be torn to shreds.

She'd only come because it was Ophelia's eighteenth birthday, and if she didn't, they'd never let her hear the end of it. It would be the only invitation she'd receive for several months, since Ophelia's coming out meant rounds of parties and balls at which she would not be welcome. Her reputation had stained the family name enough—the dowager would not want her underfoot during her sister's first Season.

Taking a deep breath, she knocked, then stood back to wait for a footman to appear. She was admitted inside with the usual courtesies, her pelisse taken by the footman as the butler led her to the drawing room where the ladies of the house spent most mornings, lounging about and waiting for callers. This drawing room had the best light, the dowager often claimed—this, of course, being of the utmost importance for gentleman callers who needed to bear witness the full effect of the Lane daughters' beauty.

She paused in the doorway as the butler announced her arrival, taking in the familiar scene with a bitter taste in her mouth. Pandora lay across the sofa in a most strategic fashion, a floral shawl draping her shoulders over a cream morning gown. Her golden hair had been swept up and pushed away from her face with a matching bandeau, a few stray curls left kissing her temples. She glanced up from the letter she'd been reading to meet Cassandra's gaze, lips pursing into a pout, blue eyes showing clear disdain. Without a word, she went back to her letter without acknowledging her sister beyond that single glance.

Amaryllis sat in an armchair near the fire, her auburn head lowered over an embroidery hoop. She'd been the only one of the Lane daughters to inherit their father's burnished red hair, often leaving many to compare Cassandra's and find it lacking. The eldest of the sisters, Amaryllis had been the first to wed and now boasted three children—two of which were male, making her viscount husband quite happy.

In the center of the room, sharing a couch and poring over fashion plates and swatches of fabric, were the dowager duchess and Ophelia. The youngest Lane daughter still possessed a girlish face with rounded cheeks, limpid eyes, and the same fair coloring as Pandora. The young bucks would be after her in droves, a fact that thrilled their mother to no end.

Holding a lorgnette over her eyes, the dowager sat inspecting a fashion plate. Despite having heard the butler, she pretended as if she weren't aware that her second-born daughter stood within the room.

"This will make a lovely ensemble for your debut," she said to

Ophelia. "Though, perhaps with fewer of those frills. You're a young lady … not a table ornament."

"Oh, I quite like the frills, Mama," Ophelia said in a near whisper. "They look so … womanly."

Cassandra fought not to roll her eyes. Her sisters had been trained to speak in low, soft voices that would be 'pleasing' to a man's ear. It was the dowager's opinion that everything a young lady did was to be, in some way, aimed at satisfying a husband, both before and after the wedding. Cassandra's dissent had only been the first of many offenses to put her on the outskirts of her mother's affection—her public scandal proving the very last straw. It had been made clear on multiple occasions that she was merely tolerated because it would be unseemly to shun her completely.

"With your slight figure, so many flounces will overpower you. Trust me, Ophelia … Mama knows best."

"Of course, Mama."

The dowager did not acknowledge Cassandra until she had set the fashion plate aside. Observing her through the lorgnette still held over the bridge of her nose, her mother inspected her from head to toe. As always, her puckered lips portrayed her disappointment.

"Cassandra. How good of you to come."

She found an empty armchair near the hearth facing Amaryllis, who glanced up from her embroidery with a murmured 'good afternoon'.

"I could hardly miss Ophelia's birthday," she said before offering her youngest sister a tight smile. "You look lovely, as always. How does it feel to be eight-and-ten now?"

Her sister sat up and squared her shoulders with a smug grin. "Ever so wonderful. We've been planning my wardrobe for the upcoming Season. I've already been measured for my court dress."

Cassandra tried to muster excitement over it for her sister's sake—but it proved difficult when thoughts of her first Season made her sick to her stomach. It had begun with white gowns and dreams of making a good match, and had ended in pain, blood, and humiliation.

"How wonderful," she managed.

"Would you like to see the design? I've got the plate right—"

"As if such a thing would ever interest your sister," the duchess cut in with a huff. "Honestly, Ophelia, you know how little Cassandra cares for fashion."

This, she said while giving Cassandra's carriage dress a critical gaze.

"Or anything having to do with her appearance," Pandora murmured under her breath without glancing up from her letter.

Amaryllis giggled, head still lowered over her embroidery.

Cassandra stared back at the dowager, who seemed quite proud of her little barb, while Ophelia sat staring at both mother and sister with wide-eyed fascination. Her youngest sister did not possess as much venom as Pandora and Amaryllis, but was not without her own capacity for cattiness. It would only grow worse once she'd been introduced to the *ton*, taking on all those undesirable traits that left Cassandra at a loss for female friends. She hadn't had very many to begin with, but after her public humiliation, even her fellow wallflowers had abandoned her to stand on the outskirts of every soiree she dared to attend alone.

"I'm sure you will look quite lovely, Ophelia," she said without looking away from her mother's piercing stare. "Of course you will have to forgive me for missing your presentation and coming out. But I am certain you'll have a wonderful time."

The dowager raised an eyebrow. "It is good of you to admit that your presence would be an unnecessary distraction at such an important event. By the time we reach Ophelia's presentation, the talk ought to have died down completely. We wouldn't want to do anything to resurrect it and overshadow your sister's first Season."

Cassandra gritted her teeth. She'd thought enough time had passed that it would stop hurting for her mother to care only about the impact of all this on her sisters. No one had ever cared about her anguish or her fears. No one had fought for her, so she'd been forced to fight for herself.

"While I can hardly control what the *ton* chooses to concern themselves with or gossip about, I can choose not to appear where I am not wanted."

"You were hardly wanted to begin with," Pandora muttered, this time daring a glance in her direction.

Cassandra met her sister's stare, her jaw aching now from the strength it took to keep from blurting out every foul epithet on the tip of her tongue. That would only paint her as the villain, and her mother would have yet another reason to deride her.

Lifting her chin, she gave Pandora a sly smirk. "I can confess to not knowing how it feels to be as wanted as *you* are, sister. Your husband, your friends ... the string of paramours you collect like flowers from a meadow. How ... popular you've become over the years."

Pandora gasped, while Ophelia choked on air and Amaryllis snickered into her embroidery. The dowager scowled, looking as if she wished to deliver a scathing set down. But, to do so would give credence to the fact that Pandora had wasted no time taking on a string of lovers after providing her husband with his heir. The girl wasn't as discreet as she thought, and there were whispers aplenty about her. The hypocrisy of it all annoyed Cassandra to no end. Pandora was universally adored despite her escapades due to her status as an earl's wife, daughter of a duke, and the beauty that would allow her to get away with murder.

Turning to Amaryllis, who smirked in amusement while staring back and forth between her and Pandora, Cassandra snorted.

"How fares the viscount, Amaryllis?" she asked, not bothering to temper the sharpness of her tone. "I hear he's been seen about town quite often with that woman—an opera singer, is she not? Oh, but you should not worry. She isn't *that* beautiful, and despite what the rumors say her bosom isn't really so exceptional."

Amaryllis gaped like a fish plucked from a stream, her eyes widening as Cassandra's jab struck true. Across the room, the dowager made a low sound of disapproval, while Pandora shook her head and murmured something about Cassandra being 'an insufferable ingrate'. Ophelia flushed and pinched her lips together, and Cassandra couldn't determine whether her sister wanted to giggle or utter something in Amaryllis' defense.

The chiming of the long-case clock echoed through the cracked door of the drawing room, proclaiming the hour to be near three in the afternoon. Rising from her chair, Cassandra smoothed her hands over her skirts.

"Well, that was a lovely visit, wasn't it? I regret to take my leave now, but I have a friend I must call upon today. Shall I see you all at dinner?"

Without waiting for a response, she spun and made for the door, unable to help a little smile as she breezed into the corridor. As she approached the staircase, she heard Amaryllis' voice floating out behind her.

"As if the little witch has any friends."

"Now, now, Amaryllis," the dowager chided. "Let us not stoop to such levels of ill-mannered behavior. If she wants to ..."

Her mother's voice faded completely as Cassandra threw open the front door and rushed down the front steps. She was so grateful to be free of the house that she didn't bother going back inside for her pelisse. It had likely been stored in her room along with the other items she'd brought from Suffolk. Lila would be busy hanging things up, airing things out, and doing her best to make Cassandra feel at home in what used to be her bedchamber. Despite the maid's efforts, Cassandra would never feel at home within the walls of Penrose House ever again. Truly, she hadn't felt she belonged since the death of her father, who hadn't favored one daughter over the other.

Had he stilled lived five years ago, he would have been her ally instead of a tormentor twisting the knife in an already festering wound. If she'd come to him in tears with virgin's blood staining her gown and her full account of what a young lord had done to her in the back of a carriage, he wouldn't have asked Cassandra what she'd done to bring the attack upon herself. She wouldn't have been chided for allowing herself to be alone with a male suitor, or berated for crying over something that had been, according to the dowager, entirely her fault. When the duke went to confront Bertram's father about the incident, he would never have accepted a bank draft in exchange for his silence, nor would he have told Cassandra it was the best a girl of her plain looks ought to expect.

He would have pressed for charges to be brought against Bertram himself—if he could have kept himself from beating the young lord half to death, that is. He would never have allowed the *ton* to treat her poorly, would have given the cut direct to anyone who dared.

The current Duke of Penrose had been kind, doing everything he could to help ease her way ever since knowledge of Bertram's misdeeds had become common knowledge. But, despite the title and all its power and influence, he wielded it with none of her father's command or ruthlessness. He concerned himself too much with appearances, just like her mother, and there was only so much he would do to help her.

Papa, how I miss you.

Wrapping her arms around herself, she picked up the pace—partly to reach her destination faster, and partly to outrun the unpleasant thoughts of what life without her father had meant for her. It had hurt, losing him two years before her own coming out. Being without the man who had served as her confidant and champion when she'd needed him most had only exacerbated that pain.

She liked to think he would understand what she'd been forced to become, the mantle she had taken up as a defender of people who had no one to fight for them. If the duke would have used his influence to help those who needed it, then she could engage the tools in her own arsenal to do the same. Perhaps he would disagree with her methods, but in the end he would understand that there was simply no other way.

Glancing up, she found that she had neared her destination—the home of her friend, the Widow Dane, on Half-Moon Street. Amaryllis had not been wrong; she did not have many friends. In truth, there were only a handful—Lady Olivia Gibbs and the other women who had been victimized by Bertram, Millicent ... Robert.

Robert?

Could she consider him a friend? Thus far, she'd fucked him twice and spent every hour of the past sennight thinking of when they might repeat the experience. Their conversations had been strained and filled with pregnant silences. She felt certain she confounded him as much as she aroused him, which must be quite the muddling combination. And, she ought to know, because she'd been wrestling with those same conflicting feelings since their night at the White Cock. Thus her reason for visiting Millicent in the middle of the day. She'd taken care to arrive hours after noon, as her friend was known to keep late hours and sleep straight through the morning. By now, she could expect Millicent to be up and dressed, perhaps preparing to set out for Hyde Park. The Ravishing Widow loved nothing more than to drive her open air barouche down Rotten Row during the fashionable hour and scandalize the *ton* with her presence. Unlike Cassandra, Millicent wore scandal like a badge of honor, eschewing the rules of polite society and doing as she pleased. While many hated her for it, others adored her, and she proved a popular figure amongst the beau monde, as well as a polarizing one.

Such a life wasn't meant for Cassandra. She hadn't enjoyed excessive attention before Bertram, and had discovered during the trial and resulting fallout that she was even more ill-suited for it. Retreating to Suffolk had been the best thing for her, and she'd come to enjoy the peace and quiet of the country, the invisibility it offered her.

Before she could climb the front steps of Millicent's townhouse, the door swung open and Peter appeared on the threshold. He did not wear his footman's livery, his dark hair covered by a hat, the hem of a greatcoat swirling about his legs. He smiled when he spotted her.

"Lady Cassandra, what a pleasant surprise," he said as she ascended the steps. "Come for another sparring lesson? I was just on my way out to run an errand for my lady. But, I should return shortly."

"Perhaps another time," she said with a chuckle. "I've actually come to speak with Millicent. I assume she is in."

"She is," Peter replied, gesturing toward the half-open front door. "I just finished helping her dress, though there's a bit of time yet before she'll be on her way. I'll send word for her to meet you in her drawing room."

Cassandra didn't bat an eyelash at Peter's openness in allowing her to know he acted as a body servant of sorts to Millicent. Her friend's eccentricities were known far and wide, though only her close friends were privy to all the scandalous details. Peter had come to Millicent as a servant, and despite their arrangement as lovers, he insisted on being allowed to continue serving her. And so, outside his duties as a footman, he dressed her the way a lady's maid would—a convenient arrangement considering he spent most of his nights in her bed. While Cassandra couldn't say she fully understood the mechanics of their relationship, she knew that her friend was happier with him than she'd ever been. In the end, that was all that mattered.

Peter ducked back inside to confer with another servant before turning back to her. "Go right in. Mistress will be down in a moment."

"Thank you, Peter."

With a tip of his hat, he was gone, his long legs carrying him down the steps. Cassandra made her way inside. Another footman in brilliant red and gold livery was there to greet her, a smile lighting up his handsome face. He was tall and well-built, his shoulders straining at the seams of his coat. Her friend liked to be surrounded by only the finest of things, and that included the best-looking footmen in all of London.

"Good afternoon, Lady Cassandra."

The footman extended a gloved hand toward the open door to Millicent's favorite drawing room.

"Her Ladyship will be with you in a moment."

"Thank you," she said.

The room had shocked her to no end the first time she had entered it, but now it only felt familiar with its red walls and erotic art. The paintings and statuettes depicted men with women, men with men, women with women, and all manner of orgies. Her favorite pieces, a white marble sculpture near the hearth contained so many bodies in various positions that the limbs appeared like writhing snakes winding through and around one another.

She did not remain alone for long. After a few moments of warming her hands before the fire, Millicent entered the room dressed for her daily ride in Hyde Park. The widow looked as ravishing as ever, wearing a military-style spencer complete with frog fastenings across the bust, and gold braid coiling over one shoulder.

The high collar of her carriage dress caressed her jaw, and its ruffled sleeves showed at her wrists. Stylish nankeen half-boots peeked out from beneath her hem, and she wore a man's bi-corn hat with a large purple plume draping to one side.

"Cass, my love," she said, closing the door and coming across the room to embrace her. "I had no idea you were in Town."

"I've only just arrived," Cassandra replied, bussing her friend's cheek. "Penrose House was as miserable as ever, and I much prefer your company."

Carefully pulling a gigantic hat pin free of her hair, she removed her headwear and laid both upon the seat of an armchair. "Can I send for tea and cakes? You must be famished."

"I am not hungry, thank you, and I think I need something a bit stronger than tea."

Moving toward the sideboard, Millicent lifted one of several crystal decanters. "Brandy it is, then."

Cassandra made herself comfortable and waited for Millicent to pour their spirits. Her friend joined her on the sofa, handing her one of the tumblers.

"Now, then, tell me how you've been getting on. Are you settling into your new home? Doesn't it feel so delicious to live on what used to be Fairchild property and know it will never house one of *them* again?"

Cassandra issued a dry snort. "It's bloody fantastic, though Mother would call it unladylike to feel such glee over another family's misfortune."

"What nonsense. I would like to be left alone in a room with a locked door with your mother for five minutes. I'll show her unladylike."

That got a laugh out of her. "I should like to see that. Honestly, I do not know why I bothered to visit. It is Ophelia's birthday, and of the four of them, I do not dislike her quite as much as the others. That is sure to change once she's had a proper debut. At which point I will write them all off and continue to enjoy my solitary life as a wealthy spinster."

"Enough about them," Millicent declared with a wave of her hand. "Tell me what you've been up to since the White Cock. You did not tell me much about your evening with Mr. Stanley other than how enjoyable it was. I take it you've not been living as a monk since then?"

At Cassandra's hesitation, her friend raised her eyebrows and clicked her tongue.

"Come, Cass ... what good was going through with it if you do not intend to do it again?"

She cleared her throat, clutching her tumbler between both hands. "It isn't that I haven't repeated it. I have ... very recently, and with Rob —Mr. Stanley—again."

Shock appeared on Millicent's face for a moment, only to be replaced with amusement. "Well ... it would seem that our friend Robert was a more than satisfactory lover the first time around."

Thinking of the things he'd done to her with his pretty mouth and skilled fingers, Cassandra grew hot.

"Satisfactory is a mild word," she hedged. "And, as it happens, his family estate borders Easton Park. He is my neighbor now."

"How convenient."

"Is it? Or is it a complication I do not need? We were supposed to spend that one night together and part ways without a look back. Now ..."

"Now, he's close enough that you could have him whenever you wish. Providing he's amenable to such an arrangement."

Robert's glassy blue eyes appeared in Cassandra's mind, heavy-lidded with desire and wild with desperation. She'd been hard-pressed to forget his fervor, the desire that had grown and swelled between them until it enveloped them in a torrent of primal ecstasy.

"Yes, but Robert strikes me as a romantic," she argued. "I chose him for my first time because I knew he would submit to my demands. He did that, quite better than I'd expected."

"It sounds as if the two of you are well matched. You have certain needs, and he is capable of fulfilling them. That sort of connection doesn't come often for women like us. What is the problem, dear?"

Cassandra drained what was left of her brandy and sighed. "The romantic part ... It will become a problem if I allow this to go on, I know it will. He is ... too sweet, and ... and he keeps saying these things about my hair and my eyes, and ..."

"Perhaps he simply finds you attractive, Cass," Millicent said, her voice low and soft as she gave Cassandra a pointed look. "Not all compliments are lies."

"I am no beauty, and that is the truth."

"You do not find yourself beautiful. Shallow men who do not know how to look beyond the surface may not either. But Robert might be different."

"None of them are different!" she snapped, tearing her gaze away from Millicent's and staring off across the room.

She was uncertain why she was lashing out at her dearest friend, but something deep within her had rebelled at this notion that Robert might be special somehow. Perhaps his hidden desires spoke to the part of her that enjoyed being in control. That didn't have to mean anything beyond the meeting of cock and cunt.

Clearing her throat, Millicent shifted until she sat closer to Cassandra. "I certainly do not mean to pry or push you into something you may not be ready for. But, darling, would it be so horrible to let yourself enjoy it? It can be difficult to find a lover who can give you exactly what you need—especially when those needs are as singular as the ones you and I have. He only has to be the first, he does not have to be the last, or the only. As for that romantic streak you spoke of … you could make it clear that you want none of it. It is possible to engage in such a liaison without involving matters of the heart. I've done it many, many times."

Cassandra glanced up to meet Millicent's gaze and sighed. "You're right, of course. I'm sorry, I … I don't know what I was thinking. This is all so new to me, and the last time I let a man ply me with pretty words …"

She swallowed down the bile rising up in her throat at the thought of Bertram. Her hands clenched around the glass until she feared it might crack, yet she could not seem to ease her grip. The rage and revulsion she felt at the mere thought of the man who had ruined her had never abated, even after all these years.

Prizing the glass from her grip, Millicent took one of her hands and squeezed it. "You are in control, Cass. If Robert is open to the sort of arrangement you want, then I see no reason why you cannot indulge. Aside from the fact that it could help you to heal, it will also be a smashing good time."

She laughed and glanced up to find Millicent grinning at her, a mischievous glint in her blue eyes. "You are right, as always. Why shouldn't I have my fun? The men of our acquaintance certainly do!"

"That's the spirit. Now, why don't you come with me? After our ride in Hyde Park, you simply must accompany me to Bond Street. There is a hat in the milliner's window I've been salivating over for weeks. Oh, and there's a marvelous little coffee house I want to take you to. They have the best scones I've ever tasted. By God, you aren't wearing a coat! Come, you can borrow one of mine."

Letting Millicent take her arm and guide her from the room, she put Robert from her mind for the time being. Upon her return to Suffolk, she would make it clear that she was open to an affair of sorts. If he wanted the same thing, there was no need for any more of this worrying and thinking. For the first time in her life, Cassandra was free to live her life as she pleased. The entire *ton* despised her anyway ... there was no longer any need to have a care for propriety.

Robert Stanley would be hers for as long as she wanted him.

A FEW NIGHTS LATER, Cassandra stood in a crowded ballroom drinking watery lemonade and trying to keep her prey for the evening within her gaze. She had wished to return to Suffolk days ago, and wasn't ashamed to admit to herself that it had a lot to do with her desire to see Robert again. She spent her days thinking up inventive ways to give him more of the pleasure-pain he seemed to enjoy, and her nights stroking herself to climax while imagining every filthy thing she'd do once she got her hands on him again. When her mother and sisters began to vex her, she simply allowed her mind to wander to the carnal imaginings that dominated her thoughts as of late. If they wondered at her secretive smiles, they did not bother to ask. Not that they'd ever ask anything about what interested her, or what she thought. It brought her a great deal of amusement to imagine shocking them with the sorts of things she got up to when no one was looking.

Her plan to journey home had been waylaid by the arrival of an invitation to a ball at the home of Lord and Lady Gilbanks. The newly wedded couple had opened their new townhome to every member of the *ton*, it seemed, and the invitation had been for all the Lane daughters as well as the dowager. Lady Gilbanks was the daughter of a wealthy nabob who'd sought to elevate his family's standing in society by using a substantial dowry to help her nab a titled husband. He'd struck gold, and his daughter was now a countess. Because this would be her first event as Lady Gilbanks, she seemed determined to stuff her ballroom with as many bodies as possible. Inviting controversial people such as Cassandra and Millicent ensured the affair would be packed, as no one could resist congregating in order to gossip and stare down their noses at those who'd fallen out of their favor.

There was only one reason Cassandra had opted to attend, and he was standing near the dance floor amongst another group of gentlemen. They waited for the orchestra to begin playing so they could collect their first partners for the night.

Sir Wilfred Downing.

Unlike her past targets, this man was not a rapist. At least, she had no knowledge of any such crimes. However, Cassandra had seen the bruises Lady Downing tried to cover with powder and rouge, the careful mincing steps she'd taken when Cassandra had spotted her walking in Hyde Park. The moment her eyes had connected with the other woman's, she had seen it. She had known.

Sir Downing was beating her. It showed in the way she cowered whenever he looked in her direction, the way he grabbed her arm whenever she spoke out of turn—his grip hard enough to leave fingerprints. Cassandra had watched them in Hyde Park, had followed them home from the theater the night before last. Lurking in the shadows, she'd listened to him berate his wife for speaking to another man during the interval for too long.

As she sipped her lemonade and watched him laugh and smile, surrounded by others of his ilk, her fingers itched for the hilt of her knife. She already knew the word she would carve into his chest, could smell his blood and hear his screams and pleas for mercy. He'd probably piss himself, the coward. Men like him tended to fold like a deck of cards when confronted with someone who did not cower in fear at the sound of their raised voices.

The affair had only just begun, so she settled in for the long night ahead. Taking up her usual position amongst the other wallflowers, she listened in on the various conversations around her. It never ceased to amaze her the sorts of things people would speak about in public when they thought the din of other conversations were enough to keep them safe. But, as usual, no one noticed her standing amongst them, silently pressed against the wall.

As she expected, all gossip revolved around the highwayman terrorizing the Great North Road.

"Have you heard?" a matron in a silk turban whispered to a friend. "There hasn't been a single robbery for at least a fortnight!"

The companion wafted a painted fan before her face. "Of course there hasn't been. I knew the Masked Menace would turn coward once the Runners began investigating. The brute is probably too frightened to show himself for fear he will meet his match in them."

Cassandra hid her smirk behind her glass and remained half-hidden by a potted plant while she listened to the two women gossip.

"I suppose it's now safe to travel the roads at night," said the matron. "That Menace fellow will dance the hangman's jig in a month or less, mark my words."

The lady with the fan shuddered. "I hope so. What sort of blackguard terrorizes the innocent that way? He must be a perfect beast!"

"Hmph! He certainly is, and the sooner he is caught, the better. I've heard more than my fair share of debutantes romanticizing him, making him out to be some sort of dashing hero. What utter nonsense!"

"Ridiculous!"

Cassandra moved on, ducking her head and pinching her lips to keep from laughing aloud. As she moved through the crowded assembly, handing her empty glass off to a footman, she caught snatches of more gossip about the highwayman.

"I hear he's a giant … well over six feet tall!"

"A man who was robbed by him says the villain disappeared into thin air. He's a demon, I tell you!"

"He must be dead if he hasn't turned up in an entire fortnight. Fell off his horse and broke his neck, I'd wager."

Each claim was more outlandish than the last, making Cassandra's shoulders shake with barely contained mirth. The way the *ton* could take a bit of gossip and twist it into the most outlandish tales never ceased to amuse her. The truth was never as grand as what they could conjure in their minds, and stories of the highwayman were no different.

She neared the dance floor now, her gaze falling onto Sir Downing's back and latching on. The dancing had begun, but he didn't have a partner for this quadrille. So, he remained within the circle of his acquaintances, oblivious to her nearness or the plans she had in mind for when she finally got her hands on him. Pretending to watch the dancers, Cassandra kept her ear attuned to the conversation happening amongst Downing and his friends.

"I'd be careful if I were you," one of the men said while extracting a snuff box from his breast pocket.

"Just because the roads have been quiet these past weeks does not mean it is safe."

"He's right, you know," said a portly man with a quizzing glass held in one gloved hand. "Her Ladyship and I are off to Scotland to visit her ailing mother tomorrow—but only once the sun has risen and we shall only travel while there is light. One cannot be too careful in times such as these."

Downing waved a dismissive hand. "This Menace fellow does not frighten me. Besides, if the gossips are to be believed, he has either died, hidden away in an act of cowardice, or descended back into Hell."

He shared a chuckle with another man, but the fellow with the quizzing glass did not seem amused or convinced.

"Until I see him swinging from the end of a rope myself, I shan't believe he is gone."

"I say, Hollis, you fret like an old woman."

While the others burst out laughing at Downing's little quip, Hollis stared down his nose at them through his quizzing glass.

"Hmph. Call me what you will. If I'm an old, fretting woman, then at least I'll be a living one."

"Calm down, old chap," Downing drawled. "The man's a common thief, not a murderer."

"Not yet, he isn't," Hollis retorted. "The moment someone refuses to hand over their valuables, he's a dead man. And we'll see who's laughing then."

"I say again … I am not afraid of the Menace. I've business in

Devon and must leave tonight. I refuse to allow that blackguard to have me quivering like some schoolgirl. Let him try me if he will … I keep a blunderbuss under the carriage seat and would wager he's never been faced with something like that."

Cassandra rolled her eyes and shook her head, the man's bravado setting her teeth on edge. If it was the last thing she did, she'd have him sniveling and begging like the recreant he was. She only wished his friends could be there to witness it.

Moving away from Downing, she reclaimed her spot along the wall and waited for the ball to end. She followed him with her gaze, never letting him out of her sight. She watched as he drank, danced, and chatted his way through the ballroom, counting the minutes as the hour approached midnight. The affair would go on for a few more hours at least, but Downing seemed ready to depart, bidding his friends a good evening and edging toward the exit.

Cassandra followed at a sedate pace, weaving through the bodies packing the ballroom in his wake. She took her time, secure in the knowledge that no one would watch her movements. Heads had turned upon her arrival, but the *ton* seemed to have grown bored once they realized she would do nothing more than linger on the fringes of the crowd. While she had not earned her way back into their favor—and had no intention to—it seemed talk of her scandal was finally beginning to die down as other bits of news had begun making the rounds.

She waited while her wrap was fetched, keeping an eye on the open front door as Downing passed through it. A carriage pulled to a stop before the front steps, and Downing trotted down with a spring in his step. By the time she'd bundled herself against the cold and followed, he was gone, his vehicle threading through the others clogging the street. She did not rush, nor did she fret over losing sight of him. The crest etched upon the carriage door would be enough. She knew where he was headed, and what route he would take. He would not escape her.

Randall approached in her own carriage, so she swept down the front steps and made her way toward it on swift feet. Without bothering to wait, she threw the door open herself and leaped inside before giving the driver his instructions. Once enclosed within the dim interior of the carriage with only the sparse light of gas street lamps shining through the parted curtains, she reached for the parcel she kept hidden beneath the seat.

The long ride through London gave her plenty of time to shed her ballroom finery and exchange it for her ensemble composed entirely of black pieces. Only a white shirt offered relief from the darkness of her breeches, waistcoat, boots, and coat. It all became engulfed by the domino she clasped over her shoulders, shrouding herself in the color of the night. She spent the ride using a whetstone to sharpen her dagger and ensuring her pistol was properly loaded. When, at last, the carriage rolled to a stop, Cassandra hid the weapons on her person and reached for the black mask she used as a shield against her identity. A wide-brimmed hat completed the ensemble, turning her from Lady Cassandra, known spinster, into someone else entirely.

Randall hopped down from his perch as she let herself out of the carriage, her domino swirling about her legs. He'd stopped the carriage within the same thick outcropping of trees he always did, the darkness and foliage more than enough to keep them out of sight. Neither spoke as they went about their work, having done this enough times that communication proved unnecessary. Randall knew and approved of her mission, and had never once balked at acting as her accomplice. They could both hang for this, but the driver had never seemed concerned about such things.

"He cannot be too far ahead of us," he murmured as he handed her the lamp. "You'll catch him up in no time. Are you armed?"

"As always," she replied, holding up the lamp so that he could unhitch one of the horses.

Randall made quick work of the harnesses, freeing one of the pair of stomping, snorting beasts before handing her the reigns. "Take care, my lady. I heard drivers about the mews gossiping about how the magistrates have been conspiring with the Bow Street Runners to set up patrols along the road."

"So I have heard," she replied. "Do not worry, Randall. I will return before you know it. Keep a sharp eye on your surroundings and remember the plan. Should you find yourself set upon, you are not to wait for me. Do what you must to return home safely. I will meet you there."

She blew out the lamp and set it aside, while Randall went down on one knee, combining both hands into a cradle for her foot.

"I've told you time and again, my lady … I will not abandon you."

Bracing one hand upon his shoulder, she placed her foot into his hands and vaulted up onto the horse's back. Riding without a saddle had taken some getting used to, but she'd come to enjoy the freedom of it. Now that she lived alone in the country, she would enjoy riding this way more often, with no one about to tell her it was not proper.

"If we are fortunate, you will not have to," Cassandra declared.

Before Randall could reply, she was off like a shot, the long-legged Arabian galloping toward the road with one press of her heels. She bent her head to avoid the snare of tree branches, taking care to scan her surroundings. Her mask and hat obscured her vision a bit, but a high, full moon offered enough light for her to do what needed to be done.

Her domino flew out behind her with the whipping of the wind, stray tendrils of her hair caressing her face and neck. There were no vehicles just ahead of her, but Downing had to be out here. He'd expressed his plan to leave for Devon straightaway, and his bold claim that he did not fear the Masked Menace told her he would not do the prudent thing and travel from London along some other route. No, he would want to prove to himself, and everyone else, that he was no coward. Cassandra intended to prove otherwise.

She drove the Arabian at breakneck speed, watching for any sign of the carriage, listening for any approach that might be determined as threatening. She had no desire to harm a Bow Street Runner, but did not intend to let herself be put in irons either. She would do whatever was necessary to save herself should it become necessary.

At last, she caught the glimmer of light ahead—the yellow glow of a carriage lamp. She spurred her mount along faster, steadily gaining on the vehicle moving at a steady clip. Keeping hold of the reins with one hand, she palmed the butt of her pistol, but kept it shoved into her waistband. She wouldn't draw it until she was certain she'd overtaken the right carriage.

As she pulled alongside it, the moon illuminated the carriage's side, giving her a glimpse at Downing's distinct crest. She jerked her weapon free, pulse racing as the thrill of a hunt nearing its conclusion rushed through her. She would make Downing regret ever laying a hand upon his wife, make him pay for every bruise, every bloodied lip, every harsh word.

The driver spotted her and gave the ribbons a snap, calling out for her to cease, to turn back. She would do no such thing. He tried to outrun her, but her single mount was not encumbered by the weight of a carriage loaded down with trunks, so she gained on them with ease. The driver seemed in a panic now, hurling epithets while doing his best to outpace her.

Within seconds, she had pulled ahead of the carriage. She yanked her reins left, turning her horse directly into the path of the carriage.

Lifting her pistol into the air, she fired it twice, the thunderous crack of the shots throwing Downing's horses into a frenzy.

Her own mount reared up on its hind legs, but she gripped him tight with her thighs, hands clutching the reins in a white-knuckle grip. He calmed in an instant, falling back onto his front hooves and prancing in a swift circle as she murmured a few soothing words before returning her attention to the carriage. The driver shouted at the horses, while Downing's muffled bellows emanated from within. The beasts reared and whinnied their outrage, jerking against their harnesses.

Leaping down off her horse, Cassandra took off toward the carriage at a run. She'd practiced this with Randall many times, perfecting it before putting her skills to use for the first time. Having done this enough times now to do it with little thought, she moved without hesitation. The driver clambered down to meet her in an ill-fated attempt at protecting his master. Cassandra delivered a swift kick to the center of his chest, sending him against the side of the carriage. He fell against it with a gasp, the wind knocked from him as the vehicle rocked from the force of his weight. She moved fast, not wanting to give him the chance to strike back. Raising her pistol, she brought it down upon his head with all her might. He cried out, then crumpled at her feet in a heap, blood trickling from a wound on his temple. She gave him a little kick to ensure he was out, before stepping over his prone form and approaching the carriage.

She hesitated a moment when reaching for the door, realizing that Downing had gone silent. Recalling his bold claims at the ball, she decided it was better to be safe than sorry. Opening the door with a swift yank, she used it as a shield, darting behind it just before the blast of Downing's blunderbuss thundered out into the night.

"Show yourself, you son of a bitch!" he bellowed, the carriage rocking as if he made to exit.

Cassandra pushed the door with all her strength, grinning when it bashed against Downing's body and sent him reeling back inside. She heard the heavy thunk of the blunderbuss falling to the ground, and crouched to pick it up before entering the carriage. She hurled it as far away as possible, not bothering to see where it fell along the dark road before turning back to the man splayed on the floor of the vehicle.

He held his nose, which had been bloodied by the door, rolling about while he let loose a string of curses. She bounded inside and knelt over him, withdrawing her dagger from its place in her boot.

Pressing the tip against the base of his jaw, she grinned. "Oh dear … I'm afraid you have quite ruined the theater of my persona. I am supposed to say 'Stand and deliver!' … but, well, you can't exactly stand just now, can you?"

To his credit, Downing did not flinch away from her knife.

Instead, he sneered at her, his lips drawing back to showcase blood-stained teeth.

"Well ... I'll be damned. The Masked Menace ... a woman?"

She shrugged one shoulder, keeping the knife pressed against his throat. "Funny how that bit of information is conveniently left out of the rumors that get spread about me."

Downing spat at her, his blood splattering her domino and a few flecks of it finding its way onto her cheek. Then, he growled and lashed out at her, attempting to wrap a hand around her throat. She reacted with lightning speed, bringing her knife up and slashing, halting the momentum of his hand as the blade found his wrist. He screamed as blood spurted from the wound, wetting his face and staining his cravat. Taking hold of the injured wrist, she squeezed, drawing a tortured cry from him and another gush of warm blood.

"There, now you've attempted to overpower me and learned a very valuable lesson. If you strike out at me, I strike back—and I can assure you, I will be far more ruthless about it than you."

"You bitch," he rasped between swift breaths. "You fucking bitch ... I'll kill you!"

Cassandra snorted. "And how do you propose to do that when you can barely land a blow before I've cut you to ribbons?"

His other hand came up toward her, but she swung her dagger once more, this time landing it in the center of his palm. A high-pitched scream emanated from him as the blade stabbed clear through one side of his hand and protruded through the other. Clapping her palm over his mouth, she loomed over him, leaning down so close she could feel his harsh breaths against her cheek.

"Trying to strike me again? What ungentlemanly conduct. But then, I should expect nothing less from a man who beats his wife black and blue."

The whites of his eyes flared wide in the dark.

"Yes, I know all about how you keep Lady Downing in her place," she said with a sneer, removing her hand from his mouth.

"What has my wife to do with any of this?" he sputtered as she began loosening the knot of his cravat. "You are a highwayman! My valuables should be of far more interest to you than her. The watch in my fob pocket is worth—"

"I care not for your baubles, though I will help myself to them when I am done on principle alone. I am a highwayman as you said, so to leave without your jewels would be unseemly. However, you and I are going to have a bit of a talk first … about what I'm going to do to you for raising a hand to Lady Downing, and what will happen should I ever come to find you've done it again."

He attempted to fight her off as she used his cravat to bind his wrists together, but the dagger stuck through one hand made it a clumsy effort. Eventually, she had him subdued again—his wrists bound, and the handkerchief she found in his coat pocket stuffed into his mouth. He screamed around the fabric when she pulled the knife free of his hand, then went limp on the carriage floor.

Cassandra made quick work of opening his waistcoat, cutting away each ornate button with a flick of her dagger. Then, she cut his shirt down the front, exposing his torso. His chest heaved as he stared up at her, shaking his head as if to silently implore her.

"How many times did Lady Downing beg you?" she asked, tracing the tip of her knife across his chest in a threat of things to come. "How many times did she plead for mercy only for you to ignore her and take your impotence out on her?"

He strained upward, his face darkening in the moonlight as a vein in his forehead began to pulse and throb. He growled through the handkerchief, but she merely pressed a hand against his forehead and forced him back down.

"I can assure you, Sir Downing, no matter how much you beg, or plead, I will not stop until I'm good and damn well ready to. Shall we begin?"

Pressing the tip of the dagger against her starting point, she dug in and dragged it over his flesh. His visceral screams echoed out into the night as she worked, his blood welling in each cut and trickling back into his clothes. With a humorless smile, Cassandra cut and cut until he passed out from the pain, head lolling on his shoulders.

When she was finished, the word she'd chosen for him stood out in stark, crimson relief against his pale skin.

ABUSER.

While he lay unconscious, she quickly relieved him of his ring, tie pin, snuffbox, and pocket watch. She discovered a purse within his coat that contained several Sovereigns, and a few folded bank notes. She pilfered it as well, tucking all his belongings into her own breast pockets before leaping down from the carriage.

Her Arabian waited nearby, nickering and pawing the ground with growing impatience. Downing's driver remained unconscious, so there was no one to impede her as she threw herself up onto the horse's back and sped off into the night, disappearing under the cover of darkness with her domino fluttering behind her like a dark banner of death.

CHAPTER 7

Robert leaned back in his chair, one leg propped on a footstool and an ironed copy of the *The Examiner* spread over this thighs. His father sat upright in bed, eyes glittering with excitement as he listened to the latest news and gossip straight out of London. The papers were days old by the time they reached Suffolk, but the baron enjoyed the news anyway—particularly the bits of scandal and gossip he no longer heard firsthand. Being trapped in a sickbed meant he must live vicariously through Robert, and the stories his son carried back to him whenever he could.

"After several weeks without a sighting, it would seem the Masked Menace has reappeared," he told the baron. "An anonymous man has reported being waylaid by the criminal some three nights before the publication of this column. He reports that the Menace knocked his driver unconscious, then bloodied his nose and injured his hand before making off with a pocket watch, a ring, a ruby tie pin, and a silver snuffbox."

"Good Heavens," his father murmured, running a gnarled hand over his balding pate. "It seems this Menace becomes more violent with each new report. I suspect it will not be long before he's killed someone."

Robert shrugged, glancing at a caricature of the Masked Menace. In it, he wore an ill-fitting opera mask over a contorted face drawn in the likeness of a demon. A pair of massive horns curled up from under the brim of a hat, while a long, forked tongue slithered from a mouth sporting spiked, jagged teeth. He held a gun in one taloned hand and a dagger in the other.

Robert tilted the page to show the baron, who chuckled at the drawing.

"The stories about him are overblown and exaggerated," Robert murmured. "The violence increases with each telling because it sells papers."

"He is still a dangerous criminal," the baron replied. "I will be glad when the Runners have brought him to heel. The roads and its travelers will be safer for it."

"I could not agree more, William," said Lady Stanley as she bustled through the open door. She carried a tray holding the baron's lunch, as well as a pot of tea and a few cups resting on saucers. Pausing to kiss Robert's brow, she then turned to deposit it on the bed beside his father. "I cannot stress how happy I am that you have not seen fit to return to London," she declared as she went about pouring tea. "The road is no place for decent people during times like these. I shudder to think the danger you were in coming back from London all those months ago."

Robert wanted to point out that the highway robberies hadn't begun until after he'd returned from London, but held his tongue. She'd only maintain that he had been in danger somehow. There could be no arguing with her when it came to the matter of his health or safety. He glanced up to find her holding a cup and saucer under his nose, the earthy scent of tea wafting up his nostrils. His stomach turned and he cringed when she forced it into his hands—even though she knew he detested tea.

"Drink up," she insisted, turning back to lace the baron's cup with lots of milk the way he liked. "It's been cold today and you need to keep warm. Besides, tea is good for the constitution."

He stared into his cup with a sigh, knowing this was a battle he'd rather not wage with her. "Yes, Mother. Thank you."

Taking a careful sip, he grimaced at the taste of it. It was tantamount to blasphemy for an Englishman to dislike tea, but he had never been able to pretend he liked the stuff. He could never understand the fascination of the British with tea when coffee tasted so much better.

"Here you are, William. Mind you don't make a mess of your nightshirt."

"Of course, Rosie," his father replied, accepting the tray into his lap.

His mother took up her own cup and saucer, remaining perched on the edge of the bed while his father began tucking a linen napkin under his chin

"I've just met with Cook to discuss the menu for your birthday dinner, William. She's going to prepare all your favorites, as well as some new French recipes she's been working on. Our guests are sure to be quite pleased with the fare."

While at first, she had insisted that her husband was too weak to leave his bed for such an affair, the baron had argued that what might be his last birthday would be worth the effort.

"It does not require much strength to sit and converse while enjoying a meal, Rosie," he'd argued. "I may not see another year, and I want for this one to be special."

So, the baroness had thrown herself into planning the affair as she did this year, ensuring that her husband's seventy-seventh birthday would be the best yet. Invitations had already gone out to several of their neighbors, though Robert could guess that at least one person had been left off the guest list.

"Who have you invited?" he asked.

"Oh, absolutely everyone," his mother declared. "The Fletchers, of course. I wouldn't pass up the opportunity for you to spend more time with Miss Fletcher again. I think she is quite enamored with you."

Meanwhile, he could not be more disinterested in her if he tried.

But, as usual, he kept his thoughts to himself.

"Of course. Who else?"

"Oh, the Rodinghams—their son was always a great friend of your brother, you know. Viscount and Lady Loring, the Fareweathers, Lady Walter … the poor dove hasn't gotten many invitations since coming out of mourning. Let's see … I invited the vicar, Mr. Clarke. Such a dear man, coming to visit with your father so often and inquire about his wellbeing."

"Anyone else?"

His mother frowned, setting her cup in its saucer and furrowing her brow. "Who else is there?"

Sitting up straight, he let his leg fall off the footstool and leaned forward, ignoring the cup resting in his hands. "Oh, I don't know … perhaps our new neighbor? You know, the one everyone in the county has shunned and ignored since her arrival? Lady Cassandra?"

The baroness sniffed and raised her chin. "With good reason. She is a fallen woman."

"She has done nothing wrong, and does not deserve such treatment."

"Hear, hear," his father mumbled around bites of bread and cheese. "The way the *ton* has carried on so, you'd think *she* was the one who debauched half of London's debutantes."

His mother issued a dramatic gasp, one hand coming up over her bosom. "Honestly, William! To say such a thing."

"He is right," Robert said, taking another sip from his cup.

If he was going to war with her over Cassandra, then he'd have to drink the bloody tea.

"She is our neighbor and should be treated as such. I've had a few occasions to speak with her and I find her to be a charming and lovely sort of person. I know you would too, if you'd try to get to know her."

The baroness shook her head, giving him a look of disapproval. "I wish you wouldn't associate with her, Robert. Her reputation would cast you in a bad light. You'd do better in the company of a woman like Miss Fletcher."

The urge to throw his teacup against the wall came over him, but he pushed it down. He took a deep breath and fought to remain calm. His mother wasn't completely unreasonable; he just had to think of a way to twist her thinking to fit his own agenda. He wanted Cassandra near whenever possible, and he wanted their neighbors to stop treating her like a leper.

"Well, her reputation would not cast anyone in a bad light if you would become a champion of sorts for her. If you were to invite her, show her kindness in front of our friends ... well, they'd have no choice but to follow suit. At least here in our little corner of Suffolk, she could be accepted, with you at the forefront of the effort, of course. Imagine what the vicar would think of you inviting her in, hosting her at your table."

"He's right, Rosie," the baron declared, glancing up from his plate. "You could be a shining example for our neighbors to follow."

His mother perked up, a smile softening her wrinkled mouth. The baroness loved being the center of attention; all the better if she could be perceived in a flattering way. She might not care a whit about Cassandra, but she would publicly befriend her for no reason other than to boast that she'd been the first.

"I suppose the idea has some merit," she replied. "And we are short one lady, with Martin Fletcher coming along. If I invite Lady Cassandra, the numbers will be even. Perhaps there could be a bit of dancing after dinner. Oh, William, would that not be marvelous?"

Despite not being able to dance himself, his father smiled, giving the baroness his usual look of pure devotion. "It would be splendid, Rosie."

With a smile and a nod, she then turned her attention back to Robert. "I have a spare invitation that you can deliver to her residence."

He schooled his face into an indifferent mask, while his insides erupted into a flurry of sensation at the thought of seeing her again.

She'd left for London one day after their last night together, and he'd been thinking of her ever since, waiting for her to return.

The purple bruise from her bite on the side of his neck had begun to fade to a sickly yellow, the matching one on his chest following suit. Both marks seemed to tingle as if in response to her nearness, just a short walk through the woods and past the swimming hole. His mouth went dry and his stomach clenched, his cock stirring in his breeches. Delivering the invitation would give him an excuse to have the one thing he'd been longing for the past sennight—a glimpse into her eyes, a moment to drink her in. If she allowed him anything beyond that, he would be happy.

"Of course," he said, keeping his tone even. "I'll deliver it this afternoon."

"I will go find the invitation now before I forget. This old mind is not what it used to be."

"Your mind is just fine, Rosie," the baron murmured before returning his attention to his meal.

Once she was gone, Robert reached for the paper, leaving his teacup sitting upon the footstool. As he settled back into his chair, he caught his father staring at him, an amused smirk curving his lips.

"What?" he prodded with a raise of his eyebrow.

The baron chuckled. "Oh, nothing. I was just thinking that it is nice to see you moving on. I know how difficult things have been for you after Lady Daphne."

Raising the paper so that it obscured his face, he laughed. "That's Lady Hartmoor now, and ... I haven't the slightest idea what you're talking about, old man."

"Hmm," his father mumbled. "Right. Well, I will say this one thing and then speak of it no more. Next time, tell Lady Cassandra to aim her love bites a bit lower. The one on your neck is visible when your head is turned at just the right angle."

THE AFTERNOON SUN loomed high overhead when Robert set out for Easton Park on foot, a handful of fluffy clouds offering a bit of shade. His heart pounded and his stomach flipped this way and that. He'd missed her, if he were being honest with himself. Though, in the back of his mind a part of him wondered why. Aside from the obvious pleasures he'd enjoyed with her, she proved brittle and harsh. But, he'd come to realize that her hardness was nothing more than a wall closing out the world. And who could blame her? The woman had been through hell, both due to her ordeal at Bertram's hands and her treatment in the aftermath. While the world had shunned her, she'd learned to cultivate an armor of sorts, keeping herself safe from scorn and scrutiny.

She put him in mind of a rose—a deceptively soft and beautiful plant that sported sharp thorns. Those thorns did not make her any less appealing to him. For reasons he couldn't comprehend, they only made him want to delve deeper, to peel back her layers and see what he might uncover.

He was besotted; there was no getting around that. She'd drawn him in with the mystery in her eyes, and now he was ensnared completely, caught in the thrall of her darkness.

As he neared the pond where he'd last encountered her, he glanced down to find primroses growing in bright yellow clusters along his path. Beads of dew still clung to some of their petals, their orange centers calling out to him like a sunny beacon. He crouched to pluck a handful, imagining how they would look tucked into the loose spirals of Cassandra's hair. If his luck held up, he'd get to find out shortly.

He arrived to find the gate to her small garden hanging open. It might be best to step through the gate and determine if she was in there before he approached the house.

Turning off the footpath to the front door, he veered toward the garden, clutching the envelope and his fresh-picked primroses in one hand.

A gardener's work made itself apparent as he stepped into the small space, finding newly-planted foxglove, hyacinth, betony, and hydrangea. The blooms jutted from the soil in strategic places amongst a flagstone courtyard, with rusted wrought iron benches here and there. A few stone statues filled in the spaces between flowers—angels and fairies, whimsical pieces of art that would be further complemented by the buds once they'd begun to overtake the space.

He found Cassandra seated shaded by a May tree, its branches hanging over from the outside of the wall. Its buds had yet to open, but in another month or so, the blooms would pepper the bench and the ground with white petals. She had not yet noticed his approach, her head lowered over a book, her hair gleaming with reddish tones in the shadow of the tree. She wore a simple morning gown of sprigged muslin, a robin's egg blue sash offering a vibrant splash of color. Her hair had been pulled back into a simple chignon, though a riot of curls had worked their way free to kiss her forehead, temples, and jaw.

While sitting still, she presented a far different picture than when she was in motion. Without the perpetual anger furrowing her brow and pinching her lips, she was soft and womanly. She made him want to go to his knees and rest his head on her lap, gaze up at her and watch the way the sunbeams shining through the branches lit her hair on fire. The tender feelings were completely at odds with the tempest of lust and curiosity she usually provoked. Something deep within him panged, resounding throughout his entire body.

Then, she glanced up and locked eyes with him, and her entire demeanor shifted in an instant. Her eyes hardened with a silver glint, spine snapping straight and her chin lifting a tick. All the softness had been leeched from her entire being by nothing more than the realization that she wasn't alone.

Refusing to let that intimidate him, Robert started forward.

"How was your visit to London?"

"Ghastly," she replied, her voice heavy with spite. "I am glad to be home."

He wanted to ask her what had happened, but the look in her eyes warned him off. Whatever it was, she'd left it in Town, and obviously didn't wish to bring it home with her.

"I..."

I missed you.

He bit the words back, knowing she would not appreciate them, even if they were true.

"I have something for you," he declared, handing over his offerings.

She took the cluster of primroses first, giving him a questioning gaze. His face grew warm under her scrutiny.

"I discovered them on my walk here and they made me think of you."

That was one truth he couldn't keep to himself. She stared at the flowers a moment longer but said nothing about them—or what he'd just said. Instead, she busied herself with the envelope.

"What's this?" she murmured as she slid the thick card out and turned it over in her hands.

"An invitation to a dinner party on the night of my father's birthday. Mother and I were talking, and we decided you must come."

Pursing her lips, she gave him a pointed look. "Your mother wishes to invite me into her home?"

"Well, you are our new neighbor."

She scoffed, setting the invitation aside. "And not one of *my* new neighbors has come to call since I arrived, the baroness included. Do you expect me to believe any of them will tolerate my scandalous presence?"

Robert gave her a sheepish shrug. "Everyone loves a scandal. None of them will be able to resist bragging about how they survived a night in your company."

With an annoyed huff, she rose to her feet, the primroses falling to the ground. She paced away from him, tension gripping her shoulders.

He was on his feet in an instant, reaching out to take hold of her shoulders. She stiffened and whirled on him, eyes wide as if he'd startled her.

He held both hands up and took a step back, remembering her rule against touching without permission.

"I'm sorry. It was bad of me to make light of the situation. And you are right ... our neighbors have been turning their noses up at you from afar since you arrived. But, that is why I insisted Mother extend an invitation to you. I made her understand that they're all being ridiculous, and we must be the ones to set the example. You'll be made to feel welcome, I promise."

"Yes, while they whisper behind my back and look at me as if I am some insect to be stomped beneath their heels."

"No, that isn't the way of it."

"It is!" she insisted, hands braced upon her hips. "Do you have any idea how much derision I must endure whenever I visit London? I came to Suffolk to escape that, Robert, not subject myself to more of it."

"Then rise above it," he argued, coming toward her again.

He reached out on instinct, but then paused before his hands could make contact. At the silent question in his gaze, she hesitated only a moment, then gave a swift nod. He took hold of her waist before she could change her mind, and pulled her toward him.

He wanted to revel in the feel of pliant flesh at his fingertips. She'd just allowed him to touch her in a way that had nothing to do with sex ... and it felt as if such a moment ought to be observed, exalted in. But, he was on a mission, and having Cassandra at this dinner party suddenly became imperative.

"Wouldn't you rather stop hiding for once and rub their noses in it? Arrive wearing the most ravishing ensemble and make them take notice. Force them to see you as someone who commands respect. You certainly changed my perspective of you, so I know you can make them see it, too. Make them see how little you care for their regard and they will clamor for it."

She blinked, looking at him as if he'd lost his mind. "And just what did you think of me before?"

"That you were meek, reserved. But, you are none of those things. You are strong, Cass. You are fierce and vibrant, and you've been hiding all these years. But, you cannot hide from me anymore. I see you."

For a long moment, she stared at him in silence, seeming taken aback. He had surprised himself. The words had simply come spilling out of him before he could think to stifle them. But, he did not regret letting her hear the truth. Saying what was in his heart had been liberating in a way, allowing him to be himself without restraint. It would seem being tossed over by Daphne hadn't killed the romantic living deep inside him.

"Why does it matter to you if I attend?" she asked, furrowing her brow. "I take it this is an annual event?"

"It is."

"Then he will have another."

"No, he won't."

At her confused expression, he swallowed the grief welling in his throat and pressed on.

"He is ill and has been for some time. The physicians say it is only a matter of time. We expect this to be his last."

Her expression softened a bit, and her eyes grew mournful. "Oh, I ... I'm so sorry."

He shook his head. "I didn't tell you to gain your sympathy. It is simply the truth. I should also make it clear there isn't a single person invited who I care to spend so much time with."

She smirked at that, amusement putting a twinkle in her eyes. "And here I thought you would have many neighbors to call friend. I remember you being quite popular in London."

He scoffed, rolling his eyes. "Being popular and actually liking the people around you are two different things. Very few of them bother to try to know me. This party will be full of people I hardly like."

Her gaze darted away and she bit her lip, seeming to think on his words.

"I will beg if I must," he teased, giving her a little squeeze and pulling her closer.

Her nearness had begun having the predictable effect, his senses overwhelmed by the soft press of her body and that delicious scent of oranges and clove.

She grinned, the familiar, predatory light appearing in her eyes. He trembled as she stared at him without blinking, her breasts rising as she took a deep, slow breath as if taking in his scent.

"I'd much rather you beg while you're beneath me."

Her words conjured up memories of their night at the White Cock, him arching and groaning under her, Cassandra riding him with wild abandon. His cock swelled between them, pressing against her mons through the thin layers of her gown and undergarments.

"I'll beg all you want," he whispered. "I'll beg until you've grown sick of hearing it."

Slipping a hand between them, she palmed his cock, drawing a hiss from between his teeth. "Come with me."

AN HOUR LATER, Robert lay naked in Cassandra's bed, sated, sore in places, and thoroughly satisfied. She'd led him straight to her bedchamber, where she'd begun tearing at his clothes. He'd been shocked when she turned her back so he could unbutton her gown, then faced him so he could loosen her stays. He tried not to think too much about what that could mean, how she seemed to be softening toward him. There was hardly any time for thought once she'd pushed him onto the bed and crawled over him, taking command of him as easily as she ever had.

The mark on his chest was purple again, her lips and teeth having found the exact same spot. His chest had been marred by the rake of her fingernails, the red streaks still stinging a bit. His scalp ached from her fingers pulling at his hair, his lower lip swollen from her nibbling bites.

He'd never felt better. There was something about the moments following the finish with her—a lingering calm following the storm, a sense of peace and rightness.

Of course, he couldn't tell her that, so he simply lay at her side and stared at the ceiling, eyelids drooping as drowsiness overwhelmed him.

Since it was the middle of the day and he'd be expected back at Briarwell soon, he couldn't allow himself to fall asleep. So, he turned onto his side to face her, searching for something to say so she would talk to him. He was not ready to leave yet, and she did not seem in a hurry to push him out the door.

He found her lying on her back, hands folded across her bare abdomen, gaze affixed to the ceiling, as his had been. With the curtains drawn and a fire going in the hearth, shadows danced along her profile and made her eyes look darker. Her expression remained stoic, giving away nothing. He could stare at her for hours and still never discern what she might be thinking.

Instead of talking, he buried his fingers in her hair and caressed the long coils. He'd expected her to pull away, but she shocked him by remaining still, though her eyes did shift in his direction.

"What are you doing?"

She did not sound angry or annoyed, just curious. He smiled, twining one of her curls around his first finger.

"It is called affection," he teased, tweaking the tip of her nose before going back to her hair. "Some people engage in it after intercourse. Often before, too."

She wrinkled her nose at him and went back to staring at the ceiling. "When I went to London, it was for my youngest sister's birthday. Ophelia is eight-and-ten now, and will soon make her debut."

He did not miss a beat, falling right into her abrupt change of subject. "Your mother must be proud."

She scowled, her lips puckering as if she'd tasted something rancid. "Of course she is. The dowager has always been ever so delighted by her three perfect princesses."

Robert knit his brow and paused, his fingers halfway through her hair. "I thought there were four of you."

She snorted. "Precisely. I have never been one of them, and Mother has never hidden her disdain for me. Amaryllis, Pandora, and Ophelia are beautiful. Amaryllis has Papa's red hair and a pleasing singing voice. Pandora and Ophelia are perfect English roses—blonde and blue-eyed and well-mannered. She groomed them into miniature likenesses of herself, certain that they would make splendid matches. And they did. Amaryllis is a viscountess now, while Pandora wed an earl. Ophelia is likely to be named The Incomparable during her Season and nab herself a titled and wealthy husband."

The venom with which she spat the words was laced with a pain she couldn't have intended for him to hear. He couldn't imagine feeling like an outsider in one's own family. Even though his brothers had all lead short lives, there'd never been any question that they were all equal in the eyes of their parents. William had enjoyed the few perks of being the heir, but such was the nature of duty related to titles. In every way that counted, the Stanley boys had been treated the same by their parents.

"And what of you?" he prodded.

"Before my coming out, I was told I ought to be grateful I possessed a large dowry for it was the only thing I had with which to attract a husband."

He could not mask his horror, his mouth falling open and his eyes widening as those words struck him like the most savage of blows.

What sort of mother said such things to her own daughter?

"Ophelia has always been the sweetest of us," she said quickly, as if trying to gloss over the horrible memory. "When my mother, Amaryllis, and Pandora turned their backs on me, she treated me with kindness. She tried her best, she … she showed me pity when they gave me only contempt."

He reached over her to the bedside table, where she'd placed the invitation and the primroses. Before leading him into the house, she had knelt to retrieve the blossoms. The action had made him smile, as he'd expected her to forget the flowers altogether, perhaps even stomping on them on her way through the garden.

"I am glad you had an ally of sorts," he murmured.

While he spoke, he began slipping the flowers into her hair. The stems fit in the snarls of her curls and stayed in place. He smiled at the way the splash of yellow looked against her amber locks—as perfect as he'd known they would.

"She will not be one any longer," she said, seeming oblivious to his actions. "When next I see her, the transformation from sweet, biddable girl, to catty, hateful witch will be complete."

He paused in the act of tucking one blossom behind her ear. Her face gave not a hint to how she must feel about such a development. But he discerned the lingering hint of anger and sadness in her voice.

It broke his heart.

"I'm sorry," he whispered. "She is young and does not know any better—only what she has learned under your mother's tutelage. I hope once she has gone out into the world and learned more about the people in it, more about herself, she will come to see how wrong the dowager is."

She turned her head to look at him again, her incredulous expression at odds with the softness of her unbound hair and the flowers adorning it.

"Are you always so optimistic?"

The disbelief in her voice made him laugh. "I suppose so. There are enough people in this world always looking to see the worst in others, or tear them down. I much prefer to find the bright side of things wherever I can. Sometimes, when life becomes difficult I find it is the only way to survive."

She stared at him as if he spoke ancient Greek—as if she couldn't understand such a notion. Robert was coming to see that she'd survived by going in the opposite direction. Her hard and brittle shell had protected her, and she continued using it as a shield against the world. She did not know any other way.

"I appreciate the sentiment, but forgive me if I am not so idealistic.

My mother has made it clear she will never forgive me for embarrassing our family. When Bertram's father paid her for our silence, I was expected to keep my head down and do my best to avoid bringing more shame onto our good name. It could ruin Ophelia's prospects, you see, and that was more important than anything that had happened to me."

His stomach lurched as he imagined Cassandra, young and frightened, hurt in a way he could never fathom. The thought of her having no one to turn to, no one who'd cared to seek justice on her behalf …

"Cass …"

"Mother will never let her forget that I was almost the ruin of our family. To show me any sort of consideration would cause Ophelia to fall out of her favor, and in the end no daughter wants that."

His throat constricted, the words to comfort her sitting on the edge of his thickened tongue. Even if he could say what he wanted, would she wish to hear it? She'd likely tell him to keep his platitudes to himself, and she would be well within her rights. What could he say to make any of it better?

Instead, he cupped her chin, tilting her toward him. Letting his finger trail over her jaw, he sought her mouth. She raised her head to meet him, taking control of the kiss before it even began, clamping her mouth over his with voracious intent. He surrendered to her, giving what he could without words.

She fell back into her pillow, once again avoiding his gaze.

He returned to his side of the bed, but never stopped staring at her, waiting for her to give him what she decided he was worthy of. Cassandra did not trust easily; that much had been made clear. That she'd even said this much was more than he could have wished for.

"My father was the only person I could count upon," she said after a long pause. "When he died, it was abrupt, unexpected. If I had known my last moments with him were going to be the last, I would have …"

She heaved a labored sigh, then glanced at him again out of the corner of her eye.

"For that reason, I will attend your father's birthday dinner … so someone will be there who understands what it is like to watch their father slip away right before their eyes. The night at the White Cock you did something important for me. Having a good experience after Bertram meant something. I owe you this much in return."

Shifting closer to her on the bed, he pulled her against his body.

"You don't have to give me anything in exchange for that," he whispered into her hair. "I gave that gladly and freely, and once I knew the reason I was even happier to have done it. You owe me nothing, Cass."

"Still," she insisted. "I'll do it. Tell the baroness she may count upon my attendance."

Smiling against the crown of her head, he tried not to let himself become hopeful over this. It didn't have to mean anything beyond her returning what she saw as a favor. That was all she'd make of it, so there was no reason for his heart to swell and relief to wash over him at her words.

Yet, they did.

"Thank you."

They lay in silence for a while longer before Cassandra again changed the subject.

"Your scent," she murmured, inhaling as if to draw it in. "What is it?"

He frowned at the odd question. "It is some concoction I've been purchasing from a perfumer in London for years now. It is a blend of orris root, amber, and a number of other things I cannot recall at the moment. It's called Spanish Leather."

"Hmm," she murmured, giving no hint to what she might think of it. "I'd have thought you would smell like sandalwood or Bay Rum. I vow, the men of London are forever reeking of the stuff."

He crinkled his nose in distaste. "I abhor the scent of sandalwood."

Glancing up at him, she gave him a half smile. "So do I."

CHAPTER 8

Cassandra lifted the hem of her skirts as she allowed Randall to hand her down from her carriage in the circular drive of Briarwell Manor. Inside, she felt as if a nest of snakes writhed about in her belly. Outwardly, she did her best to portray the aloof lady—the daughter of a duke who suffered no fools and would not tolerate disrespect.

In the week that had passed since Robert invited her to the baron's birthday celebration, she had talked herself in and out of coming several times. Sure, she had promised him she would attend, but he'd insisted she owed him nothing. Which meant, if she wished to back out he did not have the right to make her feel guilty for it. But … she *would* feel guilty, because she'd given her word and he would expect her.

When had his thoughts or feelings begun to matter to her?

They don't, she told herself as she approached the front steps of the manor.

If she gave him something he asked for, he'd be more amenable to the things she wanted. Heat surged within her as her mind went back to the nights they'd spent together this week—him sneaking off from the manor to walk to the dower house in the dead of night. She no longer needed to suffer for craving more of Robert's submission and eagerness to please her—not when he lived so close and was all-too willing to come calling whenever he wanted more of what she gave in return. Sleep still eluded her most nights, but as she lay abed staring off into the darkness, she thought of Robert, not Bertram.

That, more than anything, was reason enough for her to do this. She might not wish for Robert to become a permanent part of her life, but after the things he'd given her, she owed it to him to attend.

Besides, she'd meant what she told him about her own father. If she'd known the duke's final birthday was to be his last, she'd have made it special for him—spent every second of that day soaking in his presence. After Baron Stanley had died and Robert thought back to this night, she did not want him to remember it as miserable or boring. If her presence could add some sort of excitement to it for him, then she would attend the party and make the best of it.

And, she had to admit that the picture he'd painted while they stood in the garden appealed to her. Rubbing their noses in her presence, forcing them to acknowledge her while showing them all how little she cared for their regard … it sounded like the perfect way to spend her evening.

She'd spent hours on her toilette, ensuring not a hair was out of place before she set out for Briarwell in her finest evening attire.

When the front doors of the manor swung open to admit her, Cassandra held her head high and swept inside as if she owned the place. For the first time in her life, she sought to emulate her mother—a woman who could make anyone feel small with nothing more than a cool stare. Handing her satin-lined cape off to a footman, she followed the stoic butler to a large drawing room, where the other guests had already begun to assemble. It would appear she was the last to arrive, several pairs of eyes swiveling toward her as she lingered on the threshold and waited for the butler to announce her.

"Lady Cassandra Lane."

Due to her status, the occupants of the room had no choice but to come to their feet and offer her a bow or curtsy. The forced deference amused her to no end, especially once she caught glimpses of expressions telling her most did not wish to offer it. She let her delight show, a smirk curving her lips as she inclined her head in acceptance of their obeisance.

Robert approached her first, looking like something off an artist's canvas in his black evening kit and white linen. A diamond tiepin glittered against his cravat, and his eyes sparkled with glee as he took her hand and raised it to his lips. The soft brush of his lips over her gloved knuckles sent a little shudder through her. She could imagine him sinking to his knees and kissing her this way, then removing her glove and taking her little finger into his mouth.

Now is not the time, Cass!

"Thank you for coming," he murmured once he'd straightened.

"I promised I would, did I not?"

"That you did," he replied with a wide smile. "And you look … ravishing."

The way his gaze slid over her from head to toe bolstered his words. She'd had this gown commissioned on a whim but had never worn it, preferring not to call attention to herself when out in public. But, this night proved a different sort of occasion, so she had indulged in a rare act of vanity, donning it with pride and allowing Lila to bedeck her with all the finery to match.

The gown featured a satin crimson slip with silver embroidery adorning the hem, under a robe of French gauze in decadent black. The sleeves overlaid with more of the gauze gathered in elegant sweeps at her shoulders, the neckline diving a bit lower than she usually preferred to flaunt the matching rubies she'd clasped about her throat. Lila had used curling tongs to tame her natural spirals into neater coils, sweeping them off her neck and arranging them in a whimsical style that allowed a few decorative strands loose at her temples and nape. If the look on Robert's face as he drank her in was any indication, she'd achieved the desired effect.

"Come, I want you to meet my father."

She took his arm and allowed him to guide her across the room. Its occupants sat clustered near the hearth, enjoying a drink before dinner. She recognized Lady Stanley right off, her silk turban festooned with ostrich feathers giving her a commanding air. Beside her sat a rail thin man with weathered features akin to Robert's. The man had none of his son's classical beauty, but Cassandra could see parts of him in the baron's smile.

Lady Stanley stood to help him, taking his arm and offering support as he struggled to get upright. Pity for the baron pricked within her chest. He trembled slightly once he'd found his feet and offered her a wobbly smile. His sunken cheeks and weakened limbs gave truth to Robert's claim that he would not live to see another year.

"Father, may I present Lady Cassandra Lane. Lady Cassandra, my father, Baron Stanley."

The baron took her hand, his genuine smile growing wider as their gazes met. It struck her much the same way Robert's did—full of life and joy.

"Welcome, my lady, it is an honor to have you here."

She found it difficult to keep from returning his smile. "The honor is mine. Happy Birthday, my lord."

"I have been fortunate to see so many of them. Have you met my wife, Lady Stanley?"

Her gaze shifted to the old woman looking at her with a heavy measure of disdain in her eyes. "We have been previously introduced. It is good to see you again, my lady."

She sounded as if she were anything but, but Cassandra did not let that cow her. She simply gave the baroness her coolest stare.

"Likewise."

Taking her arm once more, Robert began introducing her to the other guests.

While the vicar and the Rodinghams greeted her with polite smiles, the rest were not so magnanimous. Lord and Lady Loring—a viscount and his wife who served as two of the *ton*'s biggest gossips—wore gleeful expressions that told her they couldn't wait to return to

London and report the happenings of this evening to all their friends. She silently dared them with her eyes to speak an unkind word about her, which seemed to unsettle the viscount but did nothing to ruffle his shrew of a wife.

The Fletchers all eyed her with varying degrees of curiosity and condescension. Lady Fletcher was like a mirror image of her friend, the baroness—lips puckered, brow furrowed, eyes flashing with outright dislike. Lord Fletcher seemed the most indifferent, though Cassandra assumed his face might always be set into an implacable expression of boredom. Miss Lucy Fletcher gazed upon her as if afraid she might become sullied if she stepped too close, while Martin Fletcher seemed amused by her. She narrowed her eyes at him, but he only gave her an indolent grin, meeting her challenge head-on.

The widow, Lady Walter, gave a polite nod from where she sat in a quiet corner alone, still dressed in the muted gray and lavender tones of half-mourning. Mr. and Mrs. Fareweather ignored her altogether, turning up their noses and sniffing as if offended by her presence.

By the time all the introductions were done, the butler had arrived to inform them that dinner was served. She was handed over to the baron, and found herself grateful that propriety put her in his company for the evening. She ended up being the true escort, resting one hand atop his arm and ensuring he kept his balance as they made their slow way to the dining room.

"My son must be green with envy," he whispered, leaning in close. "He does not have the privilege of taking the loveliest woman at the party in to dinner."

While flattery tended to put her teeth on edge, the twinkle in the baron's eyes and the good humor in his voice made that impossible.

Like his son, the man was difficult to dislike.

"Lord Stanley, you are a shameless flirt."

When he winked, she erupted into giggles— something she hadn't done since she'd been a debutante. If the Stanleys union had been a love match, she could see how the man had charmed his way straight to the baroness' heart.

"And you are quite a woman," he replied as they entered the dining room. "It is easy to see why Robert is so enamored with you."

Robert, enamored with her?

She glanced over her shoulder to where he stood near the middle of the line with Lucy Fletcher on his arm. He looked bored to tears as he listened to her blather on about some thing or another, but when he found her watching him he brightened, giving her a sly smile.

No, the baron couldn't mean that. Robert had invited her here as a kindness, and for his own benefit. She excited him, that much became clear whenever they were together. The novelty of their affair would soon wear thin, however, and he would grow bored with her as men were wont to do.

But then, she thought of the way he'd been watching her in the garden, the tenderness in his expression as he'd lain in her bed placing flowers in her hair. Upon rising to look in a mirror, she'd thought she looked ridiculous, her hair in a wild tumble with the blossoms throughout. But Robert had stared at her as if looking upon a goddess, remarking that the yellow primroses looked fetching on her.

Were those the actions of a man caught up in the thrill of newfound lust?

No. They were the telltale acts of a besotted man.

Damn it all, what had she done? She'd been determined to keep him at arm's length, but now here she was having dinner in his home, with his family, walking in on his father's arm.

It is only one dinner, she reminded herself. *After tonight you will return to the way things have been. Nothing has to change.*

With that thought at the forefront of her mind, she cast off propriety in order to help the baron into his seat. The last thing she wanted was for him to tip over while trying to pull out her chair.

She took her place at the baron's right, with Lady Loring and her husband directly across from her. She wasn't certain whether to be elated or disappointed that the order of things put Robert farther down the table with Lucy at his side. The other guests filled the chairs in the order they'd come into the room, with the baroness seating herself at the other end facing her husband.

Wine was poured, and before the footmen could serve the first course Lady Stanley insisted upon a toast in honor of her husband's birthday. The baron bore all the attention with a smile on his face and rosy glow in his cheeks, raising his glass before clinking it against Cassandra's then Lady Loring's. Conversation remained light over the first course of turtle soup, lamb cutlets, and venison accompanied by asparagus. She found the food to be far better than she'd expected, and enjoyed it more than the dull conversation happening on her side of the table. The baron and Viscount Loring had begun talking about the hunting to be found in Scotland, while Lady Loring cut in here and there to give her opinion on the barbarism of the sport.

Every so often, she glanced down the table to Robert, and found he seemed to be just as uninterested in the company. It was no wonder he'd wished for her to come. The downside, of course, being that they were not seated side by side. Had they been, she might have had a bit of fun with him, resting a hand upon his thigh and drawing it upward until she held him by the cock. The thought brought a smirk to her lips, but she masked it by taking a bite of venison. Whatever was being discussed down the table, everyone around the dull Miss Fletcher seemed on the verge of shoving their knives through their ears to drown out the sound of her voice.

Did the chit really think it made her more attractive to whisper in that girlish way? She wanted to throttle the girl and tell her to speak up.

By the time the first course had been taken away, Cassandra had begun to think she'd worried over nothing. Now that dinner was in full swing and the initial tension caused by her arrival had dissipated, this entire affair promised to be uneventful.

At least, until the second course arrived and Lady Loring found it necessary to draw her into conversation.

"His Lordship and I have recently returned from London," she remarked, meeting Cassandra's gaze from across the table. "While there, we happened upon your mother and that dear, sweet Ophelia in Hyde Park. What a lovely young woman she's grown into."

Cassandra paused, her fork poised over a portion of fricassee chicken with mushrooms. It smelled heavenly and she wanted to be left alone to eat it in peace, but Lady Loring was having none of it. "Indeed. I was just in Town to join in celebrating her eighteenth birthday. She's to make her debut this spring."

"What a marvelous time in a young girl's life," the viscountess said with a knowing smile.

The expression was without warmth, putting Cassandra on edge. Her words were not as innocent as they seemed; she was leading up to something.

"Yes, I am glad for her," she replied, pointedly going back to her chicken and dismissing the other woman.

But Lady Loring pressed on, leaning forward a bit as her smile widened.

"And I am certain she will be a smashing success. What, with the exceptional example of her mother and sisters to follow. Then, there is your own glaring example of what a lady is *not* to do after her coming out, so she is sure to have learned from that as well."

Cassandra went still, her fork hovering before her face with a bit of chicken and a mushroom hanging off its end. She narrowed her eyes at the viscountess, her temper flaring in an instant. The knife resting on her plate would make the perfect tool for carving the woman's leathery skin into mincemeat. She had to fight back a smile at the notion marring the woman's sagging cheeks. 'Old' upon one, and 'Bitch' on the other.

Rise above it.

Robert's words from that afternoon in the garden came back to her now, and as she glanced down the table she found everyone had gone silent to watch, her bedmate included. He watched her with a furrowed brow, his mouth turned down.

He'd been right. She had to put these people in their place and remind them that she was the blasted daughter of a duke. She would not serve as their whipping girl any longer.

Besides, she'd had plenty of experience dealing with sharp-tounged women. After all, she'd grown up with the dowager Duchess of Penrose for a mother.

With a slow, catlike smile, she held the other woman's gaze while biting the chicken off the end of her fork. She took her time chewing and swallowing, then using her napkin to dab the corners of her mouth before laying it back in her lap. All this she did while the rest of the party looked on in rapt silence, whispers of Lady Loring's comment having made their way to the end where Lady Stanley sat.

Arching an eyebrow, she let her smile settle into a sardonic smirk. "You know quite well the sorts of behaviors a debutante ought to avoid after her come out. Speaking of which, how is your daughter? I've heard the wondrous news of the birth of her son. How proud you must be of the little love ... born a short four months after the wedding."

Lady Loring dropped her fork and the utensil clanked onto her plate, while she stared daggers at Cassandra. Farther down the table, she heard the vicar mutter something about 'shocking behavior', while Lucy giggled into her hand as her mother scolded her. Robert's frown had eased, his chin raising a tick as their gazes met. Giving her a little smile, he raised his wine glass to her, then took a sip and turned his attentions back to his meal.

Giving Lady Loring another scathing glare, she went back to her food. It was the best chicken she'd ever had, and she enjoyed every single bite, along with the other offerings of the second course.

Dinner progressed smoothly from there, with her verbal set down of the viscountess serving as a warning to the others. They went out of their way to be gracious toward her for fear of earning the same treatment as Lady Loring—who sat pouting while pushing her food about on her plate and avoiding eye contact with her.

The third course saw jokes and humorous stories volleyed back and forth across the table, the wine having loosened everyone's tongues. The baron seemed in high spirits, enjoying himself in a way she'd wager he had not in quite some time. While appearing a bit worn thin as the night went on, his color remained good and he never stopped smiling—laughing at every joke and engaging his guests with stories of his youth as well as Robert's childhood.

During the dessert course, Cassandra looked up to find Robert watching the baron, a soft, satisfied grin upon his face. He looked happier than he had at the start of the night, now that he'd forgotten Lucy entirely. The girl had turned her attention to those who cared to listen to her blather on about watercolors, and Robert seemed to content himself with watching his father thoroughly enjoy his final birthday celebration.

ROBERT OBSERVED CASSANDRA from across the drawing room, where the men had joined the ladies after retiring to a separate chamber with their chamber pots, port, and cigars. He'd dreaded this part of the evening before, hating that he would be absent while she was alone with his mother, Lady Fletcher, and that hateful busybody Lady Loring. But, if Cassandra had proved anything at dinner, it was that she could defend and take care of herself.

He'd never doubted it, but she had driven the point home with her marvelous performance tonight. First, she'd appeared in the drawing room looking like a fashion plate in the crimson confection she wore, head held high. He was grateful that every eye in the room had rested on her in that moment, because he felt certain his heart had been in his eyes. How could it not be, when she so effortlessly stoked some deep, hidden part of him he'd never known existed? He'd abhorred every moment of having to tolerate Lucy's drivel, when he wanted to sit near Cassandra and his father.

Whatever they'd been talking about had kept him smiling all through dinner—which was what Robert had wanted.

Just before the men had parted ways with the women, his father had taken Cassandra by the arm and whispered something in her ear. The two had exchanged a long, meaningful glance, and for a moment she seemed taken aback. Before Robert could catch them up and find out what had been said, she was gone, slipping into the drawing room.

He'd cornered his father to ask what he'd whispered, but the baron had given him a smug smile and refused to answer.

"It was between Lady Cassandra and I, and is no concern of yours."

Instead of being frustrated, Robert could only chuckle. "I suppose you like her, then."

"Very much. She's a good woman, and perfect for you."

He'd cringed at that, despite agreeing with his father that Cassandra was absolutely perfect. The more time he spent in her company, the harder it became to part ways with her.

It was dangerous, his mounting obsession with her. She hadn't said so with words, but he read her actions loud and clear. She held him at arm's length for a reason, and would not allow him to get too close. The moment he overstepped her boundaries, he would cease to be a part of her life in any capacity.

As he watched her from where he sat near the pianoforte, he decided that a piece of her had to be better than nothing at all. If remaining in her good favor meant picking up whatever scraps she let fall at her feet, then he'd gladly do so.

A card game between his parents three other guests began in one corner of the room, while Lucy made a beeline to the pianoforte. Cassandra sat in an armchair, seeming to listen in to the conversation taking place without wishing to engage. She sipped sherry from a cut crystal glass and stared off across the room, a pensive expression overcoming her face.

Unable to stay away any longer, he made his way toward her, leaving Martin and his father to their horse talk over port. With all the furniture in the room taken up by other occupants, he was forced to stand beside her chair. Though, he found he didn't mind. He had a stunning view of her from here—the swells of her breasts at the neckline of her gown, the curve of her neck, the tendrils of hair curling along her temple and jaw.

When she raised her eyes to look at him, he tried to smile but found himself unable. There was something about the way she was looking at him, an intent gleam in her eyes. It knocked the wind from him, while his heart took up a galloping cadence, threatening to burst free of his body at any moment. He lost himself in that gaze, in the prisms of blue and gray sucking him in like some hapless fool wandering damp, foggy moors. He was sinking into the mire, helpless to save himself, battered by the storm of her rage and passion. God help him, he didn't want to be free of it. He wanted more and more until she'd consumed him completely and he became a part of her.

Taking a slow, deep breath, he blinked and fought to find his voice. They'd been staring at one another too long in silence, and someone was bound to notice.

Bracing a hand upon the back of her chair, he cleared his throat. "Have you enjoyed yourself this evening?"

He kept his voice low, though with Lucy's playing no one seemed capable of overhearing.

"I have, actually," she replied, sounding as if that surprised even her. "Dinner was wonderful, your father is a gem, and Lady Loring was ... an interesting table companion."

Casting a glance at the old woman who had suffered Cassandra's ruthless set down, he snorted and coughed to cover a chuckle. She lowered her head, shoulders shaking as she seemed to stifle a giggle.

By the time she looked at him again, he'd composed himself. The tilt of her head was so perfect that the urge to kiss her slammed into him hard and fast. All he had to do was bend over and cup her jaw, angling her a bit more to the left. His fingertips would skim her throat, his mouth touching hers and his tongue stroking her lower lip.

She seemed to have the same thought, because her gaze fell to his mouth and held, her own lips parting and her breath hitching. He allowed his hand to shift on the back of the chair, just enough to brush her hair. He took one of the spirals and smoothed it between his fingers—an action that lasted all of three seconds, but sent a wave of longing rippling through him. He wanted to pluck the pins loose and send it cascading down her back, run his fingers through it and bury his face in the strands, wrap it around his hand and tug, exposing her neck for his lips and tongue.

Bloody hell. If he wasn't careful he'd give them away to everyone in the room.

He released the curl and took a step back, breaking her gaze. He must learn to control his reactions to her in public if he wanted to preserve their secret.

He'd just worked himself up to engaging her in banal conversation fit for a public occasion, when Martin Fletcher approached.

"I say, have you heard the news out of London?" he drawled, his eyes heavy-lidded from drink. "Terribly sad business."

Robert frowned and glanced down at Cassandra, who shrugged as if to say she had no idea what Martin was talking about.

"What news?" he prodded. "This Masked Menace business is all anyone is talking about."

Martin took another sip of his port and sighed. "Lady Downing died in a tragic accident a few day past."

Robert felt the twinge of pity for the lady and her husband, now a widower. He wasn't well acquainted with the Downings, but remembered meeting the lady at Almack's a few Seasons ago. She'd been a quiet woman, sweet and a bit shy.

"How awful," he replied. "And with she and Sir Downing married only a few short years. Did they have any children?"

"They did not," Martin murmured.

His gaze fell on Cassandra, who had gone silent, hands clenching the arms of her chair in a white-knuckle grip.

"Lady Cassandra, are you all right?" Martin asked.

Robert rounded the chair to meet her gaze, but found her staring up at Martin. Her face pale and her chin trembling, she looked as if she'd seen a ghost.

She sucked in a sharp, swift breath, her voice hoarse when she finally spoke. "How did it happen? Do you know what sort of accident it was?"

Martin sobered in an instant, regret clear upon his face. "I'm so sorry, Lady Cassandra. I did not think. Was she a friend of yours?"

Cassandra stood. "No, but I … I need to know. If you heard how she died, you must tell me!"

Her voice had risen a bit, earning the attention of the other guests. The room fell silent and the card game came to a pause as everyone seemed to wonder what was happening. Only Lucy remained unaware, playing the pianoforte with that blissful expression of obliviousness upon her face.

"I believe it was a nasty fall," Martin replied, concern creasing his brow. "She tumbled down the stairs and broke her neck. My lady, forgive me. If I'd known it would upset you so—"

"Oh, God," Cassandra whispered, seeming to no longer hear him.

Pressing a hand to her belly, she seemed on the verge of collapse. Robert was on her in an instant, taking hold of her arm and wrapping one hand about her waist. He did not care about the eyes watching them or what anyone might think of him touching her with such familiarity. Something was very wrong.

"Cass, are you all right?"

"Robert, what's the matter?" his mother called out from across the room. "Is Lady Cassandra unwell?"

Smoothing one hand up and down her back, he searched her gaze, trying to understand the sudden turmoil he found there. Tears filled them as she met his stare and shook her head, her lip quivering as if she fought against the urge to weep.

"I need to leave … I cannot …"

Then, she was gone, breaking away from him and exiting the drawing room at a near run. He was on her heels before he could think.

"Robert!" his mother called out. "What is going on?"

He paused in the doorway, fighting to maintain at least an outward appearance of calm. "Lady Cassandra seems to have fallen ill. I will ensure she is all right."

"Oh, dear," the baroness replied, one hand held over her bosom. "I do hope it wasn't something she ate."

"I am certain she'll be fine, but I ought to make sure. I will return shortly."

As he ducked out into the corridor, conversation seemed to resume, Lucy continuing to pound away at the pianoforte. A flash of red caught his eye and he turned to find Cassandra making a mad dash for the vestibule and the front doors of the manor.

"My lady, your cloak!" called the butler as she rushed past him without stopping.

"I will see to her," he told the man as he gave chase.

She pushed the doors open and lurched out into the night, then stumbled down the front steps. Robert's heart thundered as he followed, reaching out in an attempt to grab her lest she fall and hurt herself. She managed to stay on her feet as she rushed across the grounds, skirts held in one hand.

"Cassandra!"

She paused near a tree and fell against it, clinging to the trunk as if for dear life. By the time he had caught up to her, she'd become distraught, her breath harsh and uneven, tears wetting her cheeks, tremors wracking her from head to toe.

"Cass, please … tell me what's wrong. Did you know Lady Downing?"

There could be no other explanation for her reaction to the news of the other woman's death. Damn Martin for his big mouth and lack of tact.

Turning away from the tree, she doubled over and wretched. The contents of her stomach spewed out over the ground as she trembled, coughing and gagging. Robert could do nothing but stand back and watch, uncertain what he ought to do for her. She'd never taken kindly to displays of pity or softer emotion, but just now he felt gutted at the sight of her like this. He wanted to make it right somehow, but first he needed to know what was wrong.

He stood back until she was finished, then reached into his breast pocket to retrieve a handkerchief. She accepted it with a shaking hand and used it to wipe her damp cheeks, then the corners of her mouth. He remained silent, waiting for her to shed some light on her thoughts.

After a few deep breaths, she met his gaze and shook her head, her watery eyes wide and dazed as if she were in shock.

"I have to leave … I have to go … I cannot be here …"

He reached out for her, but she cringed away from his touch, so he maintained his distance. She was clearly in a state of panic, but would not allow him to comfort her, leaving Robert at a complete loss.

"Cass, I cannot let you leave like this. You are overwrought, and I'm worried about you. Please, tell me what the matter is."

She wrapped her arms around herself and shook her head several times. "It does not matter. There is nothing you can do to mend it. Lady Downing, she … she did not deserve this."

He nodded slowly, still uncertain what it was about Lady Downing's death that upset her so. She wasn't known to have many friends, and he couldn't remember hearing about any connection between them. Whatever it was, she was frightening him, falling apart right before his eyes. A brittle, hardened Cassandra was familiar to him; this sobbing mess of a woman seemed like a different person entirely.

Unable to stand it any longer, he took hold of her shoulders and hauled her against him. She resisted, arching her back and pushing against his chest.

"Let me go!"

Wrapping both arms around her waist, he only held her tighter. "No."

She thrashed in his hold, her strength nearly breaking his grip. But he fought back, capturing first one wrist, then the other, and gathering them both in one hand. Wrapping his free arm around her waist, he pressed his forehead against hers and met her gaze.

"That's enough," he said, his tone firm and his grip like iron.

He'd never manhandled a woman in his life, but these felt like extenuating circumstances. If he had to use his strength to get through to her, he would.

"Stop fighting," he murmured.

She shook her head but went still, the tension melting from her limbs the longer she stood his arms. "I can't."

"Just tonight," he urged. "Tomorrow, you can raise your defenses again and shut me out. You can be strong and fight and do whatever you feel you must to survive. But right now, you can stop. I am here. Do you understand? I'm not abandoning you like this."

He felt the steel leaving her spine by degrees, her arms falling limp as he released her wrists. She lowered her gaze and let out a small sob, a tremor ripping through her body and jolting his. For the first time since he'd met her, Cassandra seemed defeated, vulnerable. Broken. That she had complied gave him no satisfaction. He wanted his fiery siren back; the woman who could command him with a word or a glance.

"Will you come with me?" he urged, tipping her chin up so she looked him in the eye. "If we remain out here much longer, someone will come looking for us. No one has to know you are still here."

Her shoulders sagged, but she nodded her agreement. Taking hold of her hand, he led her away from the front doors and toward a servant's entrance on the side of the house. He opened it and pulled her through the dark passage to a staircase leading to the upper floors. Knowing the way by heart, he did not need a taper to light their path. He had sneaked through these passages many times as a young man, not wanting to be seen on his way to the woods to meet Daphne.

Now, instead of creeping out, he was secreting someone back in.

They came out on the landing of the third floor, and he led her to his bedchamber, spiriting her inside before a servant happened by. Felix, his valet, came rushing from the open door of the dressing room, eyes going wide at the sight of Cassandra.

"Mr. Stanley—"

"Leave us," he barked, without sparing the man a glance. "Go to the stable and find Lady Cassandra's driver. Tell him that she has requested he return home without her. I will see her back safely. Tell no one what you saw."

"Of course, sir," the man replied before turning to go back the way he came. Another door closed in the distance, and Felix's retreating footsteps faded into silence.

Pulling Cassandra near the hearth, he found himself grateful the valet had just stoked it. It was cold and she'd been outdoors without her cloak. He took hold of her shoulders and found her skin still chilled to the touch. Chafing his hands over her arms, he looked into her glassy eyes.

"I have to leave you here for a little while, but only to tell them I must see you home. The party seems to be near its end, anyway, so I should not be expected back. I'll return as soon as I can."

She did not reply with words, but nodded, her stare unfocused.

With a sigh, he took her hand and led her into his dressing room, where Felix had left a bowl with hot water on the washstand.

"You can clean yourself up a bit if you'd like. Make yourself comfortable. But, do not leave this room. I do not think I need to tell you how horrible it would be for someone to see you up here."

Again, she nodded but did not speak, leveling a blank stare at the washstand. With a heavy sigh, he turned to make his exit. He did not want to leave her alone for a second, but he had no choice.

Dashing back the way he'd come, he circled back to the front of the house from the servant's entrance. He rushed back in, ensuring the butler and footmen saw him returning to the drawing room.

"Robert, there you are," his mother said.

Their guests had begun rising from their seats and exchanging farewells. As he'd suspected, the party was now at an end. His father looked exhausted but happy, his eyes bright and clear.

"Is Lady Cassandra all right?" the baron asked.

"Just a bit under the weather. I will escort her home myself. She's quite ill, and I would not feel right allowing her to leave on her own."

His mother opened her mouth as if to argue against it, but his father cut in before she could.

"Of course you shouldn't," the baron declared. "Do give her our sincerest well wishes. We hope she recovers soon."

"I will."

He turned to flee without another word, though he heard his mother through the drawing room doors.

"William, it is hardly proper …"

"…the right thing to do, Rosie, the woman is ill."

The run back to his chambers seemed to take forever, but before long he was safe behind the closed door again, the party and guests forgotten.

He found Cassandra seated on his bed, her vacant stare focused somewhere across the room. She'd taken down her elegant coiffure, leaving the neat curls hanging down her back. Her face appeared pink from a fresh scrubbing, though crying had left her eyes red-rimmed.

Coming farther into the room, he gave her as good a smile as he could manage.

"I see you made use of the washstand," he remarked, uncertain where else to begin.

If he tried to pry into what had happened downstairs, she might retreat from him again. For now, they seemed to be at a standstill, coming to a truce of sorts. He only wanted to give her what comfort he could—what comfort she would allow.

"The tooth powder also," she said, her voice still small and strained. "Fricassee chicken tastes far better going down."

He chuckled, edging closer and offering his hand. This time, she acquiesced without a fight, letting him help her to her feet.

"Turn around."

She shocked him by obeying, giving him her back. He took advantage of her assent and swept her hair over one shoulder before trailing his knuckles down her spine.

"May I?"

The need for her approval proved difficult to ignore, and he could not act until she'd given him what he needed to proceed.

"Yes," she replied.

He began opening the back of her gown, resisting the desire to bend his head and kiss the back of her neck. He had not brought her here for carnal reasons, and did not want her thinking he had. She stepped out of the gown, which he laid over the back of a chair before busying himself with her stays and petticoats. Kneeling at her feet, he removed her slippers, then slid his hands up her legs to untie her garters and pull down her stockings.

Once she stood before him in only her chemise, he went to work on his clothes. She remained placid, watching as he untied his cravat, then removed his coat. His layers fell to the floor—waistcoat, shoes, stockings. Choosing to remain in his shirt and breeches, he stepped forward and swept her off her feet. She stiffened in his hold, but he refused to set her down. He carried her back toward the bed.

Turning to bury his face in her neck, he inhaled that intoxicating scent of oranges and clove. She whimpered, but still seemed resistant to his hold, the lack of control it forced her to accept.

"Shh," he whispered against her ear. "You promised not to fight, Cass. And I'm only taking you to bed … to sleep."

She relaxed a bit, and he held her for only a moment longer before laying her on the bed—which Felix had already turned down. Climbing in after her, he lay on his side facing her. She looked younger and smaller somehow—curls falling about her head in a haphazard tumble, lips pink and pouting, eyes wide.

He reached for her again, this time wrapping an arm around her waist and urging her against him.

Again, she angled away from him like a skittish doe jumping out of a predator's reach. But, just as he had outside, he pressed the issue, wrestling her over to his side of the bed.

"I'm going to hold you, and you're going to let me," he murmured, smiling when she narrowed her eyes at him.

It would seem she was only capable of letting go of the fight in her for so long.

"I would never hurt you, Cass," he whispered before kissing her forehead, then the bridge of her nose. "You are safe with me."

Tucking her against his chest, he held onto her and refused to let go. For the first few minutes, her breathing and the rigidity in her spine told him she still insisted on resisting. Before long, her breaths slowed and her weight grew heavier against him, her limbs going slack. Tucking his chin and gazing down at the fierce bundle of a woman in his arms, he smiled, finding her eyes closed and her lips parted, the furrows in her brow smoothed away by peaceful sleep.

CHAPTER 9

Cassandra stood near a window in Robert's bedchamber as the sun rose. She'd only just awakened, an odd departure from the usual sleeplessness plaguing her nights. Horror had overwhelmed her the moment she'd opened her eyes to find Robert beside her, one arm still draped over her waist. He appeared younger in sleep, his plush lips parted and his expression one of serenity. That she'd been comfortable in his hold, warm and content, should have made her happy.

Instead, it only made her angry at herself for allowing him to get too close.

Last night, the news of Lady Downing's death had ripped her apart, and she'd been unable to think past one stunning realization.

It was entirely her fault.

She did not believe the story about the woman tumbling down a flight of stairs for a moment. Cassandra was certain Sir Downing had pushed her. Upon accosting him, her aim had been to save the woman any further torment. Instead, she'd provoked the man to retaliate, and now the person she'd wanted to defend and protect was dead.

Her fingers clenched tight around the box clutched in her right hand, her jaw clenching until it ached. Guilt had overwhelmed her in the dark of night, but now rage overshadowed it, bursting forth from her gut like the rays of the sun thrusting upward in the distance. Sir Downing had no notion what he had done. By killing his wife, he'd set his own death in motion.

As he had paid for the abuses he'd subjected Lady Downing to over the years, he would pay for this … Cassandra would make certain of it.

The sound of rustling bed sheets had her turning to find Robert had awakened. He came upright, rubbing at his heavy-lidded eyes. His open shirt displayed the purple bruise left by her lips and teeth, a brilliant blossom of color against his skin. Instead of being pleased by the sight of it, she became annoyed with herself all over again.

How had she allowed a simple affair to become so complicated?

He might take her acquiescence last night as a desire for closeness and intimacy. And why wouldn't he after she'd fallen apart in his arms and allowed him to hold her throughout the night? It was exactly the sort of thing she'd vowed to avoid, and now she had allowed him to see the parts of her she always kept hidden.

No more.

He'd been kind to her when she had needed it most, but the moment had passed. She had a mission, a cross to bear. There could be no room for him in her life, and she could not allow him to unravel her any more than he already had.

As he stood and approached her with a soft smile, she steeled herself against him, tucking away the things she'd allowed to show last night.

"Good morning."

He faltered when he noticed the small box she held, his smile fading and a questioning glance overtaking his expression. She opened it and stared down at the sapphire ring hidden inside.

"I did not mean to pry," she said, turning the box this way and that so the light glittered off the facets of the stone. "I saw it on the washstand last night, and when I went back into the dressing room this morning I saw it again and became curious."

He nodded, reaching out to pluck the ring from her grasp. After studying it for a moment, he snapped the box closed.

"It was meant for Daphne."

She expected him to display some sort of emotion over the betrothal that had never come to pass, but his face betrayed nothing.

"Did you ever present it to her?" she asked, more curious now than ever about his severed connection to the woman who was now the Countess of Hartmoor.

"Twice," he replied with a little shake of his head. "I brought it back from London and . . . I left it on the washstand, and I suppose Felix has been waiting for me to tell him what to do with it. I've been a bit preoccupied the past few months and have hardly thought of it."

His piercing gaze told her everything she needed to know. She had been the thing keeping his mind off Daphne. Before he could voice those thoughts, she pressed on, needing to keep the focus upon him.

"Why didn't you fight for her?"

He seemed taken aback by her question, brow furrowing as his gaze flitted back to the closed box in his palm. "It is difficult to fight for someone who does not want you. She wanted Hartmoor. There was no longer anything to fight for."

"But . . . you loved her."

"She did not love me," he replied. "At least . . . not the same way I loved her."

Cassandra had her doubts. She'd never been in love, and no longer had a heart she could place into the hands of someone else. Bertram, her mother, and those who had denied her sympathy and understanding had made sure of that. But, she'd always imagined that people in love were completely irrational, willing to scale mountains and swim oceans, doing whatever it took to win in the end.

"What did you love about her?"

His frown deepened, his grip on the ring tightening until his knuckles went white. "What does it matter now?"

She shrugged, turning to gaze out at the sunrise. "I cannot help but think it wasn't Daphne you were in love with at all."

He came up beside her, and she felt the weight of his stare upon the side of her face. She refused to meet his gaze, crossing her arms and keeping her eyes focused forward.

"Is that so? How could you possibly know that?"

"It is just a theory. I think you believe you loved her … but what you actually loved was the *idea* of her. This notion of holding on to something that constantly fought to be away from you. You liked the chase, Robert. You liked that she was aloof and beautiful and always out of your reach. You liked the pain of unrequited love, the tragic romanticism of pining after her."

She felt him stiffen at her side, his gaze still piercing her without relenting.

"You are confusing the dynamic I had with Daphne to what is obviously happening between us."

She stiffened, her gut clenching and roiling in reaction to his words. She pushed the sensations down, compressing them deep inside her where they could be ignored.

"There is no *us*."

He took hold of her arm and spun her to face him, jaw set in stubborn determination. "Isn't there?"

She pulled away, once again erecting the invisible barrier between them that did not allow for touching. He stepped back as if he'd felt it, his jaw hardening as he stared her down.

"Ah, we are back where we began, I see."

She raised her chin. "Where would that be, exactly?"

He scoffed, shaking his head in disbelief. "Where you use me for pleasure, but hold me at arm's length. Where you cry in my arms, but then refuse to tell me why. Where I try to show you affection and care, and you shun me."

"I never claimed to want any of that from you," she argued. "Nor have I indicated that I want anything other than your prick."

"Perhaps not with your words, but the rest of you is clearly in need of something. Will there ever be a time you will admit that to yourself? You claim I love the chase and the pain of rejection. But, what of you, Cass? What do you love? What will you fight for?"

She squared her shoulders and thought of Lady Downing lying at the bottom of a flight of steps, her neck broken, her body robbed of life and breath.

"Justice," she ground out, fighting down the wave of grief and anger washing over her.

His expression softened and he stepped closer to her, though he took care to keep his hands to himself. "Cass, I am sorry there was no one there to fight for you—"

"I don't need anyone to be my champion!" she snapped. "I fought for myself when no one else would!"

"You did, and I cannot tell you how proud I was to watch you do it. But, the time will come when there is nothing left for you to fight for. You cannot allow the past to rule your present. You cannot let it destroy your future."

She sneered at him, her insides bursting with heat and a sudden pain that made her feel as if she were being torn apart. Why did he have to poke and prod at her this way—pull forth the emotions she tried to stifle lest they destroy her?

"Of course you can say such a thing! You, who goes about blissfully unaware of what is happening right under your nose. You know nothing of what we have suffered all these years—the shame of it, the pain of losing a part of yourself that cannot be taken back. Those women meant nothing to you until you were forced to acknowledge what happened to them. *I* meant nothing to you!"

His jaw ticked, eyes narrowing as he seemed to wrestle with himself for a long moment before speaking. She wanted to strike him and push him away, tell him to leave her alone and take his sentimental notions with him. Conversely, she wanted to pull him close and kiss him, keep him for herself, give in to the things he was offering her. She was exhausted from it all, but couldn't stop now—

not when crimes like those committed by the likes of Sir Downing went unpunished.

His voice came out hoarse and low when he finally spoke. "Miss Agatha Daventry. Lady Matilda Parham. Mrs. Viola Cathorn. Miss Janet Pleasance. Lady Lily Kirby. Lady Olivia Gibbs."

Cassandra blinked, each name falling into her gut with the weight of a stone boulder. "Those … those are all of …"

"Bertram's other victims," he said with a nod. "Yes. Lady Gibbs' involvement isn't public knowledge, but knowing what I do about Hartmoor's vendetta against Bertram, it was not difficult to puzzle out. Her child bears a striking resemblance to the Fairchild family, so it was not difficult for me to make the connection."

Her jaw dropped, and shock stunned her into silence. While the trial had been long and public, creating one of London's greatest scandals, it had been months since Bertam's execution. Not only did he remember the victims, he had paid close enough attention to figure out the secret of Lady Olivia's ordeal. She had been the only one of Bertram's known victims to remove herself from the trial and opt not to testify. Her daughter had needed protecting, and the other women had been glad to do their part in keeping the truth of her parentage a secret.

"I know their names," he continued when she remained silent. "I cannot forget who they are, or the things Bertram did to them. I think of them often, in fact, and have suffered no end of guilt over my own part in all of this. Do you think I am not ashamed at having been friends with that blackguard without ever knowing who he truly was? I have not forgiven myself for it, and I may never be able to. I care, Cass. I care about them, I care about *you*."

It was happening again. Something inside her was crumbling, falling to pieces against his words. She wrapped her arms around herself and held tight, refusing to allow his words to affect her or change her course. She had begun this, and she must finish it. Those other women had stood with her, and together they had destroyed their mutual tormentor. But what of the others? What of the maids who served as easy pickings for men with salacious intent? What of Lady Downing, who had died because of her? There was nothing left for her now—only the solace of her own actions, the peace that came from doing what she could to put the Bertrams of the world in their place.

Turning away from him, she found her garments and began dressing, stepping into her petticoats and tying them at her waist, before reaching for her stays.

"I am done with you," she declared, avoiding his gaze. "Do not return to Easton Park."

"So, that is it?" he demanded, crossing toward her. "I tell you that I care about you, and that is enough for you to toss me aside?"

No, she thought. *It isn't that you care about me, but that I cannot return the sentiment.*

Aloud, she said, "Softer emotions were never a part of our arrangement. It is clear to me that this has gone on long enough."

"What is clear to me is that you are afraid."

She froze in the middle of tying her garter, glancing up to find him watching her, arms folded across his chest.

"Afraid of what? You?"

"Yes, of me ... of this thing happening between us."

She finished off the garter and broke his gaze, plucking her slippers off the floor. She'd pulled on her gown but it remained open in the back with no one to assist her in closing it.

"There is nothing—"

"Denying it does not make it untrue," he interjected. "Damn it, Cass, I am trying to—"

"To what?" she spat, straightening once she had her slippers on. "Love me?"

He raked both hands through his hair and let out a growl of frustration. "Yes!"

"Don't. I don't want your love ... not when you don't even know what love is. For God's sake, you cannot even see that what you felt for Daphne wasn't love. How am I supposed to believe that you could possibly love me? Hell, you do not even know me."

"I want to. I've been trying to. But, how can I when you will not let me?"

"Because if you truly knew me, you could never love me. It is over, Robert. Perhaps someday you will find a woman who appeals to your need to rescue and coddle her. I can assure you, I am not what you want."

She gave him her back, sweeping her bedraggled hair over one shoulder to expose the opening of her gown. A long silence dragged out between them, and for a moment she wondered if he meant to let her traipse about with her gown falling off. But, eventually he approached, closing her gown with swift, deft movements.

"Wait here," he said once he was done.

She turned to find him disappearing into the dressing room. He returned holding a pair of shoes and wearing a banyan, his shirt still hanging open. The mark upon his chest peeked out at her, a sign of her possession, her passion.

There would be no more of that now, but it was for the best. She could not tell him that it wasn't his fault—he'd simply put all his hopes in the wrong person. She was not a woman who could love or be loved. There was room for only pain, anger, and vengeance inside of her, and in the end she would have destroyed him.

No, not him … he seemed more resilient than she'd first assumed. *She* was the one who'd be destroyed if she let him in. There were parts of her she'd never let anyone see or touch, and Robert had consistently pushed against her boundaries. She could not allow him to go any further.

"At least let me see you out of the house," he said.

Without waiting for her to answer he swept toward the door, the hem of his open banyan flaring out behind him. She followed in silence, waiting for him to determine that the corridor remained empty before he led her out. They encountered no one as they moved through the servant's passage, the majority of the staff about their duties for the day.

Before long they reached the same door they'd entered last night, stepping out into the sunny morning. The air still held a bit of a chill, but it felt good as she breathed it in, letting the cold flood her throat and chest. Robert turned to face her with the sun at his back, its rays turning his hair to white gold. His expression was set in stone—mouth tight, jaw clenched, eyes mournful. It seemed as if a hundred years had passed between last night and now. It stretched like a crevice between them, growing by the second.

"I don't suppose you want me to escort you the rest of the way," he said, inclining his head toward the path leading into the woods, the one she would follow home.

"No," she replied. "I will be fine on my own."

He scoffed. "I am certain you will. Take care of yourself, my lady."

Something inside her ached at the formal way he addressed her. She wasn't 'Cass' anymore, and he was no longer 'Robert'. But this was what she'd wanted, wasn't it?

"Good-bye ... Mr. Stanley."

As she turned to walk away, it took every ounce of her will not to look back. His gaze followed her, hot on her back until she'd been swallowed up by the trees.

THE FOLLOWING DAY, Robert walked through the woods in the direction of Easton Park with Cassandra's cloak draped over one arm. While she'd told him to stay away—and he had every intention of honoring her wishes—he hadn't wanted her to go without the garment. It had remained in the care of servants overnight, and because everyone thought she'd left after her outburst in the drawing room, he'd been tasked with returning it.

"Your father is exhausted after last evening, but he was most insistent that you bring back word of Lady Cassandra's welfare," his mother had told him over breakfast.

He'd sat across from her while poking at his food, his stomach tied up in too many knots for him to eat. He hadn't wanted to speak of the woman who'd cast him aside after ripping him to shreds with nothing more than her words. However, it seemed all his mother wished to talk about following the dinner party, so he'd had to suffer in silence.

"I am glad you convinced me to invite her," she said between bites of coddled eggs. "While I cannot confess to being fond of the chit, she held her own quite well I suppose. We certainly set a good example for our neighbors, so she should have an easier time of it now."

He couldn't help scoffing aloud at that, rolling his eyes as he reached for the cup of coffee beside his plate. Cassandra, having any easy time of it? That woman wanted nothing of the sort. She'd fight the entire world if she could, lashing out with tooth and claw at anything that got too close to her.

"Whatever could be so funny?" she asked, noting the sardonic smile upon his face.

"Nothing," he'd said, wiping all traces of emotion from his face. "I am certain you are right."

The baroness had given him a curious gaze, but carried on. "Your father seems taken with her. I cannot imagine why. Such a surly creature."

Surly, stubborn, and beautiful, his Cassandra. And yes, she was his whether she wanted to be or not. She could deny it all she wished, but he knew he wasn't alone in his feelings. Things had begun to change between them, and while Robert had been ready to embrace it, Cassandra seemed intent upon running from it.

Which left him in a bit of a conundrum at present—torn between the urge to go chasing after her, and the need to protect himself from anymore heartbreak. As painful as it had been to watch Daphne choose Hartmoor over him, the agony of trying and failing to win Cassandra felt even worse. She'd latched on to some deep-seated part of him, and he'd clung right back, coming alive with her in a way he never had with anyone else.

At this point, he could cut his losses and walk away free and clear. She had pushed him away, and he could choose to honor that and stay away. Or, he could fight his way through her defenses, burst through the fissures in her walls and break them open completely.

Running a hand over his tired face, he'd found he lacked the strength to make a decision yet. She'd turned him inside out this morning.

God help him, the cruelty only made him want her more. She'd been absolutely right about him ... he craved the pain of it as much as the pleasure.

"I will go return the cloak to her now," he'd announced, rising from the table after polishing off his coffee.

His mother had frowned, her gaze falling to his plate. "But, you've hardly touched your breakfast."

"I am not hungry."

She was on her feet in an instant, rushing around the table and reaching up to place a hand over his forehead. "Are you ill? I ought to send for Dr. Dormer."

His exhaustion further exacerbated the annoyance rising within him.

"I am not ill, I just do not want to eat," he'd said, pushing her hand away.

Wringing her hands, she had looked him over from head to toe, her gaze telling him she did not believe a word of it. "Lack of appetite can be a sign of any number of illnesses. You could be—"

"Damn it, Mother, sometimes not eating only means I am not hungry!" he snapped.

She flinched as if he'd struck her, eyes going wide and chin trembling. Wonderful. He could now count her as second among the women who'd grown cross with him in the span of a few hours. Turning to leave, he decided the long walk to Easton Park would help clear his head. By the time he returned, he hoped his mood would have improved. But, considering Cassandra would not be happy to see him when he arrived, he doubted it.

"At least put on a greatcoat," she'd called after him.

"I don't need a coat!" he'd replied as he thundered through the dining room doors and out into the corridor.

It wasn't like him to brush off her concerns, but then, he hadn't felt at all like himself the past few weeks. Cassandra had gotten under his skin, forcing parts of him aside to make room for something else. That thing had no tolerance for the baroness' constant meddling and worries.

Now he approached Easton Park with every intention of leaving the cloak in the care of a servant before returning home. Inside him, conflict roiled over whether he wished to lay eyes upon her.

Passing the pond, he avoided looking at it for fear of reliving the night he'd come here to find her plunging into the depths. It would only make him want to tear the door of her cottage off its hinges and go barreling through the house in search of her. Once he'd found her, he would take her into his arms whether she fought him or not. He'd kiss her senseless and refuse to let go until she gave in.

Christ, she was driving him out of his mind even when they didn't stand face to face.

Striding up to the front door, he made use of the knocker and stood back. A footman appeared a moment later, only to report that his mistress was not at home. He'd given the cloak over and asked that it be returned to Cassandra before taking his leave.

Going back the way he'd come, he released a low, long sigh. He could not determine if he was more relieved, or disappointed at not being able to lay eyes on her.

He paused on the path, glancing toward the small stable where a man and a young boy worked to groom a black Arabian. Within the open doors of the structure he spotted Cassandra's carriage. A carriage she ought to have taken if she had really departed for London.

It was none of his affair, and she'd made it clear his interference would no longer be tolerated. Yet, as he stood there wondering where she was, a premonition niggled down his spine. Something did not feel right about any of this. The grievous state she'd been in last night had meant something, just as her sudden disappearance did. Try as he might, he couldn't brush it off as being none of his business.

Before he could change his mind, he set off toward the stable, determination quickening his strides.

The man glanced up as he approached, while the boy went on chattering about some thing or another while he brushed the Arabian's tail.

"Somethin' I can do for you, sir?"

Robert's gaze flitted to the carriage again. Had she really gone to London, or was she hiding from him inside the cottage? He had to know.

"I came looking for Lady Cassandra, only to be informed she has departed for Town. After the events of last night, I am concerned about her. She was ... not well."

The man stood up straighter, casting a glance at the stable boy. "Leon, go into the kitchen and ask Mrs. Ingram if you can have a bite to eat. I'll come get you when I need you again."

The boy silently obeyed, throwing his brush into a bucket of grooming tools before dashing off toward the house. The man then turned back to Robert, leveling a suspicious glare at him.

"You the one that sent me home without m'lady last night?"

So, this man was Cassandra's driver, then. Strange, that he was here when she was supposedly in London.

"That's right," he replied. "She was most distraught, and I did not feel right letting her leave alone."

The man approached, shoulders squared. "And just what did you do to her?"

Robert shook his head. "No, it was nothing like that. The dinner party was going quite well until one of our guests mentioned that Lady Downing had died in a tragic accident. She did not take the news well."

The driver started, eyes going wide as he stared at Robert in disbelief. What was it about Lady Downing that threw Cassandra and her driver into a panic?

"Lady Downin', you say?" the driver asked, his voice gone hoarse.

"Yes, that's right. I thought perhaps they were friends, because Lady Cassandra was near inconsolable about it. I just want to know that she is all right. She still seemed … not herself this morning."

In truth, she'd seemed more herself than ever—brusque and cold.

But, the abrupt change overnight had confounded him.

Running both hands through a mop of overgrown hair, the driver uttered a vicious string of oaths. Seeming to remember who he was standing before, he flushed.

"Forgive me, sir. I … I didn't know about Lady Downin'. This does explain things."

His heartbeat sped up, his palms breaking out into a sweat as he realized he'd been right to worry. "Explains what? Please, you have to tell me something … anything that might shed some light on what is happening. I'm worried about her."

The driver's eyes darted and he seemed to think over his words before speaking. "M'lady left this mornin', right after returnin' from Briarwell. She seemed in a hurry, didn't even want me to drive her."

Robert frowned. "She rode to London alone on horseback?"

The driver nodded, his breath leaving him in a heavy sigh. "I thought to go after her, but she … bloody hell, what could she be thinkin'?"

The frazzled thread of his patience snapped as his worry increased to panic. He took the driver by his lapels and drew him closer, nostrils flaring as he fought to get a handle on his emotions and failed. Despite not knowing exactly what was going on, he had a feeling Cassandra was in some sort of danger and this driver knew something about it.

"You need to tell me where she's gone and what she is up to," he demanded. "If she's in trouble, I need to go after her."

The man shrugged out of his hold, chin jutting in a defiant manner. "It's not for me to say. M'lady has sworn me to secrecy."

"Goddamn it, your lady needs your help!" he railed, hands clenching into fists. "At least give me something. You must know where she'll go once she's in London. I cannot stand back and allow some ill fate to befall her."

Crossing his arms over his chest, the driver inspected Robert with a critical eye. He seemed to try to determine whether Robert's concern was sincere, and what good might come of revealing Cassandra's secrets.

He softened a bit, shoulders sagging as he recognized the loyalty of this man toward his lady.

"I care for her ... deeply. I just want to help. Please, if you know anything ..."

"The name's Randall," the driver offered, his tone gruff. "And as I said, it's not my place to tell m'lady's secrets. But ... well, if Lady Downin' has died, then it stands to reason Sir Downin' is the one what did her in."

Robert reeled as the weight of the other man's words slammed into him with all the force of a blunt instrument. "How could you possibly know that?"

Randall scowled. "The sod was beatin' her, and Lady Cassandra knew it. There's bad blood between her and Sir Downin', and if she suspects he killed his wife ..."

The panic thrumming through him swelled until Robert feared he would choke on it. His heart was clutched in a vise, his hands shaking as the implications of what the servant was saying became clear.

What do you love ... what will you fight for?

Justice.

She'd all but told him what she would do, and he had missed it, too caught up in the turmoil of watching her slip through his fingers.

"Do you think she would confront him over it?"

Randall scoffed and gave him a pointed look. "If you care for her as you say, then you already know the answer to that, don't you?"

He did. Deep down he knew without a shadow of a doubt that Cassandra meant to act on her suspicions. Sir Downing's account of his wife's fall down the stairs would be believed, and no one would think to probe any deeper. If Cassandra thought there was a chance the man would get away with what he'd done the same way Bertram had gotten away with his crimes for years, she would not be able to stand back and allow it.

"Where would she go once she reaches London?" he pressed. "Can you tell me that much?"

Randall sagged, a defeated expression overcoming his face. "Penrose House would be the last place she'd go at a time like this. You might try the home of the Widow Dane. There's also a place she takes rooms in from time to time … The Pulteney Hotel, 105 Piccadilly."

"I know of it," he said before turning to stride away.

"Are you goin' after her?" Randall called out after him.

"Yes," he replied without a glance back.

Yes, he was going after her. How could he not? Cassandra might insist she was not some damsel in need of saving, but her reckless behavior proved otherwise. She might not want him right now, but she damn sure needed him. If he stood back and allowed her to go through with her plan to confront Downing, there was no telling what might come of it. If the man was not above abusing or killing his own wife, Robert did not want to think about what he might do to Cassandra.

THREE DAYS LATER, Robert stood on the threshold of Penrose House, his first stop after arriving in London. He had not even bothered seeking out his own lodgings before beginning his search for Cassandra. Time was running short, and she had been here at least a day or two longer than him—meaning she could be anywhere. The time had come for swift action, and he was done allowing doubts and fears to hold him back.

He would drag her back to Suffolk kicking and screaming if he had to; but he would not leave London without her.

Upon answering the door, the butler accepted his card and led him into a drawing room where two women sat awaiting morning callers. Fashionably dressed and groomed to perfection, the dowager duchess and her youngest daughter were as lovely as he remembered. Only, the malice and scorn he found simmering in the depths of Lady Lane's eyes proved off-putting, turning her beauty in something glacial and hard. Anger overwhelmed him at the sight of this woman, who had stood back and allowed the *ton* to make an outcast of her own daughter. The woman who had accepted Lord Fairchild's money in place of the justice Cassandra had deserved.

The dowager gave her daughter a little nudge as he came into the room, and the chit sat up straight, a soft smile gracing her face as she looked Robert over from head to toe. Her gaze irritated him, striking him as vapid and shallow. He'd never been introduced to the youngest Lane girl, but it became clear to him then that the machinations of a matchmaking mama had just come into play. As if he would have any interest in a debutante who was little more than a child.

"Mr. Stanley," the dowager said with a practiced smile. "What a pleasant surprise. Please, sit down."

Remaining on his feet, he narrowed his eyes at the dowager. "No, thank you, my lady. I am looking for Lady Cassandra."

The girl's face lit up with curiosity while the mother scowled, looking as if she'd just taken a sip of turpentine.

"Whatever for?" she spat.

He clenched his jaw to hold back the insults dancing on the edge of his tongue. After his long and tiring journey, he stood seconds away from throttling the woman.

"A private matter," he snapped. "I only need to know if she is here."

The dowager's expression became downright cold as she rose to her feet, unfolding her limbs with a stiff sort of grace. "If she is in London, she has not seen fit to show her face here. You may try the home of the Widow Dane. It should hardly surprise you that a woman like Cassandra would keep company with such a strumpet."

His fingernails bit into his palms as he turned away, needing to be out of this woman's company before he did or said something he ought not.

"I will stop in there. Thank you."

"Have a care, Mr. Stanley," the dowager called out, halting him in the doorway. "My daughter has a certain reputation for snaring men into her trap. If you are not on your guard, she will drag your name through the mud, as well."

That did it. Hang social niceties or good manners … he was now out of them when it came to this woman. He turned to face her, the force of his rage making him vibrate from the inside out.

"You, Lady Lane, might be the greatest bitch I've ever encountered."

The dowager bristled, her spine snapping straight as her face drew into an expression of fury. Meanwhile, her daughter gasped, one hand clapping over her mouth.

"I beg your pardon?" the dowager huffed.

"You heard me quite well. Your daughter trapped no one, and Bertram Fairchild and his father deserved to carry the weight of every accusation leveled against them. Cassandra was a victim in need of love and understanding, and you gave her only scorn. You should have led the charge against her assailant rather than placing the blame upon her. You should have fought them rather than accept money as payment—money that is tainted with your daughter's own blood and tears. You are a disgrace and a pitiful excuse for a mother."

The dowager seethed, her face flushing as she approached him, fists balled up as if she meant to pummel him. He stood his ground, shoulders squared, chin raised.

"How dare you?" she ground out. "Leave this house, before I have you thrown out."

He took a step forward, looming over her with a satisfied smirk at the way she backed down, uncertainty flashing in her eyes.

"Gladly. And Cassandra will never step foot over the threshold ever again, I will make sure of it."

"Good," she fired back with a vicious smile. "She is not welcome here, and neither are you. Now leave."

"Go to Hell," he muttered before turning to make his exit.

Long strides carried him into the corridor, where a flurry of servants rushed to be out of his way. They'd been listening in, and now went about their tasks while trying to pretend otherwise. The butler gave him a curious stare but said nothing as Robert barreled through the house. Without bothering to wait for a servant to see to the task, he threw the door open himself and burst out onto the front steps.

Anger at the dowager flamed hot in his belly but he pushed it down, his mind turning back to Cassandra. While he'd love nothing more than to go back into Penrose House and continue giving her a piece of his mind, his mission superseded all else. He had to find Cassandra and put a stop to whatever scheme she had cooked up.

His carriage remained where he had left it, idling in front of the townhouse.

"Where to now, sir?" the driver asked as Felix threw open the door and jumped down to place the steps for him.

"The home of the Widow Dane on Half-Moon Street," he declared.

"Aye, sir … I know the place."

He leaped into the carriage without another word, slamming the door shut once Felix had climbed in after him. Settling on the seat, he ground his teeth and stared out the window, impatient to get to his next destination. The city was coming alive for the day, Grosvenor Square teeming with people in carriages and on foot out to make their morning calls. The traffic had not thickened enough to slow their progress, and before long they had arrived at the home of Lady Millicent Dane.

Robert jumped down from the carriage without waiting for the steps and marched straight to the door. He gave no thought to the fact that they'd never been formally introduced and had no previous acquaintance. None of that mattered, not when finding Cassandra was more paramount than anything.

A footman with a Corinthian frame answered the door, giving him a curious look. Robert knew he must look like hell, his clothing rumpled from long hours in the carriage, hair tousled from tug of his fingers, his eyes darting and bloodshot.

"I need to speak with Lady Dane, immediately. It is important."

The footman held a hand out to accept his card. "I will see if my lady is in. Wait here."

He closed the door and left Robert on the doorstep, where he began to pace, too anxious to stand still. Back and forth, he tread the short distance from one end to the other, counting the seconds that passed him by. Before long, the man reappeared, holding the door open wide.

"Right this way."

He was ushered into a drawing room, the contents of which temporarily took him aback. He'd heard rumors of the Widow Dane's eccentricities, but had not expected this. Erotic art and sculptures filled a room adorned in decadent shades of black and red. The woman herself sat in an armchair with a cup and saucer in one hand, her probing gaze fixed upon Robert.

"Thank you, Timothy," she said, dismissing the footman with the wave of one hand. "Mr. Stanley, do make yourself comfortable. Can I send for tea or other refreshment? I assume you've just arrived from Suffolk."

He lowered himself onto a loveseat across from her, bracing his elbows upon his knees. "No, thank you. Forgive the intrusion, but I've come to London looking for Cassandra. I was told she might be here."

"She was here last night, actually. I offered her the use of one of my guest rooms, but she declined."

Robert bit back a string of epithets. Yet another stop that yielded nothing, more time wasted. But then, this woman was a close friend of Cassandra's. Maybe she could help shed some light onto the things he did not know.

"I need your help. I know the two of you are good friends, and perhaps she might have said something about her plans. I am worried about her ... she left Suffolk in quite a state."

Lady Dane sighed, setting her cup aside and clasping her fingers together in her lap. "I must confess to being concerned myself. In truth, I am glad you've come, Robert ... May I call you Robert? We are connected by our mutual connection to Cassandra, so formalities are not necessary. "

"Of course."

"Then you will call me Millie. Now, about Cass ... she turned up here last night, and she was quite agitated. She wanted to talk to me about Sir Downing."

It was just as he and Randall had suspected. Robert leaned forward a bit, hanging on to Millicent's every word.

"It is not common knowledge, but there has been much gossip about the baronet and his wife. I'd seen her bruises myself, and the poor woman was terrified to death of her husband. But what is to be done in a world where a woman is nothing more than the property of a man?"

"I have reason to believe Cassandra thinks Lady Downing's fall down the stairs was not an accident. Would you happen to have any information in that regard?"

She nodded, the clasp of her hands tightening until they began to shake. "Servant gossip has made its way here. My footman, Peter, reported having heard that Sir Downing and his wife quarreled right before her death. There was a great deal of noise—crashing furniture, shouting, a woman's sobs. Reportedly, she took a valise and left their bedchamber in tears, determined to be free of him. Where she intended to run, I do not know—her mother's home, perhaps. All anyone knows is that a moment later she went tumbling down the stairs head over heels. The poor thing broke her neck and died on the spot. The servants did not see the fall, but a chambermaid claims she noticed Sir Downing on the landing a moment after she fell."

Dread seized him, his stomach twisting at the image she painted. "Do you think he pushed her?"

Millicent raised an eyebrow and pursed her lips. "A man who abuses a woman the way Sir Downing did is capable of all sorts of atrocities. As a woman who has lived with such a man, I can tell you I feared for my life every hour of every day."

Robert studied the Ravishing Widow, seeing something in her he'd never noticed until he'd gotten close enough. Beneath her allure and the confidence she wore as a second skin was a vulnerability—a sadness that rested just beneath the facade. It was no wonder she and Cassandra were such good friends—they had much in common.

"Did you tell Cassandra about all this?" he asked.

"I did," she replied. "And soon after, she left. I tried to stop her, to get her to tell me what this might be all about. But, she was determined to leave. I've been wondering what she's up to ever since."

He ran a hand over his face and sighed. Having his fears confirmed brought him no comfort. He knew Cassandra must have taken rooms in a hotel as Randall suggested, and could be preparing to move against Sir Downing even now.

"I believe she means to confront him."

Millicent gasped, one hand clutching at her throat. "My God. I … I never thought of that, but I believe you may be right. Ever since the trial she has spoken often of her distaste for injustices against women. She is angry, and with good reason. We have so few tools with which to defend ourselves, and it enrages her to know there are others like her out there—more women who have been hurt but can do nothing about it."

Rising to his feet, he gave a slow nod, his mind racing as he thought of what he'd have to do next. If Cassandra was determined to ensure Sir Downing paid for murdering his wife, she would not stop until she'd seen it through.

Millicent rose as well, hands clenching her skirts. "Will you try to stop her?"

"I will," he declared. "Someone must. If Sir Downing will harm his own wife, then Cassandra will be no different."

She nodded her agreement. "You should know that she can defend herself. My own footman gave her lessons in warding off an attacker with both her fists as well as weapons."

"It is not her ability to fend for herself that worries me. Anger has made her irrational, and I fear it could get her killed. I cannot allow that to happen. Thank you for your help. I will report back when I have news."

He turned to leave, but she rounded the low table between them and took hold of the sleeve of his coat. When he turned to face her, Robert found a soft smile upon her lips.

"I knew she'd made the right choice in you," she said. "Cassandra has been hurt, and has built up her defenses as a result. It is the only way she knows to survive."

"It was you who encouraged her to find a bedmate that night at the White Cock," he said, giving voice to what he'd suspected all along. "You who pushed her to move past the pain of what Bertram did to her."

"Yes. I wanted her to be free from her fears over intercourse and intimacy. But, I think she has found so much more in you."

Robert liked to think so, too, even if she insisted upon fighting him. Perhaps that was the reason she resisted him. The walls she'd erected around her heart would not allow her to love him, to let him love her.

"Do not give up," Millicent said, seeming to sense the direction of his thoughts. "Cassandra has been let down by every person she's ever cared for except her father, and the man is dead. She will fight you every moment, but you can get through to her. Fight for her, Robert."

"I will."

She released him, and he continued on his way through the drawing room doors.

As he exited the house, he clung tight to Millicent's words, along with his own hopes. The question of whether he would fight for Cassandra was no longer one he wrestled with. He had no choice in the matter, and deep down he'd known that from the beginning.

The only thing left to be settled was how long she would hold him off before giving in. Robert had plenty of practice with patience, and this time he was more determined than ever. Never again would he stand back and allow what he wanted most to be snatched out of his grasp. He would take hold of her and keep her out of the fire, no matter how determined she was to throw herself into the flames. He would hold on to her and never let go.

CHAPTER 10

After arriving in London and situating herself in The Pulteney Hotel, Cassandra had conducted her own investigation into the death of Lady Downing. Her instincts told her Sir Downing had pushed his wife down those stairs, but she needed to be sure.

So, she'd gone to Millicent, who had let her in on the servant gossip circulating about the suspicious happenings on that fateful night. Then, under the cover of night, she had stood outside Downing's townhome and watched for any sign of movement. The moment a servant emerged, setting off on some errand or other, she had followed. Cornering the man near the mews, she'd used the threat of her knife to prod him into spilling the truth. Everything he'd told her aligned with Millicent's story—the shouting and sounds of things being thrown about, the sight of Sir Downing at the top of the stairs as she lay broken at the bottom. Paying the servant for his silence, Cassandra had let him go and shifted her focus to the murderous bastard who would now feel her wrath.

There was no room inside her for anything but vengeance and justice, her heart pounding out a cadence of bloodlust that thrummed through her body in a continual drumbeat. She'd spent the past two nights lurking outside Downing's home in Berkeley Square, watching for any sign of movement from within. His wife had been dead for over a week now, but aside from his all-black attire the man showed no signs he mourned her.

The house proved silent and still in the daylight hours, but the moment the sun went down, he would emerge, intent upon celebrating the loss of his leg shackle. He'd frequented an opium den the first evening, smoking the potent substance before falling into a wide-eyed stupor.

He'd been easy pickings then, but the sheer number of people inside the place had stayed her hand. She could not risk anyone bearing witness to what she would do once she got her hands on him. The second and third nights had seen him ensconced in a brothel in Soho Square, where he'd spent hours indulging in orgies, sharing an abundance of whores with his drunken friends. Red-faced from drink and glassy-eyed from overindulging, he'd stumble out onto the street as dawn broke the horizon and made his way home on unsteady legs.

After a third night of following him through the same series of actions, she now returned to her hotel for a few hours of rest. She would make her move on Downing tonight, putting an end to this once and for all. Her fingers had itched for the hilt of her dagger or the butt of her pistol, but she'd stayed her hand and waited for the opportune moment. Patience proved difficult, because she was as desperate to be away from London as ever.

She missed the solitude of her home in Suffolk, the quiet and peace she had found there.

She missed Robert.

Gritting her teeth, she shook her head as if to knock him loose from her thoughts. But, he seemed permanently latched onto her mind, and other parts of her she'd rather not examine too closely. The trouble was, she didn't want him trying to expose her soft, vulnerable parts. She could not afford to let him get any closer, to give him access to the things she'd locked away within herself. Letting someone get so close once had almost been the death of her, and she barely survived day to day as it was.

She would get through this. She would finish her business with Downing, then find some way to remove Robert from her thoughts for good. Perhaps taking a new bedmate would do the trick—it had certainly helped her move past the terror and fear Bertram had subjected her to. There must be someone else who could speak to her darker urges, who would enjoy playing the submissive role and turning complete control over to her. While a part of her felt no man would do it as well as Robert, she told herself it couldn't be true. In a world overrun with men, Robert couldn't be the only one she could find satisfaction with.

Letting him go had been the right thing to do. She was entrenched in darkness, awash in the sort of pain she feared might never go away. Despite her earlier doubts, she'd come to see that he was truly a man above reproach. She would tear him to shreds. Good, pure, honest … he deserved better than a woman like her.

Approaching The Pulteney Hotel, she pushed down the hood of her cloak as the heavy black of night gave way to the morning. Exhaustion sapped the strength from her limbs, and made her eyelids heavy.

Sweeping through the vestibule, she made her way up the stairs and to her suite of rooms with trudging steps. Her sleeplessness had grown worse than ever since leaving Suffolk, and she refused to acknowledge that it might be due to the absence of a certain man in her bed.

Pushing open the door to her suite, she faltered on the threshold. She blinked and squinted to make certain she wasn't seeing things—that thinking of Robert so much for the past few days hadn't conjured illusions of him. But, as she came into the room and closed the door, it became clear that what she saw was real.

He'd gotten into her rooms somehow and now sat on the bed, elbows resting on his knees as he gazed down at an object in his hands. Her throat constricted as she realized it was her mask … the one she wore while acting as the Menace. The contents of the sack she'd brought from Easton Park had been strewn over the floor, rifled through by the man who now gazed up at her with steely determination flashing in his eyes.

She clenched her teeth until her entire face began to ache, a whirl of conflicting emotions brewing deep inside her. Most acute among them, though, was anger. How dare he break into her private suite and go through her things? How dare he seek to expose the very thing she'd worked to keep a secret from the *ton*, but from him most of all.

A muscle in his jaw ticked as he came to his feet, his intense gaze still fixed upon her.

"And here I thought the greatest of my worries would be stopping you from murdering Sir Downing."

"How the hell did you get into my rooms?" she growled, reaching up to begin unfastening the cloak.

"Are you the Masked Menace?" he countered.

He did not seem intimidated by her anger or the threat of her stare as she tossed the cloak and her pistol aside before reaching for the dagger in her boot.

"I am asking the questions! How did you get in here?"

Her gaze fixed on the mask in his hands, she approached him. He had no business here, no right digging up her secrets.

He scoffed. "You know as well as I do that enough coin placed into the hands of the right person can earn a man quite a lot. I have roamed all over London looking for you, only to follow your trail here. As I've resolved not to return to Suffolk without you, there seemed no need to rent my own suite. I am not leaving, not until you tell me what is going on, not until you agree to come home with me."

Her patience with him came to an end, and she closed the distance between them with a few quick strides. He dropped the mask when her knife came up against his throat, hands falling limp at his sides.

"I thought I'd made myself clear," she said, narrowing her eyes at him. "You are nothing more to me than a hard, warm prick. What right have you to make demands of me?"

Despite the press of her blade against the vital arteries in his throat, he met her challenge head on. "You may lie to yourself as much as you please, but you cannot fool me, Cass."

She stepped closer, until the heat of his body seeped beneath her skin, sending a heady rush of potent desire through her. The sight of him on the end of her knife stoked something dark and primal within her, making her want to hear him beg and plead before unleashing every ounce of her pent up rage onto him.

"I will hear none of your sentimental drivel," she snapped, trailing her knife down his chest.

She paused just over the top button of his waistcoat. He'd removed his coat and left it slung over a chair, so brocade and linen were the only things separating the tip of her blade from his vulnerable flesh. He stiffened when she cut away the button, sending it flying across the room where it clattered to the floor.

"Cassandra—"

"Your cock is the only thing I hold any interest in," she interjected, meeting his gaze as she lowered her dagger to the second button. "So, if you aren't here to fuck, then you ought to leave. Now is the only chance you will have to escape before I've taken what I want from you."

Flick. Another button gone, skittering across the floor to join the other. He raised his chin and met her stare with an unflinching resolve.

"I told you … I am not leaving. Do what you please to me, but know that it will not be enough to chase me away."

She gave him a hard, humorless smile while cutting away his third button, then his fourth. "We'll see about that."

Tearing his waistcoat open, she sliced his shirt down the front, revealing the expanse of his chest. Her mouth watered at the smooth, unblemished skin just waiting to be tortured. He drew in a sharp breath as she skimmed the tip of her knife from the point of his pulse, over his collarbone and across one of his pectorals. His stomach clenched, his gaze growing unfocused and heavy-lidded, his breath racing as she circled the point around his nipple before teasing the nub with light flicks of her blade. It hardened against the sharp edge and he whimpered, though did not dare move as she continued tracing the weapon down his body, tickling the soft, curling blond hairs running into his breeches. The outline of his erection showed through the fabric, and she detected the heavy thump of his pulse in the hollow of his collarbone.

He trembled as she tore at his fall, yanking his breeches down until they met the resistance of his boots. His cock jutted from his body, hard and straining toward her. She took it in her fist and squeezed until his knees buckled and he had to lean against one of the bed's four posts for balance. He gritted his teeth to hold in a scream, bending at the waist and panting for air. His cock pulsed with want and need as she eased her grip.

She released it and then took hold of his chin, forcing him upright so she looked him in the eye. His head fell back against the post, chest heaving as his breath rushed through parted lips.

"You have forgotten your place," she declared while yanking his waistcoat off and tossing it aside. "I supposed you need reminding. As I've told you countless times, I am not yours to save. I am not some helpless damsel who does not know what she is doing or what she wants."

"You *do* need saving," he argued as she peeled his shirt off his shoulders and used it to entrap his wrists. "From yourself."

He grunted when she used the garment to tether him to the bedpost.

Taking up the cravat that had fluttered to the floor, she balled it up and forced it into his mouth. He offered no protest, but glared at her while clenching his teeth around the fabric. He presented the perfect offering for her—body bared, hands and feet trapped in the strategic snare of his clothing, cock arching toward her from the nest of hair between his thighs. Strands of hair fell into his eyes, shadowing the brilliant blue orbs.

Leaving him bound to the bed, she strode over to the mess he'd made of her belongings, the tip of her riding crop peeking out from within the sack. She took it up and turned to face him, her pulse racing as she contemplated using the crop on him the way she might a beast. What better way to remind him he was nothing more than flesh to her?

His eyes widened as she approached, stroking her fingers over the shaft of the crop. The fear and uncertainty she found in his gaze only added fuel to her growing anger and arousal. As always, the need to hurt and derive her pleasure from him overwhelmed her all at once, making her head spin. She settled on punishment first, his recent behavior demanding that she put him back in his place—the place she needed him to remain in if she were going to keep a tight hold on her sanity.

"You do not question me," she ground out while pressing the tongue of the crop beneath his chin. "You do not come barging into my private rooms and ransack my things, then think to demand answers from me."

She punctuated her words with the flick of her crop, landing the tongue against his left nipple. He squirmed and growled, the skin around his nipple flushing pink. He arched his back when she did it again, his eyes squeezing shut and his breath huffing through his nose. She swung the crop three more times in rapid succession, alternating nipples and making him dance, his feet shuffling as he tried to angle himself away from her blows. The red blush spread over his chest, making her want to lave his abused skin with her tongue, bite him and push his pain toward a crescendo until he'd gone hoarse from screaming.

But, not yet. Wielding the crop gave her such a heady rush of satisfaction, she could hardly stop now. There was so much of him to torment, so much perfect, smooth skin to mark.

He trembled as she smoothed the tongue of the crop down the center of his chest and stomach, ending right at his groin.

"I warned you" she purred, letting the crop trail up his cock to the tip, then back down to caress his balls. "But, this was what you wanted, wasn't it? To push and push and push until I broke. Do you see what pushing earns you, Robert?"

He flinched when she lifted the crop and brought it down on the inside of one thigh. He groaned when she hit him again on the opposite leg, then jolted when she returned to abuse the brilliant red stain from her first strike. All the while, his cock stood high and proud, thick and seeping with his seed.

He mumbled something around the cravat, his eyes glassy and unfocused now, his head sagging until his chin touched his chest. Forcing him back up by his chin, she snatched the cravat free of his mouth and tossed it aside.

"What was that?" she taunted.

He met her gaze and leaned forward as much as his shirt would allow. They were nearly nose to nose now, his breath racing against her cheek as his gaze dropped to her lips.

"More," he rasped.

A slow, aching throb began between her legs, her breasts growing heavy as her nipples tightened to an almost painful degree. She'd been all but torturing him, and the fool could only beg her for more?

"Haven't you ever wondered why no other man will do when it comes to your needs?" he said when she did not respond, his voice strained by his shallow breaths. "Why you've allowed me into your bed time and time again? It is the same reason I am ruined for all other women. I am your match, Cass … and you are mine. We are two sides of the same coin, and no amount of denial on your part will change that. So, do your worst. I want it all … your anger, your pain, your sadness. I can take it."

So, she gave it to him, not bothering to push the cravat back into his mouth as she went back to punishing him, using the crop against his chest, his nipples, his thighs, even the backs of his knees when he twisted in an instinctive move to avoid the blows. Then, she aimed the crop between his legs with a lighter hand, landing it against the target of his bollocks. His face reddened from the roar he held in, his head falling back against the post as she followed it with another tap against the reddened head of his cock. She leaned in to clap a hand over his mouth just before he screamed, the sound muffled by her palm. His eyes began to water as he met her gaze, the depths awash in both agony and ecstasy. Her hands shook from the force of this thing pulsing between them, raw and elemental and undeniable. She wanted him now more than ever, and the erection leaking droplets of his mettle onto her hand as she touched him proved he wanted her, too … despite the pain, or even because of it.

He moaned against her hand, his skin hot to the touch from the fire she'd lit in him with her crop. He thrust into the circling sheath of the fingers, leaning forward so that his forehead rested against hers. She removed her hand from his mouth and used it to tease one of his reddened nipples, wrenching a strangled cry from deep within him.

She released his cock and played her fingers over his skin, finding the places on his chest and thighs that had been marked and pressing down on them. He squirmed against her, groaning and sighing as she alternated between stroking his inflamed skin to offer relief, and agitating it with slight pressure here and there.

Cassandra could have toyed with him this way for hours, watching the part of his plush lips as he drew in a sharp breath, seeing the glimmer in his eyes as she touched and explore him in a way she never had. But, after a while it was no longer enough. She needed more from him—his mouth, his hands, his cock inside her. She'd worked herself into a frenzy beating him with her crop, and now nothing could bring her satisfaction other than claiming and owning him in the most primitive of ways.

She untied his hands from the post, giving him only a moment to shake off the shirt and work the feeling back into his fingers. She dug her fingers into his shoulder and forced him down to his knees. Then, she motioned for him to unlace her boots. While he got to work, she began unbuttoning her own clothing. She removed the waistcoat she'd donned over her shirt, then opened her fall.

"Here is where you belong," she said. "On your knees."

He kept his rapt gaze upon the opening of her breeches, hands freezing in the midst of removing her stockings. He released a deep sigh at the sight of her cunt, now exposed by the open flap. Leaning forward, he nuzzled her mound, flicking his tongue at the inner flesh. She shuddered at the heat that tongue stroke sent suffusing through her body.

He pulled away and glanced up at her, his fingers caressing down her leg as he pulled her stocking down. "Yes, but only for you. Always for you."

The impact of his words was immediate, quickening her pulse and making the need to possess him all the more acute. He was hers, even when she chased him away, even when she tried to convince herself she neither wanted nor needed him.

But, he'd been right; no one else would do, and there could be no resisting with him here, staring up at her with his bright blue eyes so filled with earnestness and desperate need. As much as he craved her cruel depravity, she craved his exquisite submission. Denying it had been futile, as here she stood giving in to the desires and sadistic impulses she inspired in him.

Letting him help her out of the breeches, she then made quick work of removing her shirt. He traced his gaze over her nudity with reverence and awe, as if kneeling before the altar of a goddess. She accepted her tribute, taking a fistful of his golden curls and urging him between her legs. He came to her eagerly, crawling closer and burying his face in her cunt with a muffled moan. His tongue slipped between her lower lips, pressing against her clit with stunning accuracy. She threw her head back, tightening her hold on his hair and undulated against his mouth. The wet heat and rough rasp of his licks sent ripples of pleasure through her body.

He slid his palms down her thighs, squeezing one and then lifting it, draping her leg over his shoulder to open her. His tongue darted inside, swirling and plunging deep, his teeth gently scraping against the distended, pulsing bud at her center. She bit back another cry, hips bucking and her insides going up in flames as he went at her as if determined to devour her whole, licking up every drop of wetness he coaxed from within her. She shattered when he latched onto her clit, sucking with strong, merciless pulls that caused her legs to shake. He cupped her buttocks and held her in place, circling his tongue against her sensitive nub and drawing out her explosive ending.

She hauled him to his feet by his hair, then pushed him onto the bed. He went down with a little huff as she freed him from the tangle of his boots and breeches.

She couldn't get to him fast enough, crawling over him before he'd gotten a chance to pull his legs up onto the bed. Straddling him, she took hold of his face and claimed his mouth, plunging her tongue in and feeding off the taste of her own arousal still lingering on his lips. He wrapped an arm around her waist and slid farther up the bed, taking her with him until they were stretched out, chest to chest and pelvis to pelvis, limbs entangled and lips locked. He threaded his fingers through her hair and held her close, returning her ravaging kiss with his own fervor, sucking and nipping at her lips. He nudged a leg between hers to part them, fitting her over his cock so all it would take was one stroke to enter her, to give them both the thing they wanted most.

He tightened his grip on her hair and pulled, lifting her head so she looked him in the eye.

"Take me," he whispered, his lips brushing against hers. "I'm yours, Cass."

She took him inside her with one swift motion, the way made slick by the attentions of his tongue. Bracing her hands on his chest, she rocked against him, rolling her hips and using the friction of his body to stimulate her clit with each motion. He took hold of her arse and urged her faster, harder, his hips raising to meet her every downward motion. She threw her head back and gave herself over to the moment, pushing aside the last of her anger and resistance.

Tomorrow, she had a mission to carry out, a vendetta to see through to the end. Tonight, she could have Robert—without thought, without worry, without reservation or fear. She'd already given it all to him, branding it into his skin for them both to see and feel. Now there was only this.

His tongue stroked a hot path from one breast to the other, then his lips latched on to suckle, drawing her nipple in deep and sending twinges of ecstasy straight to her core. She clutched his head and held him against her, burying her face in his curls and drinking in his scent, the feel of him against her, inside her.

The bite of his teeth against the tip of her breast sent a lightning strike of heat and pleasure straight to her core.

"Robert," she groaned, arching her back in wordless plea for more.

He met her gaze, cupping her breasts with both hands while her movements atop him became more erratic, her explosive ending lingering just within reach. He planted his feet on the mattress and used it for leverage, quickening his own thrusts inside of her.

"That's it," he whispered, tugging at her nipples with gentle insistence, his cock steadily stroking right against the sweet spot inside her. "Let go, Cass ..."

She was so close, panting and shaking as the building pressure within her seem to reach its zenith. The exquisite pleasure of his fingers pinching tight to her nipples stabbed through her and she spent with a shrill cry, collapsing on top of him and clinging tight as it washed through her with ten times the power of her previous spend. Robert kept up his pace, wrapping his arms around her and thrusting through her finish, strengthening each wave of her climax. He buried her faced in his neck and she gave herself over to it, the strength leaving her limbs as her insides clenched and rippled around him, the intensity of it stealing the air from her lungs.

Finally, she came back down, her breath coming out in a rush as the pounding spasms within dulled to deep twinges she felt to the far reaches of her body.

Robert was right behind her, seeming to try to dig deeper with each surge of his hips.

"Cass, I ... I'm going to ..."

She forced herself off him before he could spill inside her, crawling down his body and taking his cock in hand. He gasped when she sucked him into her mouth, drawing him deep and swirling her tongue around his head. Then, his fingers were tangled in her hair as he thrust into her mouth and released, his entire body trembling with the force of it. She accepted it all, her palate bathed with the taste of both him and herself at once.

When he'd gone still beneath her, his rough groans melting away into harsh, ragged breaths, she released him from her mouth.

Her own body surrendered to fatigue, the events of the day as well as their vigorous coupling taking their toll. She managed to crawl up beside him before she fell onto the bed with a heavy sigh, her eyes drifting closed.

For a long moment, there was only the heat radiating off him and the grating sound of his rapid breaths mingling with her own. Then, she registered movement, felt his arms coming around her and the coverlet drifting over her naked body. Instead of retreating from the shelter of his body, she sank into it, letting herself enjoy the press of his chest against her back, the tangle of his legs with hers.

Tomorrow, she'd have to fight again. Tonight, she was exhausted, worn thin, her walls cracked and crumbled due to the man who now held her in his arms.

He nuzzled her neck as she began drifting off to sleep, his breath now slow and steady against her ear, the thump of his heartbeat against her back now returned to normal.

"I love you, Cass," he mumbled before pressing a kiss to her shoulder.

She stiffened in his hold, prepared to roll away from him, to leave the room altogether and run back to Suffolk on foot if she had to. Anything to be away from him, from the words that had the power to break through the last of her defenses.

He tightened his hold as if he'd expected such a reaction. She squirmed in his grip, but could not break it—a stunning reminder that he'd always been strong enough to subdue her if he'd wished, to hurt her if it were in his nature.

"Shh, it's all right," he whispered. "You can go back to running from me tomorrow if you like. Just know that I don't intend to stop chasing you. I love you, and it won't be any less true in the morning than it is at this moment. Now, sleep ... I know you haven't been resting."

She hadn't been, and didn't even possess the strength to wiggle out of his hold. So, she relaxed in his arms and allowed him to nestle her even tighter against him, the softened length of his cock pressed against her arse. He'd be hard again before long, the organ in the perfect position to enter her from behind. But, even that did not worry her. Robert had earned her trust, and she could sleep secure in the knowledge that he would never take advantage of her vulnerability. She was as safe as she'd ever been.

Closing her eyes, she relaxed against him. Within moments, she'd drifted into a peaceful, dreamless sleep.

ROBERT SAT on the edge of the bed in Cassandra's hotel room, staring down at the mask in his hands. She had distracted him this morning, shifting his focus from confronting her over her identity as the Masked Menace, to making certain she understood he could not be chased off. He'd faced her anger, taken on her pain as his own, and melted with her into a pool of heated ecstasy. He'd slept in her bed, holding her in his arms and reveling in how it felt to be allowed such closeness.

He had roused before her, the bright light of the late afternoon sun shining through the window facing the front courtyard. Instead of awakening her, he'd lain there and drank in the sight of her, still and peaceful in sleep. Her beauty seemed different when she was at rest, her face completely still, the defensive expression she often wore wiped away. Even with dark circles showing beneath her eyes from lack of sleep, she was a dream, soft and warm and entirely his.

But, once he'd left the bed to get dressed, he began to steel himself for the fight ahead. For, fight him she would. Now that he'd dared to ferret out her secrets, now that he'd confessed his love for her, she would battle him like never before. He was prepared to stand his ground—not just for her love, but for her life, which would be forfeit if she carried on with her dangerous vendetta.

He hadn't realized how deep and dark the pit of rage and revenge she'd buried herself in actually was. As it turned out, this thing with Sir Downing represented only a fraction of Cassandra's deeds. He was not making something out of nothing—a person who rode about on horseback alone with a mask and domino in her possession proved a likely suspect. When he thought over what he knew of the victims, and that the attacks had not begun until after Bertram's trial, the evidence seemed to point vaguely in Cassandra's direction.

She needed him far more than she would admit, more than even he had realized. No matter how she tried to convince him she did not require saving, Robert believed otherwise.

She needed to be saved from her anger, from the deadly noose of vengeance, from herself.

He turned to find her stirring, a deep sigh rushing through her nose as she stretched before rubbing her eyes. Remaining silent and still to allow her to come to full wakefulness, he observed the phenomenon of her transformation. Her soft expression hardened by degrees, eyes going shuttered and mouth tightening, as if upon awakening she'd found the world to still be as dark and miserable as ever.

Blinking, she turned her head to find him sitting there, then lowered her gaze to the mask in his hands.

"Good afternoon," he murmured, drawing her gaze back up to his face.

Having settled Felix in lodgings of his own with instructions to await his return, Robert had brought only a valise with a few essentials. Thankfully, she hadn't destroyed his breeches, and he'd had the foresight to pack a fresh shirt and waistcoat. He was now as decent as he was like to get, his hair falling in disarray without Felix's pomades to arrange it into their signature tousle. He hadn't bothered to shave either, two days' worth of stubble prickling along his jaw.

"I thought to wake you and send for a meal, but you slept so peacefully I didn't wish to wake you," he said as she sat up in bed and tossed the coverlet aside.

She found her discarded shirt on the floor and bent to pick it up. Once she donned it, she turned to face him, the garment hanging to her thighs. Its buttons remained open, offering a tantalizing glimpse of her cleavage. It slipped to expose one shoulder as she sat in a chair facing the bed, hands folded in her lap as she stared him down.

"Well, I suppose I cannot be rid of you, can I?"

Despite the harshness of her tone, he grinned. "Never. I meant what I said last night."

Her gaze faltered, landing on the mask in his hands. She seemed determined to ignore this morning's declaration, as well as the vulnerability he'd coaxed to the surface once again. It did not matter that she'd taken a crop to him first, forcing him to withstand the brunt of her anger. After that, he'd gotten the same glimpse of her he was always allowed when he submitted and gave her every part of himself.

Rather than press the issue, he decided to get to the most important matter. He held up the mask, turning it over in his hands and studying the gaping holes for eyes.

"You are the Masked Menace. I questioned you last night, when in my heart I already knew. You all but told me when I asked you what you loved, what you would fight for. Justice, you said."

He paused, leaning forward and seeking out her gaze.

"The sort of justice you were denied until it was too late," he continued when she said nothing. "The sort of justice countless other women are denied. You grew tired of being the victim, of being afraid and helpless. So, you decided to fight for people who cannot fight for themselves—in the same way you wish someone had fought for you."

Her jaw flexed, her nostrils flaring as she seemed to fight against reacting to his words. Reaching across the space between them, he touched her knee, forcing her to acknowledge him. She flinched, but did not pull away from his touch. Her eyes burned with a barely contained fire, the silver streaks in her blue irises flashing like lightning.

"Will you at least tell me I'm right?" he prodded. "Tell me it's true."

She crossed her legs, prompting him to take his hand away. Settling more comfortably in her chair, she sighed.

"When Randall first came into my service, he was fresh out of mourning," she said, her voice giving no hint to how revealing this must make her feel. "I had decided I'd had enough of the *ton*'s pious judgment. With the trial over and Bertram dead, I wanted nothing more than to move forward with my life. But, you see, moving forward was all but impossible when my assailant seemed to be everywhere, all the time, haunting me. I saw him in the other men around me—some who might never have done me harm, but others who certainly would if given the chance. When I caught Randall weeping in the stables one evening, I asked him what the matter was. He confessed that while he was out of mourning, he still had not recovered from the crushing loss of his wife. When I asked him what happened to her, he did not wish to tell me at first. I think he believed it might have been difficult for me to hear given my own trauma. But, eventually I coerced him into telling me."

Her words ripped him to shreds, despite the matter-of-fact way she delivered them.

"She was set upon by two men thinking to make sport of her," she went on. "Because she was a servant, they saw her as easy prey. Apparently, she put up too much of a fight and one of them struck her. The blow to the head caused her death."

Robert flinched, his chest aching as he thought of anyone suffering such a fate. Knowing what Cassandra had endured he found himself grateful that she'd survived, at least.

"Did Randall report what he knew to anyone?"

She snorted. "His former master was one of the men responsible for her death. He is an earl whom Randall feared going against publicly. No one would believe a servant over a lord of the *ton*, and he knew that. He resigned his post, and found himself in my service. I do not think he ever imagined that his new mistress would take such an interest in avenging his wife."

Robert turned the mask over in his hands and imagined her wearing it, descending upon her prey in the dark with her eyes blazing through the slits.

"The Masked Menace was only a facade," he whispered as the fragments of what he knew came together in his mind. "You used it to strike out at men who had harmed women."

"I started with the earl, tracking him down along the road to Norfolk. Then, I found his friend a few nights later just outside Town. Taking their valuables only covered up my true aims … meting out punishment for the atrocities they thought they'd gotten away with."

"How did you punish them?"

"With the only thing men like them seem to understand," she hedged. "Threats and pain."

Thinking of what Millicent had told him, he could imagine just how she went about delivering that pain. She'd learned to fight, to use a knife and a pistol. He doubted she was above using them when necessary.

"From there, I decided that I must take it upon myself to sniff out more secrets," she said. "It is interesting, the things a person can hear when the world ignores them. I listened and I investigated, and I sought out the men who think it their right to abuse the women in their care. It was working … they were all afraid—so afraid that not one of them has revealed that the Masked Menace is really a woman. The papers do not even make mention of the things they suffered at my hand, because they won't admit what I did to them, or why they deserved it, because they are ashamed—as well they should be."

He stood, leaving the mask on the bed. "Cass, I understand—"

"How could you?" she exploded, coming to her feet as well. Her eyes flashed with lightning strikes of fury, hands balling into fists. "What do you know of my pain—you, with your perfect, pretty face, and your loving parents, and your idyllic life. The woman you loved tossing you over is the most tragic thing that's ever happened to you, and it led you straight into my bed. Oh, how horrid that must have been for you!"

Her words fell on him like physical blows, their strikes effective. She wanted to hurt him, to push him away. It was the same thing she'd done last night, lashing out in an attempt at scaring him off.

Stepping closer, he took hold of her wrists and eased her back into her chair. When she tried to rise, he shook his head, his expression telling her she ought to stay put.

"You think I don't know pain?" he rasped, the ache caused by her words coming through in his voice.

He hadn't meant to allow her to shake him this way, but her assumption rankled more than he cared to admit. It had felt like an accusation, as if she saw his lack of anguish as some sort of character defect.

"You do not know what you are talking about," he snapped. "You've no idea the pain I have felt, or the losses I have endured."

He went to his valise, which sat open on the other side of the room. He reached inside and took hold of the three miniatures he never left home without. He liked the idea of taking his brothers with him everywhere he went.

He returned to Cassandra, cradling the three frames in his hands. Her gaze grew curious as he took one in hand and extended it to her. The young face of a solemn young boy stared up at them.

"This was Andrew, the first of my brothers to die."

She started as if his words had shocked her. "I had no idea you had a brother."

"I had three," he said, letting her take the portrait from him. "I was the youngest. Andrew was only a boy when he died … an illness that presented itself as a sneezing fit, of all things. I was in the room when he stopped breathing, though my mother did not know it. Who could spare me a glance while Andrew lay there gasping and choking, his lips turning purple as he fought for air?"

Her horrified gaze lifted to land upon him, one hand coming over her mouth. "Oh, Robert ..."

"This was Jonas," he said, offering her the second portrait. "He was the second eldest and Briarwell's resident troublemaker."

He couldn't help a little smile at the thought of Jonas, despite the heavy weight of grief settling in his chest. The portrait she held did a poor job of depicting the wide, jubilant smile his brother had always worn. He didn't think there was a painter alive who might have gotten it right. The smile lived on only in the memories of those who had known him.

"What happened to him?" she asked, laying Andrew's portrait in her lap to better study Jonas'.

"He joined the Royal Navy, and on his first voyage his ship ran afoul of a storm. The vessel went down with all hands, and ... they never recovered a single body."

The corners of her lips turned down and she gave him a mournful look. "How horrible for you all ... your poor mother."

"This was William," he said, his voice growing thick and hoarse as he prepared to tell her of the final death—the one that had broken him. "He was the firstborn, the heir. He had almost completed university when he died."

Tears shined in Cassandra's eyes, but she shed none, remaining as strong as always. He felt as if he'd begin weeping any moment, his own eyes stinging and his vision going hazy.

"He gave his life to save someone else," he choked out. "A woman who was being accosted by some blackguard after her jewels. He saved her, but he was killed. He ... I know it is bad of me to play favorites, but ... William *was* my favorite. He was everything I was not —strong, brave, sure about everything. He was everything I wanted to be, and after losing Andrew and Jonas he was all I had left."

Cassandra cradled the three miniatures in her hands, the three boys who'd never grown to become men in truth. William had never gotten to tell the person he loved how he felt. Andrew had never even grown his first chin hair. Jonas had sought adventure on the same seas that had claimed him in a watery grave.

"I never understood why," he sobbed, swiping at his leaking eyes with the back of his hand. "My parents struggled for years to conceive, and lost three babes before William. Why would God give them to us, only to take them away after all that?"

Cassandra shook her head, a lone tear finally escaping her eye. "I don't know, Robert. I … I'm so sorry."

He sniffed and reeled himself back in, determined not to fall apart —not now, when he needed to get through to her. "I know it isn't the same as being raped and publicly ostracized. I cannot imagine what that was like. But, I do know pain. I know what it is to feel helpless. I know what it is to hurt in a way that can't be healed."

She came to her feet, reverently placing the miniatures on the bed before turning to him. He had expected more resistance from her, more scorn. But, she shocked him by bringing both hands over his face and moving close until their bodies touched. The surface of his skin tingled at her nearness, the need to grab hold of her and never let go overwhelming him.

"It is no wonder you respond the way you do to the pain," she whispered, stroking her thumb over his lips. "It is all you know. You were born from it, you lived through it. Pain reminds you that you're alive, that your heart is still beating, that your skin can still register the sensation of a touch—no matter if it hurts or soothes."

He nodded, lowering his head and letting her kiss his brow. The sweetness of it stole his breath away, and as much as he craved her dominance, he found himself wanting more of her tenderness, too. She allowed him so little of it, and now he needed it like a parched man wandering an endless desert in search of water.

"*You* make me feel alive," he murmured. "I need you, I love you. Please … this nonsense with the Menace and Sir Downing … let it go, Cass. Let it go and come home with me. I couldn't stand it if you were caught, or hurt, or …"

She released him, shaking her head as she backed away from him.

"I can't."

"You can," he insisted, reaching out to grab her.

She backed away from his touch. "I can't!"

He ran his fingers through his hair with an exasperated sigh. "Why not?"

"Sir Downing killed his wife because of me!"

Realization washed over him as he thought back to what Randall had told him. He'd claimed that there was bad blood between Cassandra and Sir Downing, but he hadn't made the connection until now.

"You threatened him to stop beating her. You visited him as the Menace, but he did not heed your warning."

Her chin trembled, but she raised it and snuffed out the grief that had shown in her eyes for a moment. "I went after him thinking to spare that poor woman anymore pain. He killed her in retaliation, I know he did."

He shook his head, taking hold of her shoulders and pulling her against him. "You cannot know that. If he'd been hurting her all this time, he would have killed her eventually."

"He has to pay."

"Then we will go to a magistrate."

She stiffened, her cheeks flushing as she became more agitated by the second. "Magistrates are all but useless, and you know it! The only reason one became involved in Bertram's case was because of generous compensation from the Earl of Hartmoor. Some of us do not have that much money or influence to throw around, so we use the only tools we have at our disposal."

"Cass, he could hurt you, or kill you! Is revenge worth your life?"

"Yes!" she screamed, taking hold of his lapels and shaking him.

He furrowed his brow, trying to understand, wanting to know why she had been so reckless with her own well-being. "Why?"

"I can't stop," she said, her eyes darting as she seemed to begin retreating into herself again. "I have to fight."

He tightened his grip on her arms, determined not to give up, not to allow her to go on hiding from him. "Tell me why, Cass."

"Because I didn't fight *him*!" she wailed, more tears springing to her eyes. "Because when Bertram overpowered me, I did nothing to stop him. I laid there and let him have me!"

CHAPTER 11

Cassandra clenched her hands together, staring at her interlaced fingers as her knuckles began to whiten. She hadn't meant to blurt her secret, but the words had come tumbling out against her will. The shame of her admission had stunned her into silence for a moment, and apparently it had done the same to Robert. He stood looking at her with sorrow in his eyes, his mouth turned down into a solemn frown. He seemed to be waiting for her to finish telling him why she couldn't stop fighting, why giving up was completely out of the question.

What else could she do but tell him? He'd come all this way to try to stop her without understanding her reasons. He loved her—she believed that with her whole heart. Why else would he endure her shifting moods and secrecy? Why else would he stay when she'd done everything she could to chase him away?

"We were in a carriage returning from an afternoon at The British Museum," she said, still avoiding his gaze. "We'd been courting for weeks, and he'd charmed me so thoroughly I lost hold of all my good sense. For the first time in my life, I didn't feel like the 'plain Lane daughter'. I wasn't a wallflower. The son of an earl thought me beautiful—he said so all the time. He hung onto every word I said and showed me affection whenever he could. He sent me flowers and called upon me at home, and made mention of marriage often. He was perfect … and I was in love."

She paused, taking a deep breath and swallowing the acidic bile stinging the back of her throat. She'd told this tale many times—to her mother and sisters, to Bertram's other victims, to Randall. It had been some time since relating it had put her in such an emotional state.

It was Robert. He had pried into her soul and unearthed these feelings she'd suppressed. Inhibiting it became difficult with him looking at her as if the emotions were his own.

"He made fooling people art," Robert offered. "It was no fault of your own."

Cassandra shrugged off his reassurance. It did nothing to make her feel better about letting herself fall into his trap.

"I knew better than to let him kiss me and take other liberties when no one could see. But I'd never felt desired before … never been kissed, never been touched in a sensual way. The attention and admiration paid to my sisters … all my years of envying them faded to nothing. Because a handsome, charming man who was popular with the *ton* liked me. He wanted *me* when he could have had any woman he wanted. I have to admit that the attention and the way he made me feel … it was addicting."

He nodded as if in understanding, but kept quiet, seeming content to listen.

"That day in the carriage, we were without my chaperone. I'd been paying my abigail to leave us alone, to go for walks in the park, or spend time in circulating libraries while I went off with Bertram. We'd been carrying on this way for a fortnight by then, and each time I found myself alone with him, he pushed our encounters farther and farther. I'd always insist we stop before things went too far. The fear of ruination held me back from allowing him to make love to me, even though I wanted it … I wanted it more than I'd ever wanted anything. But after we'd left the museum and he began kissing me again, touching me, trying to lift my skirts … it didn't feel right. Everything was different than it had been before, and he was not himself—or rather, not the man I'd come to know. He was far too aggressive, ignoring me when I told him he ought to stop and return me home. He'd instructed his driver to take the long route back to Hyde Park, where my maid waited for us to return. I know now he did it on purpose, to give himself more time to …"

"You don't have to do this," Robert insisted. "You don't have to talk about it if you don't want."

She shook her head and met his gaze at last. He looked as if every word of her account was making him sick.

"I have to," she whispered. "You need to understand …"

He clenched his jaw, but nodded anyway, freeing her to continue.

"It did not take me long to understand what was happening. I struggled, but he was too strong, his weight pressing me into the seat until I could barely draw breath. He told me I was a good girl for not fighting him. He knew I wanted it, so there was no use pretending otherwise."

"Cass—"

"I laid my head down and gave in," she said, her words ground out from between clenched teeth. Her eyes brimmed with tears again, but she blinked them back, determined to get through this. "I didn't scream … I fell silent after my pleas for him to stop went unheeded. I didn't kick or flail or try to hit him. I just … I yielded and let him do what he wanted."

"You were frightened," Robert argued. "He overpowered you, he would have hurt you worse if you'd fought him—we know that based off the other womens' testimony. You did what you had to do to survive."

"I was weak!" she bellowed. "Can't you see that? My body was on the line, and I laid there and let him have it … stunned into submission so fast it was laughable."

"You were a young, scared girl," he insisted. "He disarmed you, knowing you stood little chance of escape. You cannot blame yourself."

"I don't," she spat, turning away from him. "At least not for being raped. Bertram did that, and he paid for it. But, I do blame myself for being so naive, so weak. I blame myself for crying and lying there to endure the pain of being torn apart when I should have resisted."

Robert's hands fell onto her shoulders and he pulled her back against his body. She wanted to lean into him, accept the comfort offered by his nearness and his touch.

She could not afford to do that. The sun had begun to set, and the need to finish what she had started persisted. Sir Downing could not get away with murdering his wife ... and she had to do something to atone for her part in all this. Perhaps Robert was right and the man would have murdered his wife without her interference. But, she would never know, and the guilt of it would eat her alive.

She'd kept her head down and her mouth closed following Bertram's assault, believing she'd been the only one. The revelation that there were many others had been devastating, and only exacerbated her anger at those who'd known all along and done nothing. She would not stand by and allow Downing to hurt another woman, possibly even kill again.

"Injustices happen every day," he murmured, turning her to face him. "I am not saying that you ought to turn a blind eye to them ... but, you cannot carry the weight of the world upon your shoulders. You cannot avenge them all, and the way you're going about it is dangerous. If you are caught ..."

She cut him off, taking his face in her hands and capturing his mouth in a deep kiss. He gave in with a predictable lack of resistance, his arms going around her as he threw himself into kissing her back. He seemed to take this as acquiescence, and she did nothing to show him otherwise. Backing him toward the bed, she began loosening his clothes and peeling them off. He sighed against her lips as if relieved. If they were naked in bed, intertwined with one another, then she couldn't run off and get into danger. She let him think this, pushing him down on to the mattress and urging him up toward the headboard.

She reached out for one of the tasseled cords tying the bed curtains back, showing it to him with a wicked smirk that had his cock hardening against her thigh. He submitted to having his hands tied, as she'd known he would, his gaze never wavering from her as she lifted them over his head and secured them to one of the bedposts.

Then, she leaned down to kiss him again, giving it everything she had and making it last. It could be the last chance she had to taste him and experience the heady feeling of being kissed by the most beautiful man she'd ever known. It was not his face that made him so, but the kindness he'd shown her even when she did not deserve it, and his acceptance of who and what she'd become. When she pulled away he smiled at her, his eyes taking on the glassy quality of a man who's had too much to drink. He anticipated more of the torment he'd endured last night, but Cassandra had no choice but to deny him. She had somewhere to be, and now that he was tied to the bed, he could not stop her.

Leaving the bed, she returned to where she'd left her clothes, retrieving the various articles from the floor and pulling them on. Robert lifted his head, frowning as he watched her tuck her shirt into her breeches.

"Cass, what are you doing?"

Ignoring him, she pulled on a pair of stockings, then shoved her foot into one boot. He began to struggle, pulling at the bonds keeping him tethered to the bed.

"Cass … wait … don't do this."

She moved faster now, needing to leave this room and outrun the guilt making her want to climb back into that bed with him. Clenching her jaw, she pulled on a coat and buttoned it before swirling her cloak about her shoulders and pulling the hood over her head. She abandoned the mask, leaving it on the floor where Robert had dropped it last night. She couldn't be seen traipsing about Mayfair in a black mask unless she wanted to bring the city watch or the Bow Street Runners down on her own head. Besides, it did not matter if Downing saw her face … he would not live long enough to expose her.

Outside, the sun had set and twilight settled over London, telling her it was far past time for her to leave.

"Cassandra!"

She pause on her way to the door, turning back for one last look at him. He was as perfect as ever, and hers for the taking in every way she could imagine. Confusion and sadness etched his handsome face, a golden strand of hair falling over his brow, his nude body stretched out in a tantalizing display. The heaviness in her chest only grew worse, her stomach churning at the prospect of walking through this door without looking back.

She'd had years' worth of experience pushing her emotions aside in order to survive, to do what needed to be done.

"I'm sorry, Robert," she murmured before stepping out into the corridor. "But you deserve so much more than I have to give."

Without another look back, she made her way to the stairs, turning her mind toward Sir Downing. If he adhered to the routine he'd been following the past few days, she ought to arrive at his townhome just as he set out for the night. The knife in her boot and the pistol stuffed into the back of her breeches bolstered her as she stepped out of The Pulteney Hotel and onto the street, turning in the direction of Berkeley Square.

She reached Downing's townhome in less than a quarter of an hour, taking up her hiding place amongst the trees of the park at its center as the man emerged from inside. She released a sigh of relief, her heartbeat slowing a bit. For a moment, she had worried that the time spent with Robert had caused her to miss him. There were rumors that Downing planned to depart for Devon any day now, so she could not risk letting him slip through her fingers. It had to be tonight.

She crossed the street, moving fast to be out of the way of a hackney rolling in her direction. Keeping her prey in her sights, she followed him along his route to the brothel, making sure to lag behind. Gas lamps became fewer and farther between as they moved away from Berkeley Square, prompting her to remove her pistol while keeping it hidden within the folds of her cloak. There was an alley up ahead. One blow to the head and she'd stun him, another and he'd be subdued enough for her to drag him into the darkness and slit his throat. She'd rather not shoot him, as the noise would attract notice … but if she were forced to pull the trigger, she'd do so without hesitation.

She quickened her steps as the darkness enveloped them and foot traffic along the lane thinned out until they were the only two people in sight. Her fingers tightened on the butt of her weapon, her pulse racing as she prepared to attack. Gritting her teeth, she lunged for him, brandishing the pistol from the confines of her cloak.

Before she made contact, a hand hooked into her cloak from behind and impeding her progress. She struggled to stay on her feet as her body collided with a solid, male form, one hand clapping over her mouth. She grunted and screamed, the sounds of her outrage stifled by the palm making it difficult for her to draw breath.

"Well, well, well," purred a deep voice in her ear. "Looks like I've caught myself a menace."

She kicked and flailed, but fell still when something hard and blunt slammed into the side of her head. Her vision blurred and her limbs went weak. She heard the distinct clatter of her pistol falling to the ground. Another blow, and Downing's face appeared before her as her vision began to fade and consciousness slipped from her grasp.

CASSANDRA AWAKENED to darkness and a cloying humidity. As she slowly came to, she blinked and shook her head, wincing from the throbbing pain in her temple. She could remember nothing that had happened after a stunning blow to the head made the entire world fade away. As awareness returned to her, a twinging pain in her shoulders and neck exacerbated the pounding in her head. Trying to move her arms, she found she couldn't. They'd been bound together and pulled taut above her head. With only the dim light of a single lamp to see by, she realized she had been tethered to the rafters of an underground cellar. Her arms had gone numb, and her knees had been folded beneath her, the pressure of her weight making her legs throb as if pricked with dozens of needles.

She'd been stripped of all her clothes, dust and a sheen of sweat the only thing covering her skin. A cursory glance revealed that she was alone, with nothing occupying the space but a rough, wooden chair and a lamp resting on a matching table.

Hanging her head, she cursed herself for a fool. Downing had left his home alone each night, so she hadn't been on guard for another potential attacker. The man who had grabbed her had obviously been watching his friend's back, sneaking up on her before she could overtake the murdering fiend.

She needed to know who the accomplice was and where they'd taken her. The dire nature of her situation did not throw her into a panic. Instead, it only steeled her resolve. She needed to get free and end this, and she couldn't do that until one of her abductors showed his face.

Struggling to her feet, she groaned at the discomfort of the blood rushing back into her legs. Rolling her head in a circle, she tried to ease some of the stiffness in her neck. She needed to be alert and ready for when one of the men returned.

As if her thoughts had set things in motion, the door swung open to reveal two silhouettes beyond. The cloying odor of opium told her one of them must be Downing.

"You're awake," one of them said, coming toward her while his companion sank into the chair. "Good."

She squinted against the light of the lamp and made out Sir Downing's square jaw and the sweep of dark hair over his brow. She stiffened when he drew near, but held her ground, determined not to show him fear. He'd only feed off it, use it against her. The best thing she could do was keep a level head and wait for an opening.

The ropes around her wrists gave a swift jerk, and she noticed Downing controlling the tether attached to them. With a yank, he propelled her high, until only the tips of her toes touched the floor and her arms were forced to bear the pull of all her weight. She took a deep breath and kept her focus on Downing.

The man came to stand in front of her, his teeth flashing white in the darkness as he grinned, the motion hard and feral. "I knew the Menace was a woman, but I'd never have guessed it was *you*. A dowdy, freckle-faced spinster who couldn't turn a man's head without stooping to dirty tricks."

The other man gave a sarcastic snort. "Then ruins his life when he gives her the cock she was chasing all along. Venomous bitch."

Her heart plummeted into her gut as she finally recognized the voice of the other man. He had been the first victim of the Masked Menace … the first man to ever cower away from her blade as she punished him for his crimes.

The Earl of Stratford, who was responsible for the murder of Randall's wife.

The panic she'd been trying to avoid now rose up in her, making her throat constrict and her chest ache as she realized she'd been kidnapped by two cold-blooded murderers. That she still lived could only mean they would draw it out and make her suffer first.

She flinched when Downing touched her leg, but forced herself to show no other reaction, hanging limp from her ropes as he trailed his fingers up the inside of her thigh.

"It all makes sense, really," he crooned, pausing at her groin before stroking his way back down her opposite thigh. "A conniving whore who hates men … the only motive you needed to hunt us down and maim us."

Unable to keep silent any longer, she sneered down at him. "Not all men … just spineless, impotent little shits who make sport of abusing the defenseless."

With a snarl, he swung his fist, his knuckles crashing against her jaw. Her body swung from the rope, pain flaring in her entire face. Blood welled in her mouth, her lip already beginning to swell.

She raised her head to glare at him again, her teeth grinding as she imagined using her dagger to cut out his foul tongue.

"You'll mind your mouth," he snarled. "Unless you want me to shove my cock into it."

Head rearing back, she gathered every drop of blood and saliva filling her mouth and spat it into his eyes. Satisfaction flooded her when he reared away with an outraged roar, using his sleeve to wipe the mix of her blood and spittle from his face.

"If you put that foul thing anywhere near my mouth," she warned. I will bit it off, chew it to bits and swallow it."

He straightened and approached again, this time wrapping a hand around her throat. She made no attempt to move away from him, even as his fingers pressed hard enough to leave fingerprints and make it difficult to breathe. She heard the scrape of Stratford's chair, and within seconds he was beside Downing, his upper lip curled into a snarl. He brandished something that glinted in the lamplight, making her mouth go dry. It was her dagger. He must have found it in her boot after knocking her unconscious. Had he been the one to remove her clothing? Had he done so without molesting her?

She shuddered at the thought, and Stratford grinned, pressing the knife against her belly. Holding her breath, she kept still as he trailed the knife downward, holding her gaze once the tip sifted through the curls over her mons, a silent threat emanating from his dark eyes.

"You don't have any teeth here," he murmured. "There'll be no biting when I'm in your cunt."

Annoyance welled up in her, making her forget her vulnerable position and the power of two men who were stronger than her. She laughed, the sound harsh and deranged coming through her constricted throat. Her body shook, swinging from the rope as she became hysterical, eyes watering, lips stretched wide. Stratford faltered, his hand falling to his side with the knife. Downing loosened his grip on her throat.

"She's mad," Stratford muttered. "Touched in the head."

That only made her laugh all the harder, because neither of them understood. After all she'd endured, did they really think the threat of rape was the best they could do?

"You idiots," she managed between snorts and giggles. "You've got the Masked Menace in your clutches … the woman who carved the truth of your nature into your very flesh … and the best form of revenge you can think of is to *rape me*?"

She threw her head back and laughed some more, her throaty cackles filling the dark space. The two men looked at her as if both intrigued and afraid. Suddenly serious, she stared down at them with a disdainful snort.

"As if that would be enough to break me. And you men think yourself so clever."

Downing delivered another stinging blow to her face, this time with an open palm. Stratford took hold of her thigh, stopping her swinging body with a painful clench sure to leave bruises. She bit back a cry and glared at him, her eye watering from Downing's slap.

"That will be the least of your worries by the time we're done with you," Stratford rasped before pressing the dagger against the inside of her thigh.

The sharp prick of the blade preceded a searing burn as he dragged the dagger over her flesh, opening her skin and producing a font of her blood. The pain become more than she could bear and she screamed, the sound ripping from deep within her to echo off the walls of the underground room.

ROBERT NARROWED his eyes at the house in Berkeley Square from where he sat on a bench partially hidden by a massive tree. He'd kept watch from his hiding place for almost two days. He had not seen

Cassandra enter or leave the house all this time, yet knew she was inside.

It had taken him almost an hour to work his way free of his bonds, contorting his body and working at the knots with his teeth. Once free, he'd wasted no time pulling on his clothes and going after Cassandra. After wandering Grosvenor Square and the surrounding area for another hour, he'd kept an eye out for a tall, slender figure in a black cloak. He found none, his worry mounting with every second that passed without any sign of her. Returning to her hotel suite, he had waited until the sun began to rise. She'd been gone the entire night and had not returned for her things, which were still strewn about the room.

That could mean only one thing. Something terrible had happened to Cassandra at the hands of Downing. There was no time to waste. If she hadn't been killed, she would be soon. The time for waiting and worrying was over. He had to act.

Resolved, he'd left The Pulteney Hotel after sending a messenger to Felix and his driver to await further instruction.

He'd first paid a visit to Millicent, whom he hoped would have information on where Sir Downing lived. Worried for her friend and desperate to help, she'd given him the address and offered to send Peter along for help.

Robert had declined, informing her that he did not plan to confront the man yet. He needed to watch his movements and determine whether anything happened that might offer a clue to Cassandra's whereabouts.

During the night the house remained quiet, and Robert had to fight against the urge to collapse and fall asleep. At sunrise, he'd been joined by Peter, who had offered him a hunk of bread and a bit of cheese to help him keep his strength up. Together, they'd taken a turn about the park, looking for all the world like a lord and his servant out for a morning walk. They kept Downing's house within view as they walked.

"Anything?" the footman had asked.

"Nothing yet," Robert had said with a sigh.

Just then, the front door had opened and a man who was not Downing emerged. Robert had perked up, mouth falling open as the man trotted down the front steps and set off for some destination or other.

"Is that him?" Peter had asked.

"No," he'd replied. "That is the Earl of Stratford."

What had he been doing in Sir Downing's home all night? As far as Robert knew the two men weren't the best of friends, and for him to remain for an extended visit while Downing was supposed to be in mourning …

Then, he remembered Cassandra's story about how she'd become the Masked Menace. One of the men who'd raped and murdered Randall's wife had been an earl.

"I think he's Downing's accomplice."

"I'll follow him," Peter said, turning to give chase without waiting for Robert to respond.

With the footman tracking Stratford's movements, Robert remained at his post, nibbling his bread and cheese and watching the front door. No one else came or went from the house for the rest of the day. By the time Peter returned, the sun had set once more.

"Where did Stratford go?" he asked between bites of a meat pie Peter had brought.

The twisting of his stomach eased only a bit. It would never be completely calm until Cassandra was safe again. She was inside that house … he knew it.

"To his own home across the city. I went around to the servant's entrance and flirted with a scullion. He agreed to gather information for me."

Robert paused mid-bite. "He?"

Peter cocked an eyebrow and smirked. "That's right. Does that trouble you?"

Thinking of William, Robert shook his head, his cheeks flaming hot. "No, not at all. So, what did you learn?"

"Servants say the man ordered his things readied for an extended stay in Devon. He's to leave tomorrow night."

"Devon? Sir Downing has a country residence there."

Peter nodded, his expression grave. "They're leaving the city and taking her with them … where no one will ever know what's been done to her. With Downing supposedly grieving, the timing will not seem suspicious."

"We cannot allow them to take her anywhere," he declared, his appetite gone. "If they take her out of Town, she's dead."

"Well, what will we do? We could break in and attempt to rescue her tonight, but—"

"We risk walking into a trap," he finished for the footman. "Besides, Downing has loyal servants who would probably harm us to protect him. If we are injured or dead we can be of no help to her. It is too great a risk."

"Then what else can we do? Whatever you need, I'm your man. My mistress told me to see this through to the end, so I won't rest until Lady Cassadra is safe."

A plan had sprung to Robert's mind then, as if planted there by a divine source. Without question, he knew exactly what needed to be done.

"I have an idea," he said. "I'll need you to retrieve my carriage, driver, and valet from an inn and bring them here."

Peter had leaped into action without hesitation, leaving Robert to continue watching the house.

Now, as night began to fall on the second day, he became antsy to be off. Peter had returned, and now sat in his carriage across the square, waiting for him. Before Downing's townhouse, Stratford's equipage had just pulled to a stop and the man himself descended and climbed the front steps.

Robert sprang into action, moving at a sedate pace to keep from drawing too much attention to himself. There were enough people in the square to keep him from seeming out of place as he emerged from the trees.

Ducking on the front steps of a neighboring townhouse, he peered up over the stone railing and watched as servants came and went, carrying various trunks and loading them onto the back of the vehicle. Robert clenched his jaw and forced himself to remain in his place and watch. He could not act … not yet.

He needed Downing and Stratford to leave the city, giving him a better chance at subduing them. Out on the open road, there was no place they could hide.

His spine tingled as he spotted Downing, leading the way to the carriage with a hat under one arm. Robert remained as still as he could, held his breath, and waited for any sign of Cassandra. If he was going to follow them out of London, he needed to know for certain they had her in their clutches.

His stomach churned when Stratford appeared, carrying what looked like nothing more than a bundle of sheets. But Robert couldn't take his eyes off that bundle as he watched for any sign of movement, anything that would confirm his suspicions that the sheets cloaked the body of a woman held in the earl's grasp.

When the man came off the bottom step, the bundle shifted slightly, and something came falling out from its confines. A woman's arm hung limp, swinging with every one of the earl's steps. Long and slender, it seemed caked with dirt and something else. Blood?

Rage rushed through him, but determination helped him keep a cool head. He did not know what they'd done to her, but these men would atone for it. Whether the arm he'd seen was attached to a living Cassandra or her corpse, he would make sure they paid for what they'd done.

He turned and dashed across the square, spotting his carriage and making a beeline toward it.

"Follow them," he instructed his driver before joining Peter and Felix inside.

"They have her," he told them. "We'll follow them out of London and strike when the moment is right."

Peter opened the wooden chest resting on the seat beside him, giving Robert a glimpse of the twin revolvers resting on a bed of velvet.

"We are ready and will have your back until the end."

Reaching into his coat pocket, he retrieved the black mask Cassandra had left behind in the hotel room. He'd sent Felix for it, along with a few other items he would need.

"I hope you know what you are doing, sir," Felix said, seeming more on edge than Peter.

The man was accustomed to mending clothes and polishing boots, not involving himself in dangerous intrigues. Well, it would seem they must all step into roles they'd never expected to play. Robert had never thought he'd be willing to go so far for love. But then, maybe he'd never truly loved at all. Not like this … not until Cassandra.

"I do," he assured the valet. "It will work, you'll see."

CHAPTER 12

The carriage rocked and swayed as it rumbled down the road, London falling farther behind them with each passing moment. Cassandra closed her eyes and clutched the bedsheet tighter around her nude body. She ached from head to toe, and had long grown used to the steady pounding in her head. Two days spent in the clutches of Sir Downing and the Earl of Stratford, and they had yet to kill her. She wished they would get on with it. At least, if she was dead she'd be free from the pain and degradation they'd subjected her to.

She'd remained tied to the ceiling beams in that basement room, though they'd lowered her to the ground a few times a day for a few bites of stale bread and sips of stagnant water. Downing had made his intentions known, wanting her alive until he was ready to deal the final blow that would end her life.

On the first day she'd fought them, kicking and screaming, hurling every foul epithet at them that came to mind. It had earned her a beating, but not before she'd kicked Downing in the face and bloodied his nose, leaving a moth-shaped bruise spreading toward his eyes. She'd been unable to fight them both off with her hands tied, which meant while she was dealing with Downing, Stratford was able to subdue her with her own knife. Along with days' worth of dirt, grime, and sweat, her skin held several cuts—some shallow, some deep, all painful. They'd let the blood dry on her skin in crimson smears, leaving her looking like death while days without bathing had her smelling no better. She could see the mess of her hair from the corner of her eye, matted and tangled, her scalp stinging from the way Stratford had dragged her from the basement before throwing her to the ground and wrapping her in this bed sheet.

Two days of being beaten and cut, with meager food and very little water, had left her weak and unable to fight back. There had been nothing for her to do but go along with their commands, hoping it would spare her for one more minute, one more hour, one more day.

She didn't know why this instinct to survive persisted, when her fate was all but certain. It would be better to throw open the carriage and hurl herself out, hoping to be caught under the wheels. At Downing's country home in Devon, she would be subjected to even more torture. These two men represented the worst of those she had punished, the sort with no morals and a taste for debauchery. They would enjoy every moment of ripping her to pieces until there was nothing left.

She'd be dead in a matter of days, though no one would miss her … no one would care.

Except Robert.

Her stomach twisted and her chest ached at the thought of him, of all the things she'd wanted to give him. For the first time in so many years, she wished she could be someone different—the sort of woman Robert deserved. How someone as bright, sunny, and pure had come to love her, she had no idea. She only knew that with her final desperate act of vengeance she'd ruined any chance of basking in that love, of accepting it and returning it.

I'm so sorry, Robert.

She would die, and he would mourn her. In time, though, he would carry on just as he had following the loss of each of his brothers. A man who had survived so much death and pain had to be resilient. He would go on to lead a good life, free of the complication that came with loving a woman like her. His need to love and be loved would not see him living that idyllic life alone. He'd find someone else—someone as sweet and kind as him. Someone who would blush when he called her beautiful, or smile when he put flowers in her hair. Cassandra clenched her teeth at the images conjured by her thoughts. This mythical woman did not even exist, and still Cassandra wanted her dead. She wanted to throttle her, squeeze the life from her with her bare hands and claim what was hers.

He isn't yours any longer ... you've pushed him away far too many times, and now you'll die without ever telling him you love him.

Opening her eyes, she heaved a sigh. She would meet her fate, taking comfort in the knowledge that she'd had a hand in taking Bertram down before her demise. She might not have saved Lady Downing, but she hoped that her actions might have saved others. Unlike Downing and Stratford, her other targets might have learned a valuable lesson about how it felt to be a victim, to be helpless and degraded.

And Robert ... well, at least he was safe. By tying him to that bed and leaving him behind, she had kept him from being caught up in this storm of her own making. Her actions and mistakes had led to this, and now she would suffer the consequences.

She darted a glance at the man sitting beside her. Downing had fallen asleep, his head resting against the seat, mouth hanging open as his soft snores filled the carriage. Her fingers tightened around the sheet, making the gash on the inside of her forearm throb.

Could she overtake them somehow? Looking across the vehicle, she found Stratford watching, her dagger held in one hand. He pressed the tip lightly against his palm and spun the hilt, making the steel gleam in the meager moonlight streaming through the carriage windows.

"Don't even think about it," he warned, turning the knife so that the blade faced her. "I'll slice you to ribbons before you even lay a hand on him."

Cassandra narrowed her eyes and calculated the risks. Downing was fast asleep, and if she lunged at Stratford it might be a moment before he regained all his faculties. By the time he'd come to, she could overpower Stratford and take the knife before jamming it into his chest. But, she'd be too slow and weak, and if she failed ...

Cursing her weak, battered body, she sank deeper into the confines of the bed sheet. She should conserve her strength on the chance that a true window of opportunity arose for her to escape. For the moment, it seemed the only way out of this was death.

"Help me understand something," Stratford said, taking on a conversational tone. "Was publicly testifying against Fairchild not enough for you? The man you claim raped you—"

"He did rape me," she snapped. "Just like you raped Randall's wife."

Her jaw tightened until her teeth ached as she remembered the night she'd first attacked Stratford. While at the edge of her dagger he'd been hardpressed to even remember the woman he and his friend had murdered. When she'd reminded him of his sins, he'd been flippant and dismissive—which had only enraged her more.

Just now, she wondered why he and Downing were waiting to deliver on their threat to use her body as they saw fit. Thus far there had been nothing more than beatings and threats but then that should hardly surprise her. Their depraved natures would hold them back so they could toy with her, keep her on edge and strike when she least expected it.

Stratford rolled his eyes. "Hardly got the chance before the little bitch started fighting me. Killing her was an accident, but ... well it was her fault for mauling me."

Bile rose in the back of her throat as she thought of her own ordeal at Bertram's hands, the paralysis caused by fear that had kept her from fighting him. Would she have suffered the same fate as Randall's wife had she fought him?

"No, it wasn't enough," she spat, her hands shaking with the force of her anger. "It will never be enough as long as there are men like you in the world."

Stratford snorted. "I hate to sully your grand illusion, but men like me are all there are in the world."

"No," she murmured, lowering her gaze to her filthy hands. "You're wrong."

Months ago she might have agreed with him. For five long years, she'd been unable to look at any man without seeing her assailant. But then, there had been Robert. He'd proven himself to be the opposite of Bertram in every way.

"There are men who know how to get what they want without hurting others," she continued, lifting her eyes to meet Stratford's gaze once more. "They have the decency to care for people weaker than them, not abuse them. That's what a real man is. But, you wouldn't know anything about that."

Satisfaction flared within her at the way his face contorted, lips pinching, nostrils flaring as he wrestled with his anger. Leaning forward a bit, she smiled, despite the way it made her swollen face ache and her split lip sting.

"Go ahead," she taunted. "Hit me. Cut me. Prove me right about the sort of spineless coward you are. You could never take me in a fight without Downing … I proved that the night I ran your carriage down on this very road."

Instead of retaliating, Stratford slouched in his seat and gave her a chilling grin. He went back to playing with the dagger, touching its point to each of his fingers.

"I am going to enjoy breaking you," he murmured, his voice silky smooth yet as sharp as the blade in his hand. "Just wait until we arrive in Devon. You will not have so much to say between screams."

Before she could open her mouth to deliver a scathing retort, a cry arose from outside the carriage, followed by a lone gunshot.

Cassandra started, turning to glance at the carriage window. With the curtain drawn, she could see nothing, but she heard the shouts of Stratford's driver as well as the startled screams of the horses.

"What the devil?" Stratford mumbled, pulling the curtain aside just as the carriage jolted to a sudden stop. "Downing! Wake up, you fool! I think we've been overtaken by a highwayman."

Sir Downing came to with a snort, blinking his bleary eyes as he glanced about the carriage with confusion etching his face.

"What's that? Highwayman, you say? Nonsense, we've the Masked Menace right here."

"Well, apparently, there's another one."

Cassandra's heart began to race as she listened to the driver shouting at whoever approached, warning them that this vehicle belonged to the Earl of Stratford, and there would be hell to pay. He cried out before a thud rendered him silent, followed by the thump of his body hitting the ground.

Now wide awake, Downing leaped into action, dropping to his knees on the carriage floor and reaching into the compartment under the seat. Her eyes went wide as she recalled the night she had accosted him, and the shot of the blunderbuss that might have killed her had she not expected it.

She did not know who had overtaken them, but she would rather take her chances with another highwayman than these two brutes.

"Gun!" she called out just before the carriage door swung open.

The blast of Downing's blunderbuss cracked through the night, but as the smoke cleared, Cassandra could see that his shot had hit nothing but thin air.

"You stupid bitch!" Stratford bellowed, lunging across the carriage toward her.

With freedom looming within her reach now, Cassandra willed herself to gather the strength to fight. As Downing was dragged from the carriage by their assailant, she met Stratford head on, lunging across the space between them. Her bed sheet forgotten, she ducked to avoid the swing of the dagger in his hand, then slammed a fist into his midsection. Pain radiated up her arm, but she ignored it, retrieving Downing's blunderbuss and bringing it down on Stratford's head. The earl fell back against his seat with a curse, blood trickling from his temple.

"Stand and deliver," ground out a familiar voice.

She glanced up to find a man in the opening, the moonlight framing him from the top of his golden head to the drape of a black domino about this shoulders. Even from behind a black mask she knew that face, had memorized its angles and planes and the pout of that plush mouth. Tears of relief stung her eyes as he revealed the pistol he held in one hand, leveling it at Stratford.

He pulled back the hammer, the ominous sound filling the carriage.

Stratford's mouth gaped open, one hand pressed to his bleeding temple as his gaze darted from her to Robert, and back again.

"I-I don't understand … you're not the Masked Menace, she is!"

Robert's mouth curved into a mocking smirk. "Are you certain? She isn't the one standing here in a mask, pointing a gun at you."

Stratford shook his head, hands shaking as he jerked his cravat away and pulled at the collar of his shirt. Buttons went flying when he tore the garment open to reveal his disfigured chest. Cassandra's work had scarred over, leaving behind the dark slashes from her blade spelling out two words.

RAPIST. MURDERER.

Robert inclined his head, showing no response to the sight of the earl's mutilated chest. "Step out of the carriage. Now."

Stratford shook his head, jaw clenched tight. "I know she is the true Menace, and I am owed retribution for what she did to me."

"Get out of the goddamn carriage!" Robert bellowed, thrusting the gun in Stratford's face until the muzzle came up against the earl's forehead.

With the dagger back in Cassandra's hand and Robert's pistol pointed at him, Stratford had no choice but to obey. He stepped out of the carriage and disappeared, his muffled grunts and groans mingling with the thuds of fists flying. Apparently, Robert hadn't come alone.

His expression softened behind the mask when he ducked back

into the vehicle and approached her. She could hardly see his face with the moon at his back, but felt the warmth in his voice, heavy with worry and love.

"Cass, are you all right, love?"

She cried out when he took hold of her, his thumb pressing over one of the deep cuts on her arm. She'd torn it open in her last effort against Stratford and it had begun to bleed.

"You're hurt," he exclaimed, cupping her face and tilting it to get a better look at her. "They hurt you!"

"I'm all right," she said, putting her hands over his where they rested against her face. "They did hurt me, but I'll survive, and … and you came for me."

His forehead rested against hers and he exhaled, a long slow breath carrying every ounce of his relief and pain. She'd insisted she wasn't a damsel in need of rescuing. But the truth couldn't be denied. She had needed saving, and not just from Stratford and Downing. Here she had pushed Robert away, spurned his love, and still he had come for her.

"Nothing could have stopped me," he declared. "Not even you. Can you stand?"

She nodded, taking his hand as she edged toward the carriage door. Robert backed out, keeping a tight grip on her hand. Outside, things had grown silent and still, so she allowed herself to settle into relief as he led her out of the vehicle. Whatever happened next, she had Robert, here at her side.

The warm evening breeze tickled her face, and the feel of the hard-packed earth under her bare feet came as a relief after so many hours hanging from the ceiling.

The driver had been knocked unconscious, his body propped against the side of the vehicle, hands bound before him.

She found Stratford on his knees with a gag splitting his lips, Downing still on his feet but kept subdued by the large man who held his hands clenched behind his back.

"Peter?" she blurted, recognizing Millicent's lover even in the dark.

He flashed a smile at her while using very little effort to keep Downing restrained. "Hello, Cass. Millie sends her regards. You didn't think we'd stand back and allow you to be abducted, did you?"

"No," she said, looking to Robert. "I suppose I shouldn't have."

She ought to have known he would go to Millicent for help. Her friend was the only person other than Robert who understood the depth of her need for vengeance. Even without knowing exactly what she'd been up to, the two knew her better than anyone—enough to figure out her location and come up with a plan to extract her.

Another man she recognized as Robert's valet stood nearby with a pistol in hand, silently watching their captives for any sign of trouble

"Now," Robert said, reaching up to remove his mask and hand it off to his valet. "I am not one for violence, but the two of you sealed your own fates when you made off with Cassandra. After what you've done, I cannot allow you to live."

He used one hand to untie his domino and drape it over the valet's arm while keeping hold of his pistol. Downing struggled in Peter's hold, while Stratford seemed to try to speak around his gag.

"We are the real victims here!" Downing insisted, leveling a glare at Cassandra. "She accosted us, beat us, mutilated us! It is she you ought to punish, not us."

Robert raised an eyebrow at Downing. "She showed you more mercy than I would have. You should have been grateful she left you alive. Now, you've compounded your deeds by abducting her."

Downing's desperate gaze landed on Stratford, who seemed to try pleading with Robert through the material muffling his words.

"It was all his idea!" Downing declared, angling his head toward the earl. "We happened to begin talking about the Masked Menace over drinks and discovered we had both suffered the same fate. It was he who suggested we find a way to get our revenge."

"And which of you decided pushing your wife down the stairs and further injuring her would prove enough to draw me out?" Cassandra accused, stepping closer to Downing.

Irritation flared in his gaze as he stared back at her, a vein in his temple beginning to throb. "She wasn't supposed to die."

"If you are as innocent in all this as you claim, you will prove it," Robert said, before giving his valet a nod.

The man tucked his pistol into the waistband of his breeches, then proceeded to tie her mask around Downing's face, before draping him in the domino.

"What the devil are you about?" Downing demanded, struggling to get free but finding his strength was no match for Peter's.

"This man coerced you into this plan," Robert said with a bored shrug. "His idea led you to kill your own wife by accident, and now you've been caught. It is all his fault, isn't it?"

Downing gaped as Peter released him, before the valet offered the gun. The man seemed uncertain how to proceed, leery of the pistol being presented to him so freely.

"The Menace came upon Stratford on the road and killed him," Robert declared watching Downing's face closely, hand clenched around his own pistol. "That is what we, your witnesses will say if anyone asks us what happened this night. No one ever need know it was you. And if you kill the man responsible for kidnapping and hurting the woman I love … I will spare your life."

Cassandra tightened her hand around the dagger and lumbered forward. "Like hell you will."

Robert blocked her progress with an outstretched arm, but kept his gaze fixed on Downing. On the ground, Stratford began to struggle, falling onto his side, unable to right himself with his hands tied behind his back. He inched along the road like a worm, weeping and mumbling behind his gag, pleading for his life.

"Trust me, Cass," he whispered so only she could hear. "You will have your moment, and you will know when it is right."

Still glaring at Downing, she lowered her hand and the dagger with it. He was right. She'd done things her way and gotten herself into this mess. It was obvious he'd given this all a great deal of thought, and thus far his plan was working.

"How do you know I won't simply use this pistol to kill you all?" Downing asked, still reluctant to accept the gun.

He kept staring at Stratford, who continued trying to work his way across the ground away from them. He hadn't gotten far.

"There is only one bullet in it," Robert told him, before raising his own gun. "Mine has six. If you point that thing at anyone other than Stratford, I'll fill you with holes before you can squeeze off your one shot."

Downing's gaze flitted back to Robert, then Stratford, then the gun. The earl wept without shame now, his muffled pleas going ignored by everyone present. Cassandra held her breath and waited for someone to make the first move, and either throw the entire thing into chaos or put it all to an end.

"You have ten seconds to decide before I shoot you both," Robert snapped, his words edged with impatience. "Ten … nine … eight … seven …"

"Sorry, old chap," Downing muttered before snatching the gun from the valet's hand.

He raised it and fired in a matter of seconds, the bullet striking true and landing between Stratford's eyes. The earl went still and silent, his last breath coming out on a panicked wail.

Downing dropped the gun and grinned, seeming pleased with himself for working his way out of his little conundrum. But, he did not notice Robert turning to look at her, the grim expression on his face as he whispered the only thing Cass needed to hear.

"Now, Cass."

Barreling from behind him with her dagger raised, she lunged at Downing with a sharp cry. Her blade plunged into his belly, sinking deep as his blood spilled forth to drench her hand. His knees buckled as she drew it free and stabbed him again, this time in the heart. He brought both hands up over hers, eyes wide with shock and betrayal as he stared beyond her at Robert.

Coming to stand at her side, Robert gave him a sardonic smile. "I said that *I* would spare your life. I never said anything about her."

"For Lady Downing," she hissed, giving the knife a twist, then letting it go.

Downing fell back onto the ground, gasping and gurgling as his own blood welled up in his mouth. It dripped down his chin as he convulsed, his hands falling away from the knife as he struggled to draw his last breaths.

Taking hold of her sheet again, she pulled it around her body and turned away from Downing's corpse. The man had paid for what he'd done to his wife, and Stratford could never harm anyone else ever again. The two men who knew the identity of the Masked Menace were no more.

"What will we do with the bodies?" Peter asked from behind her.

"Leave them," Robert replied. "We take the driver and pay him for his silence once he awakens. He helped them make off with an abducted woman ... the threat of being exposed ought to be enough to keep him quiet."

When she turned to give him a puzzled frown, he returned her gaze with a determined expression.

"It is over, Cass," he said, extending one hand to her. "The Menace dies right here, tonight. He attacked Stratford, who fought back and stabbed him. Before he died, he managed to fire off a shot, killing Stratford. That is how the world will remember it … it is what everyone will believe. Now, you will leave here with me and never look back. The Menace is no more, and you are free to begin anew."

Cassandra gazed down at his hand, strong and clean, and offered without hesitation. Her own hand was drenched in not only her own blood, but Downing's as well.

How could he have done this for her when they both knew she deserved none of it?

But, as Robert held her gaze, she recognized the surety in the depths. He did not waver, he did not cringe away, or look at her as if she were somehow beneath him for the things she'd done. There was only love, and the acceptance he'd always shown her without wavering.

"I just killed a man."

He nodded, but seemed unaffected by her declaration. "He would have killed you first, so it stands to reason he deserved it."

How could he be so unruffled by it all? How could he not look upon her and see a woman who had put him in danger and did not think twice about murdering someone in cold blood?

"I love you," he said, as if in answer to the questions she hadn't asked aloud. "And that will never change. Now, come."

Hesitating only a moment, she reached out to take his hand. Instead of pulling away from his gentle tug, she surrendered and let him bring her against his body and wrap her in his arms.

There was nothing left to fight for or against. She could insist she didn't need saving, or she could admit that her pain and vulnerability required his affection. Her beautiful lover. Her saving grace.

Closing her eyes and burying her face in his shirtfront, she inhaled the fading remnants of Spanish Leather and sweat. She knew she must reek to the high heavens, but he buried his face in her hair and held on tight as if she'd been bathed in rosewater and drenched in lavender oil.

The relief of being safe again washed over her, and she sagged in his arms, giving herself up to oblivion as the world around her began to fade.

2 DAYS LATER . . .

Robert sat at Cassandra's bedside, elbows braced on his knees as he watched her sleep. Upon leaving Downing and Stratford's dead bodies on the side of the road, he'd taken her unconscious form into his arms and carried her back to his carriage. After the hell he was certain she'd endured, exhaustion had taken its toll. He'd held her in his lap as they rode back to Town, Peter seated across from him and Felix sharing the perch with the driver.

Relief had stolen the last of the tension from his limbs, making it difficult to stay awake. All his worrying and planning had ended, and now he was only glad it was over, to have her back with him where she belonged. They'd slept all the way back to the hotel, where Peter had left them to go in search of a doctor. The sun had not yet risen, and only a small amount of staff were on duty so late, so Robert hadn't had any trouble whisking her up to her suite undetected.

Once there, he'd unwrapped her from the dirty, bloodied bed sheet, enraged by what he found. Aside from her battered face, there were bruises along her ribs and thighs, and one of them had used the dagger on her as well. Most of the cuts were shallow, but one along her forearm and another on the inside of her thigh concerned him. They would need cleaning and stitches. He'd run for one of the night footmen and requested a hot bath for her in the neighboring sitting room.

He'd bathed her while she slept on, her head rested against the lip of the tub as he gently scrubbed her clean of her ordeal. At least, as much of it as he could touch. Without knowing the extent of what they'd done to her, he knew there could be scars embedded so deep he might never reach them.

Peter had returned with the physician not long after her bath, who had banished him and Robert back into the drawing room while he examined her. The deepest of her cuts had required stitching, though her exhaustion had allowed her to remain unconscious while the man worked. They'd been assured she would recover as long as they kept watch for signs of infection. With nothing left to do, the surgeon departed, leaving them to tend to her. By then, dawn had come, and Robert began to have a difficult time remaining on his feet. His days spent watching and waiting outside Downing's residence had begun to take their toll.

"I will return tomorrow for a report," Peter had said. "Millie will want to know how she is faring."

"Thank you for all you did to help me. Be sure to convey my gratitude to Millicent as well."

"I love my lady, and my lady loves her friend," Peter had replied, as if that were explanation enough. "She would have been devastated had anything happened to Cassandra."

Once the man departed, Robert had sent for fresh water for himself. Bathing away the past few days, he then climbed into bed beside Cassandra and pulled her nude body into his arms, careful not to agitate her wounds.

They'd slept the day away, awakening when the sun had begun to set. He'd sent for a meal, and ensured Cassandra ate her fill. She confided that her captors had only allowed her bread and water, all but starving her for two days.

He hadn't wanted to ask for more details, even as the wondering and guessing drove him mad. But, once he'd put the remnants of their meal aside and returned to the bed with her, she'd told him everything. He'd been relieved to know they hadn't molested her, seeming to want to save defilement for when they had her locked away in Devon.

As he lay there listening to her account of what had happened, he was more grateful than ever that he'd followed through with his search for her. Had he allowed himself to grow angry and spiteful over her tying him up and leaving him here, she might have suffered a fate worse than death.

She'd spent another day sleeping, waking sporadically to eat and drink before falling back into a deep sleep. Robert had hardly left her side, wanting to be near when she awakened again. He wanted her strong enough to return home, where they could leave this all behind them. Already, word must be spreading that the Masked Menace had been Sir Downing all along, as well as the Earl of Stratford's tragic death. Only those who had been present that night knew the truth, ensuring it never came to light.

He did not care what Cassandra had done ... he only wanted it to be over. If she could let go of her vengeful vendetta, then perhaps they stood a chance.

He sat up straight when she stirred with a groan, then opened her eyes. She turned to find him sitting there, pain etching her features.

Her lip had begun to heal, and the swelling in her jaw had gone down, but the bruising would need more time.

"Good morning," he murmured, offering her a smile.

She tried to smile back, but the effort seemed to hurt. "Good morning. I must look a fright."

Reaching out to gently run a thumb over her discolored jaw, he shook his head. "No. You're still my beautiful Cass."

She closed her eyes and leaned into his touch with a sigh. "There is nothing beautiful about me. I am angry and mean and spiteful. I almost destroyed your life, and I did not deserve for you to rescue me. I do not deserve for you to love me."

He frowned, pulling his chair closer to the bed. Stroking her hair, he planted a kiss upon her brow.

"None of that is true. You can be mean and spiteful, but so can most people. You most certainly have not destroyed my life. In fact, you have enriched it beyond measure. I've felt more alive, more myself, since that night at The White Cock. I was in pain, and you turned that pain into something else … something wonderful and all-consuming."

A tear leaked from the corner of one eye. "I've held you at arm's length when all you ever wanted was to love me."

He chuckled, swiping the tear away. "As you can see, it didn't work. It only made me love you all the more."

Shaking her head as if she didn't understand, she gave him a puzzled look. He moved from the chair to sit beside her on the bed, taking one of her hands in his.

"You see, you were right about me and Daphne," he continued. "I thought I loved her, and in a way I believe I did. But it wasn't this sort of love. It was … the idea of her, this woman I saw as perfect, unattainable. She was always running headlong into danger and I needed to be the one to save her, prove my love and win her heart. In the end, it was far too easy for me to let her go. Yes, it hurt. But you … when I thought of losing you I realized I would die. I would cease to exist because there is no me without you. That is real, lasting love, and it is worth fighting for."

Another tear fell, then another, then she was sitting up and reaching for him, pulling him into her arms. He felt as if his heart would burst from the joy it gave him to be accepted without reservation, to be pulled toward her instead of pushed away.

"I love you," she whispered into his hair. "I didn't want to ... I tried to fight it ... but damn you, Robert Stanley, you broke me. You tore me open and put me back together, and now there is no *me* without *you*."

He clung to her, reeling from the impact of her words. Never would he have thought to hear them from her. He had been content for her to know how he felt as he endeavored to earn her affection piece by piece, the same way he'd earned her trust. Now, he became overwhelmed by so many emotions at once, he didn't know how his body would contain it all.

Tilting her head, she offered her lips. He brushed his mouth against hers, careful not to disturb the healing wound. But, she threaded her fingers through his hair and urged him closer, engaging him in a deep, soul stirring kiss. She leaned back against her pillows, urging him to follow, her tongue sweeping against his lower lip.

His body roared to life as it always did when she touched him, but he held back with a shake of his head.

"You are still healing. I don't want to hurt you."

"I do not care," she whispered, already loosening the buttons of his shirt. "I need you, Robert. You are the thing which eases my fears and my pain ... you have been since that night at the public house. I need you to do that for me again now. Please."

Her words broke him, and he couldn't stop himself from coming down on top of her, allowing her to go on undressing him. He would never stop wanting to please her, giving her the things she couldn't find with anyone else.

She pulled his shirt off over his head, then went to work on his breeches while he crouched between her parted thighs, kissing her cheek, her bruised jaw, her neck. He was already hard for her, groaning as she took him in hand and stroked him. Even battered and bruised she was his goddess, his fierce and strong lady who could command him with nothing more than the touch of her hand.

She paused, her hand still wrapped tight around him, her other hand resting on the back of his neck. "This need I have to dominate and control ... it may never go away. I've come to realize it is part of my nature."

The words came out as if she were apologizing for her eccentricity, which only made him smile. Didn't she understand that he was her counterpoint in every way—that he would never want to stop submitting to her every demand?

"Well, that is a relief," he teased, nuzzling her nose with his. "Because that is exactly what I want from you ... now and always. I am yours, Cass ... I told you that before, and I meant it."

She smiled back at him, raising her hips and urging him closer. "Then we are well matched. But right now I need you to be in control. Love me, Robert ... take me. I am yours."

He slid into her with one smooth stroke, finding her already wet for him. The clench of her around his cock and her spoken surrender freed him. He wrapped his arms around her and took her with slow, gentle strokes, taking care to avoid creating too much friction against her injured thigh.

She closed her eyes and gave herself over to him completely for the first time, wrapping her arms around him. The pleasure of the moment surrounded them both, and before long he was panting and moaning against her neck, pressing soft kisses against her skin, plunging as deep into her as humanly possible. And still, it did not feel like enough. He would never stop trying to go deeper and deeper, until they ceased being two people and became one. He took her hands and fit his fingers between hers, capturing her mouth as climax loomed near.

She broke first, crying out and shuddering beneath him, her fingers clenching tighter until his knuckles ached. The little jolt of pain threw him closer to his end, tremors wracking him as he fought for more time.

But then, because the need to give him the exquisite pleasure-pain he craved would never be far from her, she turned her head and latched onto his neck with lips and teeth. With a roar and one final thrust of his hips, he released inside of her, shaking and fighting for breath as it spiraled through him with overwhelming force. He seemed to fly free of his body for a moment, a heady dizziness sweeping over him as his vision went hazy. Then, he collapsed on top of her with a heavy sigh, the brand of her bite mark warm and perfect against the side of his neck.

TWO WEEKS LATER ...

Robert made his way through the trees, inhaling the pure, clean scent of the outdoors. Night had fallen hours ago, and he was anxious to see Cassandra. Only one day had passed since the last time they were together, but he felt as if it had been an eternity.

They'd returned from London a few days after Cassandra's harrowing incident. As he'd suspected, the deaths of Stratford and Downing had set London ablaze, the papers filled with varying accounts and exaggerations. The case of the Masked Menace continued to baffle them all, but as Robert and Cassandra had agreed, the mysterious highwayman died that day and would never reemerge.

She had confessed to feeling a certain peace about it.

"By taking justice into my own hands, I only made matters worse," she'd said to him during their carriage ride home. "There are simply too many ways I could cause more harm to the people I want to protect. I ... I think what's more important is that women like Lady Downing and the others come to see that they must fight for themselves. It was not easy when I did it, and the consequences may follow me for the rest of my life, but I will never regret it. Maybe what we did can prove to others that they have the power to do the same."

He'd been relieved to hear that, considering their newfound happiness. He didn't want anything to destroy that. To lose her would crush him, and he only wanted the future to hold hope and life, not despair and death.

Leaving her at Easton Park and returning home had been difficult, when all he wanted was to spend every spare moment he had with her. But, he'd needed to look in on his father and reassure his mother. He had assumed she'd be worried sick over him leaving for London so abruptly, and he'd been right. She had fussed and fretted over him, demanding to know where he had been.

After the hellish time he'd had, the last of his patience with her had dissipated. After having yet another cup of tea thrust into his hands, he'd snapped.

"For the love of God! How many times do I have to tell you I don't like tea?"

She'd jumped with shock when he stood and slammed the cup back onto the tray she'd brought to him. One hand over her bosom, she'd stared at him as if he'd gone mad.

"Robert, what on Earth has gotten into you? Are you ill?"

He'd ducked his head before she could check his brow for fever, heaving a frustrated grunt. "I'm fine. In fact, I'm better than I have been in some time. I'm in love with Lady Cassandra Lane and I intend to make her my wife. That is what I was doing in London, Mother. She left, and I went after her and refused to return without her."

She blinked several times, her mouth gaping and shutting several times as if she searched for words. "You must be ill, delirious with fever. You are spouting nonsense!"

"No, the way we live is nonsense," he countered, reaching out to take hold of her shoulders. "Mother, I love you … but, your constant worrying and coddling must cease. I'm not a boy anymore. William, Jonas, and Andrew were young and we lost them. It hurt … it hurts every day. But we cannot let it make us afraid."

Tears filled her eyes as she stared up at him, trembling in his hold. "I am afraid every day … all the time. Every morning when I wake, I fear I will enter your father's chamber to find he has stopped breathing. When you are not here, I dream about you dying in horrible ways, each time different than the last. Since you were a boy you've died a thousand deaths in my dreams. Do not tell me not to be afraid! When your father is gone, you will be all I have left."

Pity overwhelmed him; his mother meant well despite being overbearing. He understood her dread all-too well. It had held him back from so many things in life.

"I don't have to be all you have left," he said, gentling his voice. "There could be Cassandra, too. There could be children. Don't you want to be a grandmama?"

She gave a wobbly smile at that. "Of course I do, but—"

"No," he interjected. "No buts, no maybes, no speculation over death or loss or the future. William didn't know he was going to die … but before he did, he enjoyed his life. He reveled in London and went to university and rushed headlong into saving a woman's life because it was the right thing to do. Jonas didn't know he was going to die, but he lived every day like it was his last. He craved adventure and chased it wherever it would take him. And Andrew … he was just a boy, but there seemed to be the soul of an older man inside him."

The baroness laughed at that, her smile widening through her tears. "He never wanted to stop learning new things."

"Exactly," he'd replied. "I don't know when I'm going to die, or when you or Father will die. I don't want to know, and I refuse to spend every day worrying about it. I may never understand why we survived and they didn't, but while we are still in this world we have a chance to live life the way they did. To learn new things, and chase adventures, and revel in the exciting. That's what I want … and I want it with Cassandra, and you, and Father for however much time there is left."

She'd collapsed into his arms and wept, clinging to him as she always did. But this had felt different. Instead of feeling as if she were holding him back, Robert felt in the depths of his soul that she was finally setting him free.

"I love you, my dear, sweet boy," she had said, patting his cheek. "You have always been the light of my life, my pride and joy. I never thought any woman could be good enough for you. I still believe that."

He'd laughed, reaching into his coat to offer her a handkerchief. "You haven't come to know Cassandra yet. When you do, you'll see she's perfect for me. You were right about Daphne. At least, about her not being the woman for me. But Cass … she's the one, I can feel it. I love her, and so will you."

The baroness had given him a skeptical look, but said no more. The rest of the day had passed with an excruciating slowness, but he'd been forced to wait. Cassandra wouldn't be expecting him until evening, and he'd needed the time to think over what he would say. She had confessed her love for him … but would she marry him? After all that had happened, she might still need time to grow accustomed to this new life—a life in which she was not the Masked Menace, where Bertram no longer haunted her, and where she was free to be and do whatever she wished.

But, he couldn't wait any longer. He felt as if he'd been waiting his entire life for her. Whether she agreed to marry him or not, she would never be rid of him. He'd beg her every day if he had to.

He knew how she loved it when he begged.

Before stepping into the clearing where the swimming hole lay, he crouched to pluck a perfect primrose from the ground. It's yellow petals spread to the moon, vibrant and beautiful. With a smile, he proceeded along his path.

He hadn't expected her to meet him here, but there she stood on the water's edge. She wore a forest green gown that flowed about her legs in a gossamer curtain. Her hair had been taken down, hanging in amber ringlets down her back. The impact of her eyes as he neared took his breath away. Her bruised face had begun to heal, the swelling gone and the purplish tinge giving way to greenish yellow. But through all that, he saw her.

He'd never be able to look at her again without thinking her the most beautiful creature in the world.

"I've been waiting for you," she said, coming forward to meet him. "There is something I want to tell you, and I thought it appropriate to do so right here, where you saved me."

Gazing out over the water, he recalled watching her go under and the fear that had clenched his throat when she didn't resurface. "But, you weren't drowning. You didn't need me to come in after you."

"Yes, I did," she whispered, gazing at the pond. "You see ... when I would come out here to jump into the water, it was to contemplate death."

He tensed, his pulse accelerating as he remembered his suspicions from that night.

"I used to sink as far as I could and think about giving myself over to the water," she continued. "I wondered if the silence and the stillness in the depths was what life after death might be like. I wanted an end to the fear, the pain, the rage. But then ... you came in after me and pulled me out. You challenged me and made me question if it might have all been worth it."

Cupping her face with his free hand, he inched closer until he registered the scent of oranges and clove, until the heat radiating off her body seeped into his skin.

"And was it worth it?"

She nodded, then turned her head to kiss his palm. "It was ... it is. I want to live, Robert. I want the fear and the pain, but I want the joy too. I want the happiness. And I want it all with you. That night of your father's birthday ... Do you want to know what he said to me?"

"Very much."

She smiled at him, plucking his hand from her face and clutching it in both of hers. "He told me he knew he wasn't long for this world. He said that when he was gone, he wanted to know that you would be taken care of ... that you would have something to live for. He told me that he had a feeling I was it. At the time I found the idea preposterous. I was still fighting you ... fighting us. But, now I know he was right, because I want to be the thing you live for, the reason you smile

... and I need you to be all those things for me. I want to be with you for all my days."

His mouth fell open as he found himself momentarily stunned. "Are … are you …"

"Asking you to marry me?" she replied with a little laugh. "It's a bit unorthodox, I'll admit—"

"It's perfect, because I came here tonight to ask you the same thing."

It was her turn to look stunned, her gaze falling to the primrose in his hand. He raised it between them, twirling the stem and watching the way the moonlight illuminated the petals.

"Last year, I went to London with a ring, thinking I would come back with the love of my life," he said, turning his gaze to her. "I didn't return with what I wanted, but along the way I found what I *needed*. You. Every part of you, even the parts you don't like. I love them all, because they all make up the different facets of the person I adore. I don't have a ring tonight, but ..."

He took hold of her left hand, looping the stalk of the primrose around her third finger. She grinned as he tied the stem into a knot so that the blossom lay like a jewel would.

"What I do have is a true and lasting love for you," he said, taking her hand and placing it over his heart. "I have myself to give to you for the rest of my life … and I have a surety that our life together, no matter how difficult it may be at times, will be one worth living. Marry me, Cass."

Her smile faded as she stared into his eyes, her hand still pressed against his pounding heart. In her gaze, he saw all the emotion she'd previously shuttered away from him. He saw every painful moment of what was behind her, but also the glimmer of hope for what lay ahead.

"Yes," she murmured, wrapping her arms around his neck. "I'll marry you."

He took her into his arms, one hand cupping the back of her head.

Fingers tangled in her hair, he angled her head for a kiss. Her mouth moving against his with an urgency that gave fuel to his own insatiable desire. He didn't think there could ever be a day she stopped affecting him this way.

Breaking the kiss, he rested his forehead against hers and met her gaze. For the first time in his life, uncertainty about the future did not seem so daunting. He held forever in his arms, and come what may, he knew that was one thing that would never change. It was the one thing that could never die.

EPILOGUE

THREE MONTHS LATER ...

Robert paused in the doorway to his mother's favorite drawing room and peered inside, a soft smile curving his lips at what he discovered. The baroness sat on a loveseat with an embroidery hoop in her hands. Beside her, he found Cassandra holding a similar hoop. Her graceful, dexterous fingers worked a needle through the fabric with an ease born of practice.

The two had become fast friends, and as he'd predicted, his mother had come to like Cassandra.

On the day he'd brought his betrothed to Briarwell to announce their engagement to his parents, he had settled her in this very room to go fetch them. His mother had been apprehensive, still worried over what their impending marriage could mean for the reputation of their family. Robert had done his best to assure her that everything would be all right. Marriage would erase the stain of her ruination, and their shocking match would replace past gossip about her. No one would have predicted such a union, and he supposed they would be the topic of drawing room talk for at least another year.

He'd led the baroness to this room and paused on the threshold. "Mother, this marriage is happening. You must accept it."

She had frowned, but nodded. "You are not like yourself Robert ... you are different now. I suppose I would have her to blame."

"I'm more myself than ever, so you would have her to *thank*," he'd corrected. "Now, go in there and get to know your new daughter-in-law. She will be part of our family now and I want the two of you get along."

She'd issued an impatient huff. "And if we do not?"

He'd given her a teasing grin. "There's always the Outer Hebrides for you."

"That isn't funny," she'd grumbled.

But, she had taken herself into the drawing room and pasted a smile on her face for his benefit. As he'd stood outside the room, he had watched her discover that Cassandra had been studying the embroidery work she'd left lying on the couch.

Cassandra's voice had flitted out to him, soft and tentative. "This is lovely. I wish I knew how to do such fine work."

His mother had been shocked to learn his future wife did not possess a skill for embroidery. "Goodness, child! Did your mother not instruct you?"

Cassandra's face had fallen at that, the pain of the dowager's rejection still as acute as ever. The baroness seemed to register it, and from that moment on she found herself a new person to coddle. Now, when Cassandra visited, his mother was ready with tea and biscuits, and embroidery hoops for practice. The two talked and laughed together, and his mother fell seamlessly into the role of mother to a woman who had been lacking one all her life.

As he watched them now, with his wedding day looming ahead in a few, short weeks, he felt a contentment he'd never known. His father's health hadn't improved, but the man spent as much time with them as he could, reveling in seeing his son happy at last.

Turning away from the drawing room, he decided to let them have their time together. He'd have Cassandra all to himself tonight, when he stole away to visit her at Easton Park. He could hardly wait until they were wed and she came to live at Briarwell. That way, he would not have to sneak around to be with her. After being whipped with her crop and fucked within an inch of his life, he would prefer to curl up in his own bed with her and sleep, not traipse about the woods with a sore arse.

He entered his study. On the desk lay a letter from Daphne, sent from her new home in Scotland. He and Cassandra had agreed to invite her and Hartmoor to the wedding. He'd enclosed a personal letter along with the invitation, asking after her welfare and wishing her well. She had written back, thanking him for helping her reunite with Hartmoor. She'd also reported the impending birth of their first child, news that might have hurt him months ago but now only made him happy.

She might have broken his heart, but she was one of his dearest friends in the world. In the end, he was grateful for her, because she was the reason he now knew what true love was.

Sinking into his chair, he winced and shifted, taking pressure off a particularly tender spot. Cassandra had left a welt with her crop, and the flashes of pain when he sat only brought back memories that made his cock harden to unbearable limits. If he wasn't careful, he'd have to go rushing into that drawing room, drag her to his bedchamber, and seek relief between her thighs.

Instead, he focused upon penning his letter.

Dearest Daphne,

Cassandra and I are elated to hear that you and Hartmoor will be in attendance at our wedding. We often speak of how, in a way, you and the earl are responsible for us finding one another and falling in love. I could not be more grateful for that, or to have you as my friend.

Congratulations on the coming birth of your child. That is wonderful news! I could not be happier for you, and I mean that with all of my heart. When we were children, we often spoke of what we thought would be the perfect life. Do you remember that? We spoke of marriage and children and happy days spent with the people we loved. It brings me joy to know that you've begun the journey toward your perfect future. Rest assured, Cassandra and I are well on our way.

You will be surprised to know that she and Mother have been getting along famously. I know it hardly seems possible, but I swear to you, it is true. Once I made it clear that the two of them must get along, she made every effort to befriend Cassandra. So, I thought you'd like to know that, for now, I have not had to send her off to the Outer Hebrides. Time will tell whether that decision will stand.

I look forward to seeing you and the earl at the wedding. Until then, rest well and take good care of your growing babe. Have you considered any names yet? If not, do consider Robert for a boy. It is quite a good name, I think. I am certain Hart will love it.

All my love, save the majority of which I give to my darling Cass,

Robert

ALSO BY VICTORIA VALE

The Scandalous Ballroom Encounters Series

A series of standalone books centered around the scandalous private lives of the London ton.

Book 1: Masquerade

Book 2: Marriage Most Scandalous

Book 3: Tempting Two

Book 4: Submitting to the Marquis

Book 5: Dominating Mr. Darling

Book 6: Her Beautiful Bastard

The Villain Duology

A Regency Dark Erotica duet set in the wilds of Scotland.

Book 1: The Villain

Book 2: The Dove

Book 3: The Butterfly

Book 4: The Damsel

Prequel Short Story: Hart

ABOUT THE AUTHOR

Sexy heroes … sassy heroines … electrifying erotic romance. Victoria Vale has written over two dozen Romance and Young Adult novels under various pseudonyms. As a lover of erotic romance, she enjoys nothing more than a sexy hero paired with a sassy heroine, flavored with a dash of spice and lots of heat. A wife and mother of three, she enjoys reading (of course), cooking, sewing … and other activities that aren't appropriate for inclusion in a biography.

www.eroticromancebyvicki.com

Made in United States
North Haven, CT
29 November 2021